1000

Attack of the Bounty Hunters

Steven Gordon

Clifford Croft Press, New York
www.CliffordCroft.com

First published on paper in 2004

For information, contact Clifford Croft Press
http://www.CliffordCroft.com

ISBN 0-9749652-0-0

Library of Congress Control Number: 2004090847
Books by Steven Gordon

The Clifford Croft Series
Attack of the Bounty Hunters
The Invasion of August
The War Admiral's Fleet
Death to the Insects!
Nightfall on August
Rise of the Standard Imperium
Still The Most Dangerous Game
Infiltrator
The Essential Mindreader
Escape from Altera

Other science fiction by Steven Gordon
Clashik Cube
Unexpected Wizardry
Future Park

Other books by Steven Gordon with fiction, but no science
Redweld Warrior
Finish Line

This book is dedicated to
Beaver the Pomeranian
"Ow Wow Wow!"
Good dog!
(Search Google for "Space Pomeranian".
Click on the first entry)

Forward: Who are the Graftonites?

They were the most fearsome gunmen in the galaxy. Everyone knew what they were capable of. People trembled in their presence. All it took was the mere mention of their name.

The Graftonites.

It was a curious world, Grafton II, at first an uninhabited, lush planet. It was several years before the first settlers started to notice something different about themselves. Their reflexes started to speed up. They could move and dodge more quickly, and of course, shoot more quickly as well. At first, that skill was largely used for hunting.

But as time passed and their new found abilities matured, word spread about what the Graftonites were capable of doing. Graftonites suddenly found that their abilities were in demand on other planets. Suddenly, the life of a hard working pioneer had little allure for these settlers, compared to the life of adventure and excitement (and not to mention enrichment) that the galaxy had to offer.

Fifty years later, the four most common professions on Grafton were pretty much set for centuries to come. In order of popularity:

Bounty hunter.

Gunman.

Mercenary.

Killer.

Graftonites became feared throughout the civilized galaxy for their exceedingly quick reflexes. But as individuals they were only a threat to those they had been hired to capture, or kill. A capable Graftonite gunman could take on three or four other soldiers, outdraw them, and kill them all before any could fire a shot.

But what would it take to stop an army of Graftonites? They would be almost unbeatable.

It was fortunate that the Graftonites, fiercely independent by nature, had never organized. Each one did his or her own thing.

At least, until Mo Quandry came along.

In a stadium on Quandry's personal property, he stood on a stage, surrounded by hundreds of cheering Graftonite gunmen in the bleachers. Quandry was a tall, dark haired man, with a single scar running down the side of his face. He had a certain hardness in his brown eyes, a hardness uncommon even for a Graftonite. He wore the blue denim that was the popular dress of all Graftonites, with a blaster holstered to one side, and a traditional Graftonite weapon, the slicer, holstered to the other.

"My friends," he said, standing before the gathering of assembled Graftonites. "Our time has come! No longer will we be content working for the sheep, living off the pocket change they pay us for running their errands while they get fat and rich. Why settle for a handful of credits when it can all be ours!"

The crowd roared.

Quandry started pacing. He seemed to be looking through the crowd, picking out individual faces. "The sheep have nothing but scorn for us. But even more than that, they fear us!"

The crowd roared again.

Quandry suddenly stopped moving. "As proof, see the spy they have placed in our midst!"

He snapped his fingers, and two Graftonites were instantly at his side. Quandry pointed, and a very surprised looking spectator in the audience found himself surrounded by Quandry's men.

"Bring him up here!" said Quandry.

The spectator was brought to the stage. One of the guards handed Quandry the spectator's blaster.

"Who sent you to spy on us?" Quandry boomed.

The man looked frightened, but said, "I... I am no spy."

Quandry stood for a moment, as if considering that answer. Then he looked at the man's blaster. "Not a bad weapon."

Almost quicker than the eye could see, Quandry fired off a series of shots with the man's weapon. They exploded all around him, only inches from the man's hands and legs.

Quandry aimed the blaster at the man. "Now, who do you work for?"

"The L-league," said the man.

"You see!" said Quandry. The crowd roared.

"We will no longer do your bidding while you skulk in the shadows, like a coward!" said Quandry. The crowd roared again.

"If you want to confront us, you must do it face to face!" said Quandry. He tossed the man his blaster, and took several steps backwards. "Draw."

The man sweated, but didn't raise his blaster.

"Are you afraid?" said Quandry.

"I don't want to fight," said the man, now trembling.

"Nevertheless, by trespassing on my property, and spying, you've picked a fight," Quandry roared. "Look how cowardly the sheep is!"

The crowd roared again.

"Now draw," said Quandry, staring the trembling man down.

"You can outdraw me. You have faster reflexes, I wouldn't stand a chance," said the man.

"All right," said Quandry. He slowly drew his own blaster, and laid it down on the ground. Then he drew his slicer, a long, thin foil. He thumbed a contact on it, and the foil glowed as a thin energy field enveloped the length of it.

"Now you have no more excuses," said Quandry. "Draw."

Still trembling, the man didn't raise the blaster. He took a step backwards.

"You have exactly three seconds before I come after you," said Quandry. "One... two..."

The man raised his blaster, and fired. But he might as well have been moving in slow motion, for Quandry dodged out of the way of the blast, raised the slicer, and gave a quick, horizontal slice with his blade.

The man didn't even have time to scream. He fell to the ground, in two distinct and separate thuds.

Quandry raised his glowing slicer into the air.

"This will be the fate of all sheep who oppose us! Let us take from them what is rightfully ours!" he yelled. "Together, we will rule the galaxy!"

"Victory!" he shouted.

"Victory!" the crowd shouted back.

They shouted it over, again and again, as Quandry continued to excite the crowd. With their super reflexes and gunfighting abilities, who would be able to stop them?

Chapter 1: The Column Gets Involved

The League of United Planets was the most powerful coalition of colonized planets in the galaxy. It was administered by an elected government on the planet August and stood for human rights and democratic representation. A very large bureaucracy administered its programs and a slightly less large military defended it. In addition, the League had a number of external intelligence agencies working for it.

Stellar Intelligence was the largest, most well known, and most respected agency--and the least competent.

At the other extreme, the most capable intelligence agency was one without the staff or the resources or even the public relations of Stellar Intelligence. What it did have was superb operatives. This agency was simply known as the Column.

And in the Column, the most capable agents were known as Level One Agents. There were traditionally only eight of those, who were known, for a very obvious reason, as "The Eight." And of those eight most capable agents, perhaps the very most capable agent in all the League was at that moment performing vital work... in an insane asylum.

For the first time in a very long time, superspy Clifford Croft was almost at a loss for words.

"...just because," Croft finally said. "Do I really have to explain why it's a bad thing to light someone's clothes on fire?"

Croft was speaking to one of the Column's gamma operatives, a fire starter named Red Sally who could literally start fires with her mind. They were deep underground, in a secure sub basement in Column HQ on August.

Sally glared at Croft, her blonde hair turning a hint of red as the room temperature around her rose slightly. "It's not like I actually hurt someone."

"I don't think the deputy secretary appreciated the first degree burn on her right arm," Croft said.

"First degree? That's nothing," said Sally dismissively.

"She's an important government official, and important government officials don't appreciate being lit on fire," Croft persisted.

"It was an accident," said Sally.

"Was it?" Croft said. "Or was it just coincidental that her jacket burst into flame when she asked if you were emotionally stable?"

"I am emotionally stable!" Sally shouted, wisps of steam coming out of her blonde hair, which was starting to look more and more red. "And I only lit her jacket on fire, if she had only taken it off promptly, she wouldn't have gotten a scratch!"

"The point is that the deputy secretary should never have needed a fire safety course in order to visit here," Croft said. "And you need to learn that."

"All right, I'm sorry," said Sally. "I won't ignite anyone again."

"You've promised that before," Croft said. "The doctors think you need some practical training."

"I don't care what the doctors think!" Sally snapped.

Croft snapped his fingers and took a few steps back from Sally. Attendants in metal fire resistance suits and visors came running forward, on cue, carrying large books. They stood between Sally and Croft, and held the books up, all around Croft.

"What's this all about?" said Sally. "Say, those are my books of poetry!"

Red Sally was well known in the institute for writing feverish poems, mostly involving fire.

"So they are," Croft said. "Consider this an object lesson in controlling your powers."

"What do you mean?"

"I have some frank things to say to you," Croft said. "And I have some concern how you will take it."

"I can take some constructive self-criticism, I suppose," said Sally guardedly.

"Good," Croft said. "Because remember that your books are surrounding me." The orderlies in the fire protection suits held up the books.

"First let's start with your temper," Croft said.

"Who says I have a temper!" Sally yelled.

"Everyone," Croft said. "And I'm not only talking about the people you've injured. People are afraid to be around you, Sally. They think if they say the wrong thing, they'll burst into flames."

"Lies!" said Sally, her hair half-red, and positively steaming now.

"So nothing I could say could cause you to start a fire, then?" Croft said.

"No!" said Sally.

"Well then, Sally, let us talk about your poetry," Croft said. "Have I told you that I have actually read some of it?"

Sally's expression turned grim.

"I can't say I think much of it," Croft said, in a carefully modulated tone that was just the slightest bit derisive.

Her hair was all red now.

"Your poetry has no rhythm."

A curtain of steam rose from her.

"And all you do is write about fires. That gets old, real quick," Croft observed.

Sally glared at Croft.

"And for another, your spelling and grammar are awful. What educated person spells conflagration with a u?"

The air in the room became sweltering hot.

Croft could see that things were reaching a boiling point, perhaps literally. It was time for the final push. "I read some of your poems to the guys upstairs, and they actually laughed at the amateurish-"

Sally screamed, and a jet of flames shot out from her hands. The orderlies cringed, even in their fire protective suits, as did Croft. But the flames shot backwards, not forwards, engulfing an unoccupied table and a set of chairs in flames. The flames shot out again, and again and again, as Sally glared at Croft, perspiration running off her brow.

Finally, Sally started gasping, and the flames stopped. Orderlies rushed forward with fire extinguishers.

Sally wiped some of the perspiration off of her face. "You see?" she said. "I never touched you. I can control it."

"Why am I here?" Croft wondered aloud.

Croft was still wondering this as he left the gamma section and went to the Column HQ cafeteria. A fellow operative named Preston was there.

"How did it go?" Preston asked him.

Croft shrugged. "The usual."

"Why did you get picked for this assignment?" Preston asked, vocalizing a thought that had been on Croft's mind.

"The Chief volunteered me," Croft said. "I told her one of the doctors should do it. I'm not a psychiatrist."

"What did the Chief say?" Preston asked.

"She said she wanted Sally trained and she wanted someone who could get an aggressive reaction from Sally, and she said I was very good at that," Croft said.

"She thought you'd be good at getting Sally angry?"

"No, just people in general," Croft said.

"Um," said Preston. He suddenly sniffed in Croft's direction. "I take it the lessons in fire control aren't going well."

"What makes you say that?" Croft asked.

"Well, for one thing, your clothes smell of smoke," said Preston.

Croft sniffed his clothes, and made a face.

Croft's wristcomm beeped. Startled, he looked at it; it was the Chief calling. He didn't answer it.

"What are you waiting for?" Preston asked.

"You don't suppose she could already have been informed about some minor non-structural fire damage in the institute?"

"You'd better answer it."

Croft did so. The Chief was not calling about the fire damage. She was calling him, instead to an unscheduled meeting in a certain conference room.

When he arrived the Chief gave him her warm and familiar glare. Mitty Benchly was new to the job of director of the Column, but she had quickly taken an instinctive dislike to Croft. She was a shrewd, elderly looking woman with the eyes of a hawk.

"Mr. Croft," she said, giving him a warning glare. "The Chief of Staff will be joining us at this meeting," she said, indicating a dignified, middle aged man sitting in a fine, eight piece suit, flanked by aides. The aides only wore six piece suits. They were obviously less important.

Croft paused. The Chief evidently expected a response, and she probably wouldn't appreciate a witty one.

"That's, uh, very nice," Croft said carefully.

The Chief glared at him.

"Hello, Mr. Chief of Staff," said Croft.

The Chief of Staff, seeing that Croft was a mere employee, gave him the slightest of nods. It oddly reminded Croft of the same kind of greeting he used to get from a mutant shetland pony he once owned.

"Have a seat," said the Chief sharply. "Lights!"

The lights dimmed. "This briefing will be led by our second deputy chief analyst for sector intelligence, Sylvia Tane," said the Chief, indicating a young blonde woman. "You may begin, Ms. Tane."

"What is this about?" Croft whispered to the Chief.

"Be quiet and find out," the Chief advised. She raised her voice. "Ms. Tane, we're waiting."

"Ah, yes," said the young woman. She pressed a button, and an image of a blue-green world appeared on the holoprojector. "You are all undoubtedly familiar with Grafton II. It's a planet notorious for its gunmen for hire. Until now Graftonites have operated individually for different employers, some working against our interests, some working for them, but most engaged in activities unrelated to our interests."

"Until now," the Chief prompted.

"Ah, yes." Another holoimage appeared, this one a moving image showing Graftonites in battle, firing blasters as they ran and weaved across the area in view. They moved so incredibly quickly that their images blurred, only solidifying when they stopped to momentarily steady their aim.

"This holo transcript was taken from Grafton IV, another planet in orbit around Grafton. The inhabitants from Grafton IV aren't members of the League, but rather are independent, like Grafton II. Unfortunately, they don't have the speeded up reflexes of their neighbors on Grafton II," said Tane.

"What we're seeing, gentlemen, is an attack on the Zytrilium depository on Grafton IV," said the Chief.

"Groups of Graftonites are occasionally hired to stage armed raids," said one of the generals. "As long as it doesn't concern a League world, why do we care?"

"Because when the Graftonites took the Zytrilium, they didn't leave," said the Chief. "They stayed behind and took over the entire planet."

That started some murmuring in the audience. That wasn't typical Graftonite behavior.

"Next image, please!" the Chief said, taking over the presentation.

The image of a dark haired man appeared on the screen. "This is Mo Quandry, the leader of this new group of Graftonites," said the Chief. "As far as we can tell, he's the one who organized this invasion." There was more background chatter at the mere mention of the I-word.

"Invasion, gentlemen. There is no way to minimize it," said Benchly. "If the Graftonites are getting organized, and have started to invade a neighboring planet, who is to say whose planet will be next? A League planet, perhaps?"

"The Graftonites are formidable fighters, but we outnumber them more than a thousand to one. They only have one planet with a population of what, 50 million?" said one of the generals.

"Actually, the figure is closer to eight million," said Tane, the analyst.

"Eight million! What is that against a population of hundreds of billions?" said the general.

"And they have no space force to speak of," said an admiral. "How did they even get to the planet they're invading?"

"According to our remote sensors, they used a civilian transport, escorted by fighters. No more than 300 Graftonites were involved in the invasion," said the Chief. "And Grafton IV, their target, has a population of 40 million."

"You're saying that 300 Graftonites took over a planet of 40 million?" said a general. "That's impossible."

"Facts on the ground would indicate otherwise," said the Chief. "They have a quite solid hold on Grafton IV."

"Have we spoken with their government, sounded out their intentions?" one of the civilians asked.

"There is no government," said the Chief.

The murmuring increased.

"What do you mean?" said the civilian who had spoken up earlier. "Every planet, even a small colony world, has to have a government. "

"There is no government," the Chief repeated. "Tane?"

"There is no planetary government," Tane repeated. "You have to remember, these are fiercely individualistic people."

"Impossible!" said one of the Admiral. "Who provides for planetary defense?"

"The citizens do. Nearly every citizen has their own airfighter, and quite a number own spacefighters," said Tane.

"Who provides for social welfare?" a civilian analyst asked.

"The citizens provide for themselves," said Tane. "All essential services are privatized. Living on Grafton isn't a cheap proposition. That's part of the reason that the planet's so underpopulated."

"What about schools?" This question came from the Chief of Staff.

"They're privatized," said Tane.

"Privatized?" said the Chief of Staff, looking puzzled. "But who sets the curriculum? Who instills the citizen's duty, the social conscience, the sensitivity training-"

"They don't seem to do that very much. Besides basic reading and writing, I do know they train a lot with guns," said Tane.

"Maybe that's when they get the sensitivity training," Croft muttered.

The Chief of Staff looked incredulous. "Children training with guns? What about the justice system, police?"

"There is no justice system, or police, or laws," said Tane. "There is no crime, legally speaking."

"But… what if one civilian gets robbed, or attacked…."

"Then that citizen can use his gun and hunt down the attacker," said Tane. "That's another reason that Grafton II is underpopulated. If you're not good with a gun you don't tend to last long there."

"How does the population respond to murders?"

"If a particular killer incenses the locals with his choice of targets, locals can band together to hunt him down," said Tane. "There is a limited form of local government. Water, sewage, and roads are provided by limited local authorities, the equivalent of county governments here. They function by assessing a property tax, which is set on a sliding scale based on the property owner's fighting ability."

"Fighting ability? What does that have to do with anything?" a civilian asked.

"The county authority hires as its tax assessor a gunman, the best it can find, but usually someone with average or slightly above average gunfighting skills. The tax assessor goes from home to home assessing the property tax for each establishment. Before the assessor sets the tax, he takes into account how formidable the owner of the home is. Because the owner can appeal the ruling by attempting to kill the assessor."

"How barbaric!" said the civilian.

"If the tax assessor/gunman knows he's a faster draw than the owner, he assesses a relatively high fee, figuring that the owner will find it more reasonable to pay than to go up against him. If the gunman thinks the owner is faster than him, then he assesses a relatively low amount, figuring that at such a low amount the owner won't think it worthwhile to kill someone he hasn't been paid to kill."

There was a lot of murmuring now in the conference room.

"So there's no central government at all?" asked one of the generals.

"Sometimes Graftonites get together to discuss issues. When a lot of Graftonites, say a 100 or more, get together, it's called a Grand Meeting, or Grand Gathering," said Tane.

"And that's all the government they have?"

"About a hundred years ago there was a movement to get a lot of Grand Meetings together to elect representatives to form a national government," said Tane.

"What happened?" a civilian asked.

"The delegates met, but given their fiercely individualistic nature, they could only agree on two things, and disbanded," said Tane. "One of them was their planetary national motto, 'Live Free or Die'.

"What was the other thing they agreed upon?"

"Not to allow guns in the debating chamber," said Tane.

The murmuring grew louder.

The Chief raised her voice to cut over the side discussions. "We have an embassy on Grafton, of course, to represent the interests of our people there, but very little information about the current situation."

"What about our Column operatives on Grafton?" said one of the generals. "What do they say?"

The Chief pressed a button. An image appeared of a man, lying on the ground with a burn in his forehead. "The agency chief doesn't say much."

"Neither do his deputy operatives," the Chief added. The image expanded to show two other people in a similar condition. "Meanwhile our embassy staff are huddled in their offices, afraid to come out. Since they don't have a government of their own, the Graftonites don't think much of the concept of diplomatic immunity, I'm afraid."

"Where do we go from here?" asked the Chief of Staff.

"We need more information about this Quandry and his intentions, and what the situation on the ground is," said the Chief. "That's why I'm going to send another agent in."

"One agent? Will that be enough?" said a general.

"I'm sending the best," said the Chief, looking meaningfully at Croft.

Ten minutes later Croft was seated in the Chief's office. He started in with his first question even before she took her seat.

"Why do I always get the suicide missions?" said Croft.

"You're one of the Eight," said the Chief. "You're one of our leading trouble shooters."

"It's funny that I never hear about any of the other seven being sent on these one-way missions," said Croft. "Why don't you send a Graftonite?"

"I would, if we had a Graftonite operative, but we don't," said the Chief.

"Why don't we hire one? We've done it before."

"Because I need feedback from one of our own, not a Graftonite operative," said the Chief. "We've been trying to hire a Graftonite to accompany you, but anti-League sentiment is on an upswing there, undoubtedly thanks to our friend Mo Quandry, and we'll be lucky if we do find someone by the time you land there."

"Do you really expect me to outgun a Graftonite?" said Croft.

"You'll have to rely on your cunning," said the Chief. "You'll be dressed as and will pass as a Graftonite when you're in public. When you meet with people in private you'll have a different cover, as a League diplomatic official."

"I'm going to pose as a Graftonite? Who thought up that crazy idea?" said Croft.

"I did, Mr. Croft," said the Chief coldly. "Mr. Croft, may I be frank?"

"By all means."

"I don't like you," said the Chief. "I don't like your frivolous, headstrong ways. I've read your lengthy service records; my predecessors found you irritating too. But you have an uncanny knack for survival, and that's something we need here. If it will help stroke your precious ego, we're sending you in because we think you have the best chance for survival."

Croft paused. "That's very flattering. But if you're going to send me there, I'm going to need some help."

"I was actually thinking along the same lines," said the Chief. She appeared to changed the subject. "What did you think of Ms. Tane's presentation?"

"It was good, what little you let her give," said Croft.

"She's very knowledgeable about the Graftonites. One of our top analysts in the area," said the Chief.

"Are you suggesting I take a non-operative on a mission?" said Croft, suddenly comprehending. "I'm going to have a hard time enough protecting myself, I can't babysit-"

"I'm not suggesting anything," said the Chief. "I am ordering you to take Ms. Tane. Your service record indicates a tendency to disregard cultural norms and a failure to appreciate local culture-"

"We're not talking about a touristy visit here-"

"Silence!" the Chief thundered. "You will take Ms. Tane and that is the end of it. I need to find out what the Graftons are up to and we need to understand their culture to understand them. Ms. Tane will provide invaluable assistance. Now, is there anything else?"

Croft opened his mouth, closed it, then opened it again. "Yes. A gamma operative."

"Denied. Gamma operatives-"

"-are limited in number and strictly intended for critical A-1 missions," said Croft. "I know, I've heard it all before. If the Graftonites are planning to invade other planets, I'd say that's priority A-1."

The Chief paused for a moment, considering. Then she looked up at Croft, sighing. "Who do you want?"

Croft also considered for a moment, then he said, "A telekinetic would be nice."

"A telekinetic," said the Chief, punching some buttons on her keyboard. "You say it as if we had a whole warehouse of such operatives available." She pressed another button and the holoimage of two faces appeared in the air.

"The Clapper and the Bopper," Croft groaned.

"Which will it be?" said the Chief.

Croft considered, trying to decide which one was less brain damaged. Gamma operatives had special abilities, but almost all of them had "personality quirks", some more serious than others. The Clapper had a tendency to clap his hands continually, which was irritating, but was not nearly as annoying as what the Bopper did.

"The Clapper," said Croft.

"Very well," said the Chief. "There's a freighter leaving tomorrow. We've booked special passage for you."

"Thanks," said Croft. He got up, and turned to go.

"Croft?"

"Yes?"

"I want regular reports. I intend to run your mission myself. There are to be no headstrong actions without consulting me. Are we clear?"

Croft sighed.

"Are we clear?"

"Yes, I will only take headstrong actions that meet with your approval," said Croft, feeling very much the child.

The first thing that Croft did after leaving the Chief was to send a quick message using his wrist comm. Then he started deeper into the complex towards one of the most heavily guarded section of the base--the Gamma section. He had been there just a few hours ago to administer Red Sally's "therapy", and now he had to return there once again.

His ID was checked several times at several checkpoints staffed with heavily armed guards, before he finally found himself in a large room filled with screaming, shrieking individuals.

Croft tried to filter out the noise.

"No, no, it's my toy, mine, mine, mine!"

"I must have 15 raisins with my dinner, not 14, not 16, but 15!"

"Do they thank us? Does anyone ever thank us? No, no gratitude."

Croft tried to blot it out as he approached a trainer in a white uniform. He asked her a question. She pointed to a room down the hall.

Croft had just reached the door when a flame spurted out of the open doorway, almost burning him. He jumped back, waiting for the flame to subside, before entering.

"Hey, what do you think you're doing?" said Croft, seeing Red Sally as he entered. "You almost burned me!" So much for the morning training session.

"Told you (clap clap) you might burn someone (clap clap), told you (clap clap)," said a skinny man to one side of the room.

"Sorry, I didn't see you," Red Sally grinned, a sheen of perspiration on her head as her hair color slowly turned blonde.

"We just had a lesson in controlling your powers this morning," said Croft. "Didn't any of that stick with you?"

"What lesson?" said Red Sally, looking momentarily puzzled. And then, frowning, she concentrated. "Oh, you mean that."

Croft turned to the Clapper. His real name was Robert Clerk, but to everyone here he was just the Clapper. "I'm here on a mission."

"Mission?" said the Clapper. His eyebrows perked up, and he looked excited, like a pet promised a walk outside.

"We're going to Grafton," said Croft. "Have you heard of Grafton?"

"Is it pretty?" said the Clapper.

"Very pretty," Croft assured him, automatically falling back into liespeak. Actually, though, Grafton II was mostly untamed forest woodlands and mountains. It really was pretty. But the truth wasn't foremost in his mind right now. "Come along now."

Croft was successfully escorting the Clapper to the door when Red Sally said, "Take me with you!"

"Not possible, Red," said Croft.

"Why not?"

"This is going to be a dangerous mission-"

"Dangerous?" said the Clapper, his face contorting.

Oh oh, wrong thing to say. "Dangerous for Red, not for you," Croft corrected. "We're going to a planet of people who like to pick fights. With your temper-"

"Who says I have a temper!" said Red Sally. Steam rose from her hair, which started to turn faintly red again. The room grew warm.

"Sally, you're not going to win an argument by committing arson," said Croft. "And if you create a tantrum and start a fire again, I'll have you put in the ice room."

"Oh...." The heat started to dissipate. She took a few steps forward. "Take me with you. Please!"

"No," said Croft.

"Please!" said Sally again.

"No!" said Croft, wagging a finger at her. "Stay!"

Sally stopped.

"Good girl!" said Croft, in a rich voice intended for puppies. "We'll send you a holocard." He turned to the Clapper. "Let's go."

As they left the facility Croft inured himself to the screams and yells. But one voice in a forest of conversation caught his ear. "Never grateful, never grateful, no.... do not try the first hamburger, not the first one, Croft!"

But when Croft turned to find the person who had spoken, he was gone.

Two hours later, after dropping off the Clapper and running some other errands, Croft made his way to the roof, on the 392nd floor. It was only there that one could appreciate the majesty of August, the capital of the League and the Alliance, one great city of skyscrapers spread out over most of a continent. Here, near the palace at Sarney Sarittenden, the bulk and height of the buildings were especially dense.

The sun beat down at him and the wind whipped at his body as he walked on the crunchy green turf. A man in a chef's hat stood cooking on the far side of the roof, on an old fashioned grill. Croft slowly walked towards him.

"Really, Levi, I don't know what you see in all this," said Croft.

"I like outdoors," said the man. His name was Levi Esherkol, and he was one of the most brilliant scientists working for the Column. But he also liked to cook. Levi pressed down on the meat, and the dripping juices raised a fire which surrounded the burgers. "Ready, I think."

"Levi, I don't have time for this."

"Always time for quality food," said the cook. He handed Croft the hamburger. The smell was delicious. Croft's first instinct was to bite into it, but then, remembering something he had heard, lifted the bun and looked at the burger. "Levi!"

"What?"

Croft showed him the burger. There was a bug mashed on top of it.

"How that get there?" said Levi. "Sorry." He took it away and gave Croft another.

After careful inspection, Croft bit into it. It was really good.

"Eh? Eh?" said Levi, watching his expression. "Use specially flavored hickory chips. You like?"

"Um," said Croft, chewing a bit and then swallowing. "I like, I like. But Levi, about the problem I commed you about-"

Levi looked down at Croft's boots. "I look in service, file, your boot size 10.1, correct?"

Croft nodded.

Levi reached behind the grill and handed Croft a pair of black boots that looked identical to the one that Croft was wearing. Levi looked pleased with himself. "I even got color right!"

"Yes, Levi, but I already have boots, and how is this going to protect me from Graftonite gunmen?" said Croft. "I was expecting some sort of portable forcefield-"

"Don't have portable forcefield, certainly not on short notice," said Levi.

"What do you have?"

"Look in boot," said Levi.

Croft raised the right boot and looked inside, but only saw darkness.

"No, left boot!"

Croft did the same with the left boot, but only saw the same thing.

"No, not look!" said Levi. "Feel!"

Croft started to put his hand in, but Levi grabbed his arm.

"Gently!" said Levi.

Croft, nodding, cautiously put his hand in. He felt an unfamiliar lumpiness on the roof of the interior of the boot.

"The padded area?"

Levi nodded. "Gas injector. Step on foot with other foot, and injector will send compressed gas injection through skin."

"What kind of injection?"

"Accelerant. Experimental," said Levi. "May accelerate bodily functions fast enough to temporarily compete with Graftonites."

"May?"

"Experimental," said Levi. "Works on chimps for short periods."

"Chimps," said Croft. "Will this make me faster than the Graftonites?"

"Not sure," said Levi. "Depends on your bodily chemistry, and formula."

"Maybe I'd better ask a chimp," said Croft.

"One more thing. Watch out for side effects."

"What side effects?" Croft asked.

"Dizziness. Maybe some nausea," said Levi. "Not likely life threatening. Only lost one chimp."

"Only one?" said Croft.

"Not directly related to serum," said Levi. "Chimp fell off roof. Wrong to test it up here, but was nice sunny day."

"Oh," said Croft. "It still sounds dangerous. Isn't there anything else-"

"Best can do on short notice," said Levi. "Do you have few weeks?"

"No."

"Then all I can give."

"Well, that's all I can ask for, I guess," said Croft. "I'm bringing the Clapper, maybe that will help even the odds."

Levi gave a short laugh, as if Croft had said something amusing.

Croft turned to go, but was called back after only a few steps.

"Croft?"

"Yes?"

"Looking for new meat recipes, Graftons famous for. If time, can you-"

Croft thought about the danger the Graftonites posed to the galaxy, and he said, "You bet, Levi. Recipes. Priority one."

Actually, Grafton really was famous for its meat dishes. That was one of the many useless things that Croft learned on the tedious trip to Grafton II. Sylvia Tane was a veritable fountain of information, telling him much more than he wanted to know about Grafton. Croft had actually briefly been to Grafton once before, very briefly, but he had to admit that Sylvia knew a lot more than he did.

"Did you know that over 90% of the population are dedicated carnitarians?" said Tane. Carnitarians; that meant they only ate meat.

"No," said Croft.

The Clapper sat quietly, watching the conversation, clapping softly. He generally only clapped when he was nervous, or bored, or if the weather were just right.

"They refuse to eat fruits or vegetables," said Tane.

"Fascinating," said Croft. "Is there anything in your database that tells us how to win a gunfight against them?"

"Gunfight? You're not planning to challenge any Graftonite, are you?"

"No," said Croft. "I was thinking of the other way around."

"It is not uncommon for Graftonites to challenge others to gunfights, but only if they feel insulted, or if they don't get what they want," said Tane. "My advice is not to insult any of them and to give them whatever they want."

"I wonder if any of our late operatives insulted the Graftonites," said Croft.

"I did notice from the holoimages that all of them had their blasters out," said Tane. "If someone challenges you, simply refuse to fight."

"Haven't you ever heard of Graftonite killers? They'll kill me whether I defend myself or not," said Croft.

"Well, certainly, there are some of those in Grafton society. But there is also a strong cultural belief in the fair fight."

"The fair fight?"

"Yes," said Tane. "That all gunfights should be one on one. That a Graftonite shouldn't be attacked by surprise, or sniped at long distance."

"A code of conduct for a planet of killers," said Croft dryly.

"Don't dismiss it so casually, Mr. Croft," said Tane. "I've read of instances of Graftonites who disregarded the rules who were hunted down and killed by their neighbors. Some of them take these things very seriously."

"What about the Graftonites who hire themselves out as killers?"

"Yes, they also have a code of conduct, of sorts," said Tane. "But their victims are almost always non-Graftonites, so the same rules may not apply. But as long as no one has been hired to kill you, you should be all right. After all, you're a sheep."

"A what?" said Croft.

"That's what Graftonites call non-Graftonites. Sheep. It's meant as a visual metaphor for the weak, those unable to defend themselves. It's meant disparagingly, but actually may help us," said Tane.

"How?"

"Well, sheep are looked down upon, but they're also pitied. If someone simply killed a sheep without cause, his neighbors would look negatively on that," said Tane.

"Uh huh," said Croft, aware that despite what Tane said, any Grafton could kill them for any reason he wished. Then another thought struck him. "But we're not posing as off-worlders, as least not in public. We're supposed to be posing as Graftonites, so we won't even have that theoretical protection."

"Well, that was the Chief's idea. I can't be responsible for that," said Tane.

The Clapper clapped twice.

It was going to be some trip.

Chapter 2: Basking in the Hospitality of the Silencer

Croft drew his blaster lightning with lightning speed, appraising his opponent in the mirror who drew just as fast as he did. Studying his stance for a moment, he holstered his blaster and drew it again.

"You won't need to do that," said Tane. "We're going to pass for Graftonites. Nobody's going to challenge us."

Croft gave a short laugh. "Graftonites are always challenging each other."

"They only challenge people who they think are weak," said Tane. "They don't challenge each other unless it's over something really important. Since we will be posing as native Graftonites, we shouldn't have any trouble."

"No trouble," Croft repeated. He drew his blaster again. This time, he thought he was slightly faster. Good. He turned away from the mirror and set his blaster to the test setting. Tensing again, he drew his blaster and fired immediately, hitting a crate some twenty feet away. Not bad, but not good; he had been aiming for the crate above the one he had actually hit.

"No matter how much you practice, you'll never be as fast as the natives," said Tane.

Croft hadn't told her about the accelerant that Levi had given him. It was still experimental, Levi had said. Only to be used as a last resort. Croft wasn't enthusiastic about injecting a barely tested drug into his system, but if he were faced with a Graftonite killer, he would have no choice.

"A more productive use of the time would be spent reviewing the data on Grafton," said Tane. "We will be landing on Regular in just a few hours."

"Regular?" Croft said idly, continuing to practice quickdrawing, firing, and reholstering his weapon.

"Their capital, and, it appears, their only city," said Tane. "If you can call a locale of only 50,000 people a city."

"Only 50,000 people? And that's their only city?" said Croft. "What about the other almost eight million Graftonites?"

"They're all spread out, all over the countryside," said Tane. "You see, it's things like this you should be learning, and not playing with your weapon. I can help."

"You want to help?" said Croft.

"If I can," said Tane.

"Can you move right over there?" Croft asked, indicating the crates he had been targeting. "I need to practice on a human shape."

When the freighter touched down, Tane said, "I hope you spent at least some time figuring out a course of action. The Chief's initial orders are to find out more about this Quandry and what his intentions are, but we have been given some latitude in how we approach this. I suggest we begin by reviewing the local media database-"

"Fine, you do that," said Croft. "But I didn't come all the way here to review their local media database."

"Then what do you plan?"

"First we pick up our contact," said Croft. After substantial effort Column had ultimately succeeded in hiring a local Graftonite to accompany them for a premium. Given the anti off-worlder sentiment, it was lucky they had found anyone at all. His name was Tallas Carper, and that was all Croft knew about him.

"And then?"

"We'll drop by a friend's place," said Croft.

"May I remind you that we're here on official business," said Tane.

"I think you just did," said Croft.

Croft and Tane stepped out onto the tarmac at the Regular Spaceport. Although it was the largest spaceport on the planet, it didn't have connecting tubes to the arrival terminal as most spaceports did. Most of the traffic that came through Regular was cargo freight; if Graftons needed to travel off-planet, they used their own spacefighters or small transports.

A mile away, Croft appeared in the crosshairs of a sniper scope.

"I have him," said the slightly accented voice. "They did send Croft, as we predicted. Shall I kill him?" the sniper asked.

"Fool!" said his superior, a woman with light brown straight hair whose eyes flashed as she grabbed the sniper rifle away from him.

The sniper and the other members of the observation team looked up at her with surprise.

"Don't you think it would be the tiniest bit suspicious to kill Croft in so public a place?" said the woman.

"Yes Major, but-"

"And don't you think that at this range a kill would be far from certain? You might only wound him, and put him on alert."

"Yes Major, but-"

"And wouldn't it be wiser to first find out what he's doing here, and what his mission is, before liquidating him?"

"Yes Major," said the sniper. "But you are only observing our mission and so I thought-"

"What you most obviously did not do was think," said Major Nancy Kalikov of the Slurian Special Tasks Bureau (STB). "Follow him, learn what he's doing and what he knows. Once we find out what he's up to, then we may kill him."

They entered the arriving building. To Croft's surprise, there was no customs inspection. Tane had told him that their luggage wouldn't be inspected, but he hadn't believed it.

"Customs inspections only occur when there are governmental regulations and tariffs regarding imports and exports," said Tane. "There are no such rules. This isn't even a public spaceport. It's privately owned."

But there was one line they had to stand in before they left the spaceport. When they got to the head of the line, a bored looking Graftonite said, "200 credits."

"200 credits? For what?" said Croft.

The Graftonite looked at him oddly. "Import tax."

"But how can there be an import tax if there's no government?" Croft asked, forgetting for the moment that he was supposed to be playing the part of a native Graftonite and if he were a native he would have known about such things.

The Graftonite, who, like all Graftonites was armed, sighed. "This spaceport is a private facility. Nothing here runs for free. "

"But 200 credits, simply for the ability to walk out of here?"

"If you're poor, don't come to Grafton," said the Graftonite. His hand casually went down to the area around his holstered weapon. "Are you saying that you're challenging the entry fee?"

The Clapper's eyes grew round.

"No," said Croft quickly, paying for him and Tane and the Clapper.

"Thank you," said the Graftonite coldly.

As they stepped out of the terminal Croft found himself blinking in the bright morning sunlight. Everyone around them was wearing blue denim pants and jackets, almost as if it were a national uniform. Of course, given the ruggedly individualistic nature of the Graftonites, there could never be any such thing as a national uniform.

Croft, Tane, and the Clapper were clad in blue denim too, all part of the Chief's plan to have them pass for Graftonites.

"Where's our contact?" said Croft, looking around. There were a few Graftonites standing around outside the terminal, but none made eye contact with them. Croft keyed up a picture of Tallas Carper on his personal data unit, then looked around. He didn't see anyone who looked like Carper in the area.

"I told him when we were arriving," said Tane.

"Did you also tell him to meet us here?" said Croft.

"I think so," said Tane. After a pause, as she tried to reconcile her memory with what she wanted to believe, she said "I presumed that was self-evident."

The Clapper clapped twice.

Croft sighed and rolled up his left sleeve to reveal his personal comm unit, while simultaneously pulling up the comm code for Tallas Carper.

In seconds he was speaking to their contact.

"My name is Clifford Croft," said Croft.

"How alliterative," said the stone cold voice on the other end.

"We're here, at the spaceport in Regular," Croft said.

"Good to know," said Carper.

"Why aren't you here?" Croft asked.

"I haven't received the first installment of my payment," said the even voice.

"Our arrangement was to pay you on a weekly basis, at the end of the week," said Tane, speaking into Croft's comm.

"I'm altering our arrangement," said Carper. "I want to be paid a week in advance, effective immediately."

Croft put his hand over the comm unit. "Are you sure you couldn't find anyone else?"

Tane shook her head. "No one wants to work for off-worlders right now."

Croft took his hand off the comm unit. "Just a moment."

He took another device out of his pocket with a small keyboard, and started typing away. Then, a minute later, he returned to the wrist comm. "Done."

"Just a moment," said the voice. Then, "Confirmed. What are your instructions?"

"How long would it take you to get to the Regular spaceport?"

"About four hours."

Croft sighed. "Forget it. Just meet us at the following address," he said, providing him with a specific location. After signing off, he glared at Tane.

"What?" said Tane.

"We'd better go rent a groundcar," said Croft.

The groundcar, like everything else on Grafton, was expensive. When Croft tried to negotiate the price, the owner said, "Perhaps you'd prefer going to my competition."

"Where is your competition?"

"I have none," said the proprietor. "Only off-worlders need to rent groundcars, and we don't get many of those."

"But 500 credits a day is outrageous," said Croft.

"If you're poor, don't come to Grafton."

Croft sighed, paying. It wasn't his money, after all, but he disliked being gouged under any circumstances. Plus, he was sure that the Chief would micromanage his expense reports.

They drove for several hours in silence, only occasionally punctuated by brief outbursts of clapping.

"Does he always do that?" Tane said irritably after one outburst.

"Yes. I've even seen him do it in his sleep," said Croft. He stopped at a crossroads to study the onboard map (which had cost 20 credits extra per day).

Then he turned off the paved road onto a dirt road. They had a bumpy ride for the next hour.

"Roads are one of the few services handled by the local governments," said Tane.

"Obviously they haven't quite finished the job," said Croft, as the groundcar skimmed over a bump.

"Their financial resources are quite limited, as I mentioned earlier," said Tane. "As I told you, their only source of revenue is a real estate tax on homes with-"

"Inferior gunmen, I know," said Croft.

After another hour they arrived at turn off the road which had a big sign that simply read, "Keep out." And then, in much smaller letters underneath, it also read, "Bodies of intruders will only be returned at next of kin's expense."

"I think we're here," said Croft, carefully checking the map again.

"Your friend lives here?" said Tane.

"Friend is a strong word," said Croft. "I'm not sure Graftonites have friends. Call him an acquaintance." He drove the groundcar past the sign.

"Are you sure he won't consider us intruders?" Tane asked anxiously.

"Oh, he just puts up that sign to scare people," said Croft. "The Silencer is a pussycat."

"His name is the Silencer????" said Tane. "He sounds like a professional gunman."

"I hear he spent millions on focus groups to find the right name," said Croft, with a straight face.

A moment later they came upon an enormous ranch house surrounded by evergreen trees. Rows of colorful flowers were planted in front and exotic butterflies hopped from one petal to another.

A Graftonite stood on the porch.

Croft, Tane, and the Clapper cautiously got out of the groundcar.

Instantly the Graftonite's blaster was in his hand, though Croft hadn't seen him draw it.

"I guess you can't read," he said simply.

"Wait!" said Croft, raising his hands slowly in the universal surrender gesture. "I'm here to see the Silencer."

"Who are you?"

"I'm his friend," said Croft, directly contradicting what he had said to Tane only minutes earlier.

The man gave a hoarse laugh.

"What's so funny?" Croft asked.

"The Silencer hasn't got any off-worlder friends, sheep."

"He does have one, and his name is Clifford Croft," said Croft. "If you kill me without asking the Silencer first, he'll be very angry with you."

The man noticed Croft's tone and paused for a few seconds, obviously weighing the pros and cons. Would the Silencer really be upset if he shot this intruder? Or was this stranger bluffing?

There's no telling what might have happened next if another voice hadn't interrupted the gunman's train of thought.

"Ted! Put that blaster down," said a woman who had stepped out of the front door onto the porch. "What did I tell you about shooting people without permission?"

They turned to see a woman with brown wavy hair. She was wearing the traditional Graftonite blue denim jeans but also a brown leather vest, the first non-blue color they had seen anybody wearing since they had arrived. She also wore two pearl handled pistols, one holstered on each thigh.

The Graftonite immediately lowered his gun. "The Silencer's standing orders are to shoot-"

"And my standing orders are to get their names first."

"I've already gotten his name," said the Graftonite. He nodded to Croft. "This sheep claims he knows the Silencer."

"He does," said the woman. "And it's not polite to call our guests sheep, at least not to their face." She turned to Croft, and gave a real smile. "Clifford Croft, what a surprise! What brings you here?"

Croft turned to face the Silencer's wife, Annie Oakley. It was not the name she had been born with, of course, but as the winner of the gold medal in the Galactic Trick Shooting competition five times running she was entitled to be called whatever she wanted.

"Hi, Annie. I'm here to see the Silencer. I need his help," said Croft.

"John's a bit busy right now getting ready for a mission," said Oakley. "But I'm sure he can spare a few minutes for you. Follow me."

They followed her into the spacious house through a maze of rooms. They arrived at a room filled with equipment and provisions where a tall, thin man with dark hair was filling up a rudsack. He happened to be facing away from them when they entered.

"John, I have some unexpected guests to see you," said Annie.

"Tell them I'm not here."

Croft cleared his throat. "It's a bit too late for that."

The Silencer turned around, allowing surprise to show on his face, but only for a moment. "Croft. What are you doing here?" he said, as he continued to pack.

"I need your help," said Croft.

"Sorry, I'm off on a mission," said the Silencer. He looked over at his weapons rack, picked out two blasters, and weighed one in each hand, as if deciding which one to bring. Frowning, he made a decision, putting both in the rudsack.

"This is important," said Croft.

"So is my mission," said the Silencer.

"What is it?" said Croft.

"Bounty hunt," said the Silencer.

"I'm talking about preventing a war."

"I'm talking about collecting a big fee."

"I see," said Croft. "John, I'm here to talk with you about Mo Quandry-"

"He's no concern to me," said the Silencer.

"He will be if he plunges Grafton into war against the League."

The Silencer closed the rudsack, lifted it up, and turned to Croft. "As long as he stays off my property, doesn't try to take a cut of my bounty, and keeps away from my lovely wife, I really don't care." He walked past Croft to Annie, and gave her a perfunctory kiss.

"Bye killer," he said to her. "I'll see you in two weeks, maybe ten days if things go even easier than I expect."

"I'll see you, John," Annie said, watching him go. She seemed awed for a moment, but when the Silencer left the room, she quickly snapped back to the present. "I'm sorry John was in such a rush, Clifford. Would you like a drink before you go?"

They sat out on the porch drinking vorsk, a coarse local liquor that burned Croft's throat after the first sip.

"So you're here about Mo," said Annie. "It's no surprise, really."

"What's it all about, Annie?" said Croft.

"He's been stirring people up, saying we aren't getting true value for our labor," said Annie. "He says that we're the best fighters in the galaxy, which is true, of course. But the controversial part he's talking about is upping our compensation rate."

"How, by unionizing?"

Annie laughed. "We already have the bounty hunter's guild. No, Quandry is saying we should simply go out there and take what we want."

"Like he did on Grafton IV," said Croft. "Only he didn't simply rob the planet, he actually occupied it."

"Yes, that was unusual," said Annie. "His people have effectively taken over. They collect the taxes, tariffs, and fees, and are getting quite wealthy, I'm told."

"How many people does he have there?"

Annie shrugged. "50, maybe 100."

"He controls an entire planet with only 100 people?"

"I suppose," said Annie. "You look surprised."

"Well, you people are fearsome warriors, but can 100 of you really stand up against a 100,000 man army? Or a blockbuster bomb?"

Annie laughed again. "You think in such conventional terms, Clifford. Yes, if you lined up 100 of us against 100,000 of you, we'd only manage to kill a few thousand of you before we were taken down. However, that's not the kind of war that Quandry waged."

"What kind of war did he wage?" Croft asked.

"You'll have to ask him," said Annie. "I wasn't there."

"You seem remarkably unconcerned," said Croft. "Don't you care if Quandry drags Grafton into a wider war?"

"I'm not involved," said Annie. "In fact, 99% of Graftonites aren't involved."

"What?" said Croft, looking surprised.

"Oh, he has his supporters, and a lot of sympathizers, maybe, though since they don't take many polls here, his level of support is hard to tell," said Annie. "But if you're asking how many blasters he has behind him for action, well, it can't be more than a few hundred, maybe a thousand or two."

"So you think we're blowing this out of proportion," said Croft.

"Not at all," said Annie. "He's gaining strength all the time; even I can see it. And a few thousand Graftonites can conquer a lot of planets."

Croft still couldn't understand how a handful of Graftonites, however skilled they might be, could take over an entire planet. It was a matter that merited further investigation.

"But things didn't really start going crazy until Rel Cadwalader was killed," said Annie.

"Cad--who?" said Croft.

"Cadwalader," said Annie.

"Who is he?"

"Who was he," Annie corrected. "A bounty hunter. He was gunned down a few weeks ago."

"I would think that can happen in your line of work, even to a Graftonite," said Croft.

"Yes, but it's seldom done by one's own employer," said Annie. "Rel did the mission, but when he went to collect his bounty, his employer tried to cheat him, only paying half. When Rel refused to accept it, he was gunned down."

"Ouch," said Croft. "But I find it hard to believe that a typical Graftonite could simply be gunned down."

"Anyone can, if you have the element of surprise, and five people jump out of an alley with guns blazing," said Annie. "That was the other galling thing about it. It wasn't a fair one on one fight. It was a surprise hit, and five on one at that. That really rankled people almost as much as the hit itself."

"What do you mean?"

"On Grafton when someone calls out someone else, it's almost always one-on-one," said Annie. "It's considered sportsmanlike. The combination of Rel's employer first trying to cheat him and then kill him in such an unsporting way enraged people here. They kept broadcasting holos of the hit over and over on the local networks. It was only a few weeks later that Quandry riled up enough supporters to invade Grafton IV."

"There was a holo recording of the death of this bounty hunter?" said Croft.

"Yes, I think it was recorded by a security holovid," said Annie. "I'm surprised you don't know all this already, this is all public knowledge; don't you have any operatives on Grafton?"

Croft, remembering the images of the dead operatives, said, "We have some, ah, holes in our surveillance network."

Annie was about to reply but suddenly frowned as a groundcar pulled up in front of the ranch. Her hand instinctively snaked down to one of her pearl handled pistols. She wasn't expecting guests.

She was silent, watching, as a man in blue denim with his right arm in a sling stepped out of the car. Seeing Annie, he nodded respectfully, keeping his good arm well away from his holstered weapon.

The newcomer turned to Croft. "You Croft?" he asked gruffly.

Croft nodded. "You must be Tallas Carper."

The man nodded.

"What happened to your arm?" Croft asked.

"I scratched it," said Carper, suddenly giving Croft an unexpectedly hateful glare.

"Well, the cavalry is here," said Croft. "Thanks for the drink, and the information, Annie."

"You barely touched your drink," said Annie wryly. "Feel free to give John another try when he gets back."

"I may do that," said Croft.

As she entered the house Croft turned to face his team.

"So now that we're all together, what do we do?" Tane asked.

"I think the most obvious thing to do is to pay Mr. Quandry a visit," said Croft.

"I don't think he likes off-worlders," said Tane. "That may not be very safe for us."

"Then it's a good thing that the Chief cleverly had us disguise ourselves as Graftonites."

Carper snorted.

The Clapper clapped.

"What's with him?" Carper asked, giving the Clapper a sharp glance.

"He has enthusiasm," says Croft. "Shall we go?"

Chapter 3: The Face of the Enemy

They tapped into one of the local online information networks (for a fee, of course--nothing was free on Grafton II), and quickly discovered that Quandry was holding a Great Gathering on a ranch in the middle of the continent the following day. It was too far to go by groundcar, so they had to rent passage on a private transport. With a maximum of prodding, Carper located a transport they could rent. Croft steeled himself for the outrageous price they had to pay and simply billed it to one of the Column's unmarked accounts, but he knew he'd have a lot of explaining to do to the Chief afterwards. What kind of spy had he become when he had to spend half his time filling out and justifying billing forms?

During the trip out Croft tried to size Carper up. He studiously avoided eye contact with all of them, finding a bulkhead much more interesting to stare at. He also defied all of Tane's attempt to start a conversation with him.

"So, what do you normally do for a living?" said Tane.

Carper glared at her. She timidly stared back. When it became obvious that she wasn't going to look away, he said, "I answer stupid questions."

"I'm just trying to be friendly," said Tane.

"Be anything you like," said Carper generously.

Tane looked at the cast on his arm. "Does your injury hurt you?" said Tane.

Carper turned to face her. "What are you implying, sheep?" he said his voice cold. His good hand strayed close to his holster.

Tane started to tremble. "I… I…"

"Are you saying I'm weak?"

"No, most certainly not!" said Tane.

Carper relaxed his good arm, and some of the tension seemed to evaporate.

"Are we paying extra for attitude?" Croft asked.

Carper turned to glare at him now.

"The only reason I'm asking is, because if we are, I'm happy to say we're getting our money's worth," said Croft.

It was a very long and quiet trip in the transport after that.

When they touched down in a small, private clearing, they rented a groundcar. They drove to an estate of a wealthy rancher who was permitting Quandry to use his estate for the Grand Meeting.

"As it is a Grand Meeting, or Great Gathering, as it is sometimes called, there could be anywhere from 100 to 500 people here," said Tane, as they entered a small stadium on the grounds.

"Doesn't sound so large," said Croft.

"On a world of only eight million, with such rugged individualists, it's considered significant," said Tane.

The bleachers filled up rapidly. They looked for seats.

"Watch it, sheep," said a Graftonite, pushing past Croft.

Croft checked his anger, probably saving his own life. He saw some available seats and went for them, but by the time he got there another Graftonite walked right in front of him and sat down. "You're blocking the view, sheep," said the Graftonite, staring at him.

They eventually found seating on the upper edges of the bleachers. As they sat down a pair of Graftonites sitting in front of them turned around and looked distastefully at them. "I didn't know they allowed your kind here, sheep."

Croft looked at his denim clothes, and turned to Tane and muttered, "This disguise is working really, really well."

Just how were the Graftonites able to determine that they were off-worlders just by looking at them? Croft resolved to find out.

He tapped the man in front of him on the shoulder.

That was a mistake. The man whipped around, his blaster pointed at Croft.

No one spoke for a moment. The man waited for Croft to draw. Croft slowly raised his hands and gave a watery smile.

"You got a death wish, sheep?" said the Graftonite.

"I just want to know what makes you think we're off-worlders," said Croft.

The man snorted, shook his head, and turned around to face forward.

Croft looked at his companions; Tane looked frightened out of her wits; the Clapper looked idiotically content; and Carper looked like he wished he were somewhere, anywhere else.

In a few minutes the bleachers were filled. Croft took a quick count of the audience; there were well over 1000 people there. Maybe Annie Oakley had underestimated Quandry's appeal.

A tall, dark haired man with a scar running down the side of his face stepped out into the arena, flanked by several guards. He had a blaster on one hip and a slicer strapped on the other. His image was amplified on holograms projected above and around the arena.

Croft recognized him immediately. It was none other than Mo Quandry. Quandry stood there for a moment, boldly basking in the attention of the crowd.

Immediately, there were wild cheers from the audience. The cheering went on for a while, until Quandry gestured with his hands for it to subside. Reluctantly, the audience went silent.

"Thank you, my friends," said Quandry. "As many of you know, I'm a man of action, not words, so let us get down to business. By now you have all seen the following."

The large floating holograms suddenly showed a grainy side street. A Graftonite could be seen standing there, in the middle of the conversation.

"You can't be serious," said the Graftonite. "I delivered on my end of the contract. Now you pay up."

"I'm afraid I can only afford to pay half," said the man the Graftonite was speaking to. While the Graftonite's features could clearly be seen, the other man was largely off camera-- only his hands and body could be seen.

"That's not acceptable," said the Graftonite.

"I was afraid you might say that," said the man.

Suddenly, the image they were watching panned wide to show the image of blasters poking out of several surrounding buildings. They discharged almost simultaneously, even as the Graftonite was drawing his weapon.

The Graftonite fell to the ground, his eyes open, as blood dripped from his body. Dark boots walked by his face.

"If I had known Graftonites worked so cheaply, I would have hired more of you," the figure chuckled.

There were screams and roars in the arena as the image faded. It took Quandry several minutes to quiet them down far enough so that he could be heard over the amplification system.

"You see!" he yelled. "They didn't even give him a chance! That's the way the sheep fight!"

He was greeted by more yelling and jeers.

"But now see how we fight!"

A new holographic image appeared, that of Graftonites running and shooting in a different setting. Dimly, Croft guessed that these must be scenes of the invasion of Grafton IV. The Graftonites there didn't have the accelerated reflexes of their cousins on Grafton II. But they did have a substantial standing army. How did these Graftonites conquer the planet so easily?

The answer wasn't forthcoming from the holo that was being showed. Graftonites jumped and shot and ran rapidly, moving almost too quickly for the holo to record. But what they were shooting at and what the overall tactical position was couldn't be determined. The images were also put together from small clips, making it difficult to clearly see the larger picture. Intentionally so?

But the clips served their purpose.

"See what happens when we unite, when we take the fight to the sheep!" said Quandry.

There was a thunderous applause.

"There will be no more jobs for piddling fees, no more exploitation of our labor!"

There was more applause. The Clapper, unable to restrain himself, started joining in.

"We took Grafton IV like it was an apple waiting to be plucked!" said Quandry.

The crowd roared again.

"But never let it be said that we do not seek peace," said Quandry.

The crowd was silent, expectant.

"I propose a new... paradigm for dealing with other planets."

There was widespread laughter at Quandry's use of the word paradigm.

"Since we are stronger, more equipped, and yes, superior, in every way, to other planets, we will suggest to each inhabited planet that they pay us a... fee, a fee for protection," said Quandry.

The crowd roared with approval, clapping wildly. So did the Clapper.

"If a planet peacefully pays its assessed fee every year, we too will leave them in peace," said Quandry. "But if they do not, they will feel our wrath!"

The crowd roared.

In a room deep inside the stadium, a group of Graftonites looked at the monitors.

"Where?" said one of the Graftonites, the one in charge. His name was Janson Rocco, and he was Mo Quandry's chief of staff.

"I had it a moment ago," said one of the Graftonite security men, panning the image across the stadium bleachers. Suddenly, he saw what he was looking for, and stopped the panning. "There!"

The image showed Croft, Tane, and the Clapper, sitting around other Graftonites. To an uneducated eye, the image didn't look odd, especially when everyone was clapping. But it was when everyone stopped clapping that the oddness became apparent--the Clapper didn't stop clapping.

"Sheep, sir," the security man reported.

Rocco snapped his fingers. "I want them removed."

"Alive?" The security man inquired.

"At least one of them, yes, for questioning," said Rocco.

"Do you care which one?" said the security man.

"Not really," said Rocco, turning away.

Two men suddenly materialized on either side of Croft and his team. "You will come with us."

The other Graftonites in the audience, who were still listening to Quandry, turned to give Croft a withering stare.

"Did we sit in reserved seats?" said Croft, giving a little smile.

"I'm not going to ask again, sheep," said the Graftonite coldly.

Croft looked over at Carper, who was carefully looking away. Perhaps their bodyguard, with only one good arm, didn't feel fast enough to take on two of his countrymen. Were they going to be taken to a quiet place to be killed? Possible, but unlikely. The Graftonites didn't seem to go in for the subtle approach. If they wanted him dead, they could shoot him right here. The other Graftonites would probably applause such a move. No, they were probably wanted for interrogation. That didn't sound very good either, but their options were limited. Croft knew he could never outdraw a Graftonite, much less two of them. All right, they would play along, for now.

Nodding, Croft got up. Tane, the Clapper, and Carper followed.

They were led to a small room without windows where a serious looking Graftonite awaited them. They weren't disarmed, which only half surprised Croft. After all, the Graftonites would probably love it if they tried to draw their weapons. The two Graftonites stood guard behind them, undoubtedly silently hoping for this turn of events.

"Who are you?" asked the Graftonite behind the desk. It was Rocco, Quandry's chief of staff.

"My, ah, name is Clifford Toft," said Croft. "I'm from Regular."

"The truth, sheep," said Rocco, in bored tones.

"All right," said Croft, giving Tane a I-told-you-so look. "My name really is Clifford Toft. I'm leading a special diplomatic envoy from the League."

"You've got some nerve showing up here. What are you doing here?"

"Assessing the situation," said Croft. That seemed to be what a diplomat would say, right? He was abruptly aware that if the man behind the desk didn't like his answers, he wouldn't leave the room alive.

"Assessing..." said Rocco, looking away as if he were thinking, weighing options, alternatives. Croft felt as if the decision came out the wrong way, he would be dead.

Rocco turned back to Croft. "And what have you assessed so far?"

"Um," said Croft, not sure how much leeway he had to lie, even for a diplomat. "I was... impressed that Mo Quandry is looking for a peaceful solution."

Rocco gave Croft a cynical stare. He considered for a moment longer. Then he nodded. "All right," he said. He snapped his fingers. His guards opened the door.

"Is that 'all right, you can go?' or 'all right, shoot them'?" said Croft.

"I think you'll find out when you get outside that door," said Rocco. "Now get out of here and hope we never meet again."

Croft got up slowly. "How can I hope we never meet again if I don't know who I just met?"

"The name is Janson Rocco. I'm Mr. Quandry's chief of staff," said Rocco.

"Really? Could you arrange a meeting with Mr. Quandry?" said Croft.

Rocco chuckled. "The only time you and Quandry will meet is if he shows up at your funeral. Now get out of here before I change my mind."

Croft nodded, slowly leaving. But he noticed that Rocco gave Carper a disproving stare as they left.

After they had left, one of the security men said, "What shall we do, boss? Shall we tell Mr. Quandry-"

"You will tell Mr. Quandry nothing!" Rocco snapped. "I don't pay you to talk."

"Yes sir."

"I will tell Mo what needs to be told. For now, simply follow them. There's something not quite right about that so-called diplomatic envoy."

Croft drove the groundcar off the grounds of the ranch. "We'll never be in danger," said Croft, his voice in a whiny imitation of Tane's. "We'll pass for Graftonites. No one will figure out who we are."

Carper chuckled.

Tane reddened. "It was the Chief's idea," she said.

"And you assured me it would work," said Croft. "It almost got us killed."

"I don't understand how they recognized us as being off-worlders," said Tane.

"Well, maybe we should ask an on-worlder," said Croft. "How were we recognized?"

There was silence in the groundcar. Croft carefully pulled over to the side of the road and turned to Carper. "I'm talking to you."

Carper gave Croft a withering look. "It should be obvious, even to a sheep."

Croft kept his anger in check. "You're an employee; answer the question, em-ploy-ee," he said, purposefully dragging out the last word.

Carper's face darkened, and anger flared in his eyes. He didn't speak for a moment, but when he did, his voice was soft. "It should be obvious. It's everything. It's the moron with the idiotic expression on his face. It's you and the woman with your defeatist body language and feeble expressions."

"If I'm translating this correctly, then, we don't act arrogant enough to be Graftonites," said Croft. "Hm, where did I go wrong?"

Tane said, "There are probably subconscious facial cues embedded in the Graftonite culture-"

"Shut up, Tane," said Croft. "The only thing that matters is the end result, which is that our cover is blown."

"We still have our secondary cover as diplomats," said Tane, not showing any offense.

"Somehow I don't get the impressions that these guys put much weight in the concept of diplomatic immunity," said Croft.

"Then why did they let us go?" Tane asked.

"I don't know," said Croft. "Maybe they're not ready to create a bigger diplomatic incident by killing a League diplomat."

"From Quandry's announcement, it sounds like he's ready to blackmail the League for a major cash infusion," said Tane.

"Yes, that's how it appeared, didn't it?" said Croft. "Or maybe he was just saying what they wanted to hear, to drum up more support for his cause. And that's not the only thing."

"What do you mean?" Tane asked.

"Isn't it curious that this incident with the murdered Graftonite seems tailor made for Quandry's purposes?" said Croft.

"Well, bounty hunters do get killed, even Graftonite ones," said Tane.

"Yes, but seldom in a way calculated to incur maximum ire among the Graftonites, and seldom is it conveniently recorded on a holodisk," said Croft. "Did you notice anything else unusual about that holoshow?"

"What do you mean, unusual?"

"Have a look," said Croft, producing his own holoprojector. He had had the sense of mind to record the event as it unfolded. Now it produced a smaller version of the shooting they had seen in the stadium.

* * * * * * * * * * * * * * * * * * *

A quarter mile back down the road…..

"What are they doing?" asked one of the Graftonites with the field glasses.

"Just sitting there, in the ground car," said the other.

"Just sitting there?"

"Yeeeep."

* * * * * * * * * * * * * * * * * * *

Another quarter mile farther back….

"What are they doing?" said one of the agents.

"The Graftonites tailing them are just sitting there, watching Croft, who is also just sitting there."

"Just sitting there?"

"Da."

* * * * * * * * * * * * * * * * * * *

The holorecording of the execution of the Graftonite Rel Cadwalader finished playing in the groundcar.

"Well?" said Croft, turning to Tane.

"Well what?" said Tane.

"The Chief said you were good," said Croft.

"Stop taunting me and tell me what you think you see," Tane snapped.

"Watch." Croft slowly replayed the events, providing the commentary.

"Here we clearly see Cadwalader's face... then the camera pans directly left... but for some reason we only see the body of his employer, not the face. If the camera went left, how did the head get lopped out of the picture? Now watch as the camera pans out to show the blasters appearing." The image replayed. "Do you see it?"

"See what?"

"There's no way a camera positioned in such a way to catch Cadwalader could also pan the entire alley. It would have had to capture areas outside of its view, or be able to see through walls," said Croft. He moved the replay forward again, to show the body of Cadwalader on the ground, and the black boots standing by the fallen Graftonite's face. "Isn't it convenient that the security cam panned down once again, so that we couldn't see the face of the attacker?"

"Maybe the security cam was a multitasking unit that took a variety of pictures, and those were the images that Quandry selected."

"Why? Why would Quandry purposely obscure the pictures of Cadwalader's employer and attackers?"

"I don't know," said Tane.

"And how do you explain the wide angle shot?"

"It could be from another camera."

"It... could... be... from... another... camera...," said Croft, slowly and derisively, like a mentally retarded person.

"Obviously, you disagree," said Tane coldly.

"Obviously," said Croft. He closed his eyes, and reclined his head.

"What are you doing?"

"Thinking," said Croft. He opened them again. "We've got to dig some more into this."

"Why?"

Croft ignored the question. "But before we do, we have one last matter to deal with." And he was looking at Carper as he said it.

Carper showed no visible reaction.

"We were confronted by two Graftonites in the stadium today," said Croft. "And you didn't lift a finger to protect us."

"Why would I?" said Carper, looking angry and puzzled at the same time.

"Hm, I don't know, maybe because we're paying you to?" said Croft.

"That's not what I was hired for," said Carper.

"Really?" said Croft. "What exactly were you hired for?"

Carper shrugged. "To be a guide."

"To... be... a... guide," said Croft, in that same slow, derisive tone he had formerly reserved for Tane. "Tane? You made the arrangements to hire him, didn't you?"

"Y-yes."

"Well?" said Croft.

"Well, what?"

"What terms did you hire him under?" Croft asked.

"He, um, was hired to guide us," said Tane. "But I presumed he would also protect-"

Croft interrupted her. "Tane, have you ever heard the old saying, when you PRESUME, you PRE-pare our SUM-mary execution?" Without waiting for a response, he turned to Carper. "All right, how much would it cost to hire you for what we really hired you for?"

"For what?"

"Bodyguard," said Croft promptly.

"Five hundred thousand."

"Five hundred thousand?" said Croft, disbelievingly.

"Five hundred thousand a day," said Carper.

"Five hundred thousand a day," said Croft, in a mocking tone.

"Payable in advance," Carper added.

"Oh, that goes without saying," said Croft, in an even more mocking tone. He paused, choosing his next words carefully. "Isn't that a bit above market rates, even for Grafton?"

"I don't think so," said Carper. "Given the anti off-worlder sentiment, I don't think you'll be able to hire anyone else on Grafton."

"But you know full well we're not going to pay you half a million credits per day."

"Yes," said Carper, giving an unfriendly smile.

"Then… why?"

"Because you're sheep," said Carper. "I don't like you. And I certainly don't want to protect you."

"Then why are you working for us at all?"

Carper raised his bandaged arm. "My last job knocked me out of commission for a few weeks. This is easy money."

"Easy money," said Croft. What was he being paid for, if not to protect them? "You've been paid for the entire week in advance?"

"Yes."

"Consider the next six days a gift," said Croft. "Get out of the car."

Carper stared at Croft. "Drop me off back at the transport."

"No, Croft!" said Tane. "The ch-" she broke off, looking at Carper. "The boss said we had to keep him on."

"We'll see about that," said Croft.

* * * * * * * * * * * * * * * * * * *

"Of course you have to keep him on," said the Chief. "He's a local, he knows the situation on the ground." The holo of her image scowled at him. Croft had rented a few rooms at a nearby ranch for the night (at skyhigh rates, of course) and was now duly reporting to the Chief.

"He's also hostile, and won't lift a finger to help us," said Croft.

"Croft, you look at everything in black and white. He may be a little antagonistic, but he can also be a source of information," said the Chief.

"I'm not keeping him on, he's just as liable to shoot me in the back."

"You are keeping him on, unless you want to be recalled immediately and subject to court martial!" she said, glaring at him.

Court martial? What did she think this was, the military? More IQ problems at the top. But Croft resisted the impulse to comment. The moment passed.

"What else do you have to report?"

"I think there's something fishy about that holovid of Cadwalader's death."

"So? What implication could that have?"

"I'm not sure, until I investigate more."

"I think your time would be better spent meeting with local opinion leaders and gauging Quandry's level of support."

"Isn't that something that the real embassy staff can do?"

"The real embassy staff are holed up in their embassy, afraid to come out. This is a job for you, Croft."

Croft sighed. "All right."

"Anything else?"

"One thing. Your orders that we pose as Graftonite hasn't worked. Not a single person has been fooled."

"A tribute to your skill as an infiltrator, I suppose," she said.

"You have a nice day," said Croft, cutting the contact. He frowned for a moment, as if listening to empty air. Then he walked silently to the door, and then quickly opened it. Tane came tumbling in, as if she had been standing by the door.

"So I guess there's no need for me to reiterate our orders," said Croft dryly.

"We're to interview local opinion leaders," said Tane.

"Yes," said Croft. "Starting with friends and relatives of Cadwalader."

"Croft, we're supposed to focus on opinion leaders."

"Who's to say that they aren't opinion leaders?"

Chapter 4: The Tragic Story of Rel Cadwalader

"Get me the station chief," Croft said irritably, staring into the small comm unit.

"The Chief is busy at the moment," said the operative at the other end. "Can I take a message, Mr..... er,"

"Croft. Clifford Croft. Level One agent," Croft.

"You're one of the eight?" said the operative. "I'm sorry, sir, just a moment."

"Bureaucrats," Croft snorted. He had been trying for the past 20 minutes to get through to someone in a position of authority at the Column branch on the planet Whenfor. Tane had done a little research and discovered surprisingly little about the death of Rel Cadwalader, but she had managed to find out that he had been killed while on a mission on Whenfor.

The station chief appeared on the comm. Croft identified himself and repeated his request. "And I need this done ASAP."

"I'm sorry, Mr. Croft, but we're a little shorthanded at the moment-"

Croft peered around the image of the station chief to see the people in the background. "Is that Preston? Get me Preston."

"Mr. Preston is preparing for-"

"Now," said Croft, in a low voice.

Preston shortly appeared on the screen. "Hey, Croftie, what's happening?"

"Preston, I need some information quickly," said Croft. "I need you to find out everything you can about the death of one Rel Cadwalader."

"Cliff, I'm on a stakeout that starts tomorrow-"

"Which dovetails perfectly with my needs because I need results by tomorrow," said Croft. "This is important, Preston."

Preston sighed, then nodded.

"Good. I'm downloading a holo and some other information which might be useful," said Croft, pressing a button. "Can you also do some digging through the Grafton database network as well?"

Preston shook his head. "I certainly won't have time for that. Why don't you ask the Database Espionage division?"

"Because by the time I get all the proper approvals-" Croft caught himself in mid-sentence. "Wait a minute, I have an idea. Croft out." He terminated the contact, and started another.

The irritated face of Levi Esherkol appeared on the screen. In the background could be seen bright sunshine, and a grill. Levi wore his white chef's hat.

"Who bothering me now-" he started to say, but then his growl turned into a smile. "Croft! How did accelerant work?"

"Much as I'm delighted to be your first human test subject, Levi, I haven't had the opportunity to try it yet," said Croft. "I'll try not to test it near the edge of any rooftops," he added, remembering what had happened to that errant chimp.

"Um," said Levi, turning to flip some burgers on his grill.

"Hard at work, I see," said Croft.

"I work hard, I deserve break," said Levi philosophically.

"Well, it's good that I'm catching you when you're just coming off a break, because I need a favor," said Croft.

"Did you get those Grafton meat recipes I ask for?"

"I'll have them right after you do a little digging into the Graftonite network," said Croft.

"I a chemist, not a-"

"Computer expert. Electronics experts, physics expert, mechanical engineering expert," said Croft. "I'll keep the list short because we're both busy. You know as well as I that you're a genius in every kind of science. You're so smart that you complete a full day of work for the Column in a matter of minutes, which is why you have so much time to putter about with your food. The only thing that puzzles me is why a brilliant mind like yours is obsessed with cooking."

"Cooking, good cooking, hardest thing of all," said Levi, applying a pinch of unidentified seasoning to the burgers. "I have to work on the mashed potatoes soon, can get to point?"

"I need you to tap into the Grafton network and find out everything you can about the late Rel Cadwalader."

"Late? You kill?"

"No, I didn't get there in time to do the honors," said Croft. "He died a particularly suspicious death."

"What am looking for?"

"Anything suspicious."

"Um," said Levi, turning again to apply the seasoning. A fire leapt up out of the grill, forcing him to move some of the burgers to the edge of the grill. Obviously, Croft had bumped up against the limits of the cook's attention span.

"Levi?"

No response.

"Levi!"

"Yes?" said the cook

"Did I mention I need this by tomorrow?" said Croft.

"Uh...."

"Thank you, Levi," said Croft, disconnecting.

He turned to find Tane standing patiently in the background. "Now, who can honestly say the Column is dysfunctional?" said Croft.

"We're supposed to be checking with local opinion leaders," said Tane.

"And so we shall," said Croft. "Have you set up that appointment with that Anderson fellow?"

"Yes, he's agreed to meet us," said Tane.

"How nice," said Croft.

"Well, you know how people here feel about off-worlders. It's amazing that anybody's willing to meet us," said Tane. "Still, as the publisher of one of Grafton's largest news services, perhaps he's a forward-thinking journalist."

"We can only hope," said Croft, his tone betraying his distinct lack of interest. "Shall we collect our baggage and go?"

"Baggage?" said Tane.

Croft opened the bedroom door, and the Clapper, a big smile on his face, rushed out, clapping vigorously.

They were able to take the groundcar to their destination, the home of the Cargon Press Syndicate. Carper knew the way there so he drove, but Croft kept a wary eye on him.

When they arrived, Croft was surprised by the strong layer of security they had to pass through--the whole building was fenced off, there were not one but four guards at the front gate, and an ugly turret, presumably for air defense, protruded from the roof. However, much to Croft's surprise, neither he nor Carper were disarmed. Croft guessed that on Grafton, politeness was more important than security.

Before they entered the building, Croft nodded to the Clapper. The Clapper gave a wide, idiotic, ingratiating smile.

* * * * * * * * * * * * * * * * * * *

Several hours earlier, Croft had come into the Clapper's bedroom. He had been smart enough to get separate bedrooms for each of them; it was well worth the expense to get a solid night's sleep away from the nearly constant clapping.

"I need your help," said Croft.

"Help?" said the Clapper, looking puzzled.

"Have you wondered why I brought you on this mission?" Croft asked.

"Why you brought me?" said the Clapper, like a parrot.

"It wasn't just for your conversational skills," said Croft.

"You like talking to me?" said the Clapper, breaking out into a great grin as he clapped again.

"Yes, it's great fun, especially with all the applause," said Croft. "But what I really need is an edge over these Graftonites, if I'm forced to fight one."

"You have Grafton man for that (clap clap)," said the Clapper.

"No, Grafton man isn't going to (clap clap) help," said Croft, imitating the Clapper as a way of peacefully venting his frustration. "But you are going to help."

"I am?" said the Clapper, surprised by the concept.

"You are a telekinetic," said Croft.

"Te-le-k-"

"No, don't try to pronounce it again, just leave the multisyllabic words and other heavy lifting to me," said Croft. "But it's occurred to me that if you can move objects, that you can also move people."

The Clapper considered. Then he nodded.

"If a Graftonite attacks me, or is about to attack me, I want you to move him."

"Move him?"

"Push him to the ground. Knock him off balance," said Croft.

The Clapper looked puzzled.

"Anything to give me an edge. I can never be as fast as they are, but if you knock them off-balance at a crucial time, that could give me the edge I need. Do you understand?"

The Clapper gave a broad smile.

"I hope you understand, and you're not just giving an idiotic smile," said Croft. "Because if an assassin gets me, can you guess who he's going to go after next?"

The Clapper considered this one... "Uh... the talking lady?"

"Before the talking lady."

"Other Grafton?"

"Before the other Grafton."

The Clappers grin faded. "Me?"

"Clap Clap!" Croft clapped twice.

* * * * * * * * * * * * * * * * * *

They entered the building housing the Cargon Press Syndicate. There was an armed guard at nearly every turn in the corridor. Croft wondered why there was a need for such heavy security. This was a press organization, not a bank.

He was still puzzling over this as they were led into Tolbar Anderson's office. He was a tall, bearded man with thinning hair. Like every other Graftonite, he wore a blaster, of course.

"Mr. Toft, sit down," said Anderson. "It's so nice to meet an off-worlder."

Tane, in setting up the interview, had used their "diplomatic envoy" persona.

"I'm surprised to hear you say that," said Croft. "I didn't think off-worlders were especially welcome right about now."

"Well, some people may feel that way, but one thing you learn on Grafton is that there's no unanimity of opinion," said Anderson. "We're too individualistic to agree on anything in very large numbers."

"That's part of the reason I'm here," said Croft. "I'm trying to gauge the level of support that Mr. Quandry has."

"It's hard to tell, we don't usually take opinion polls," said Anderson. "They're too dangerous."

"Dangerous?" said Croft.

"People don't like being annoyed with pesky questions around here, Mr. Toft," said Anderson. "I imagine you have holo marketers on your planet?"

"Well, those of us with listed numbers do," said Croft. He didn't have enough down-time at home to experience it personally; nor was his number listed. But he knew the practice of unsolicited holo marketing existed; banks of holomarketers worked 25 hours a day, calling to sell their piles of worthless junk. Holomarketing was very irritating, and numerous laws were passed against it; but that didn't slow the industry one bit.

"Just as we have no polling, we don't have unsolicited marketing on Grafton," said Anderson. "Most people will simply ignore an unsolicited contact, but then you've got your deadly 10% to worry about."

"The deadly 10%?"

"Not a precise figure," said Anderson. "But it represents the fraction of the population who will feel strongly enough to shoot the solicitor."

"Even holosolicitors?" said Croft. "What do they do, shoot the offending hologram?"

Anderson took a deep breath. "No, they trace the offending call, go down to the offices, and execute one or more of the salespeople. It's really put a crimp on the unsolicited marketing business."

"I can imagine," said Croft. "So you have the same problem with polling?"

"To a lesser degree. Polling doesn't irritate people as much as unsolicited sales pitches, but every so often you run across an angry Grafton, and, well-"

"What about solicitations from beggars?" said Croft suddenly.

"Beggers?"

"Your poor?"

"There are no poor people on Grafton, Mr. Toft," said Anderson. "If someone's poor-"

"They shouldn't come to Grafton, yes, I think I've heard that before," said Croft. "But what if someone happens to be a poor Graftonite?"

"A poor Graftonite?" said Anderson. "What do you mean?"

"Poor. No credits," said Croft. Didn't Anderson know the meaning of the word?

"Oh, that kind of poor," said Anderson, brightening. "I thought you were referring to marksmanship. No, we don't have that kind of poor on Grafton."

"You mean because you have a social safety net, welfare payments-"

Anderson gave a short laugh. "Mr. Toft, we have virtually no government, so we certainly have no payments as you describe. No, if a Graftonite is poor, he gets a job. Usually, if he's a good shot, he gets a job in our traditional export industries--bounty hunting, repossessing important objects, people removal, etcetera etcetera."

"What if he's not a good shot?" said Croft.

"Then he might get a job in our small business community," said Anderson. "Not all of us are gunmen by trade, you know."

"What if he can't get a job in your small business community? I'm surprised your lack of a social welfare system hasn't caused people to turn to crime."

"No, Mr. Croft, we don't even need police for that, the poor don't turn to crime," said Anderson.

"Why not?"

"If a Graftonite is a good shot, he can easily get a job in one of our traditional lines of work. If he's a bad shot and tries to steal from one of his fellow citizens, he'll quickly be killed," said Anderson. "The good marksmen can make more money working off-planet, and they know it. The bad marksmen won't live very long if they try to steal from the good marksmen, and they know it. It's a perfect system that leaves our society almost crime free."

"So what happens to the poor, bad marksmen?" Croft wanted to know.

Anderson gave a cold smile. "They often attempt to do something beyond their means."

There was an awkward pause for a moment. Then Croft tactfully changed the subject. "So your journalists must be from that other category, people who have turned to business and who aren't, as, ah-" he was unsure how to phrase it without causing offense.

But Anderson, understanding his meaning immediately, gave a big laugh. "You needn't worry, Mr. Toft, I don't get offended easily. But you're totally wrong; our journalists aren't gunmen who can't cut it; quite the opposite, we only employ journalists from the top ranks of our marksmen community."

"Why? Why would you need to?" Croft asked.

"Because-," Anderson stopped. "I keep forgetting. You have, I believe they are called, libel laws on your League planets, correct?"

Croft nodded.

"So if the press publishes something objectionable, a person may sue in court to seek recompense, correct?"

"Something like that."

"Well, we don't have any courts on Grafton."

"No courts?" said Croft, surprised. "Oh--you have no government, so I guess that follows."

"Correct. So since we have no way of pursuing legal remedies against reckless journalists-"

"You kill them," said Croft, immediately understanding. "The writers. That's why you have such tight security here."

Anderson nodded. "You never know when someone will get ticked off by an article. One time many years ago someone came in here, guns blazing, demanding to know who did the weather. Didn't like our forecasts."

"What did you do?"

"I shot him," said Anderson. "But only in the leg. He was obviously mentally deranged. His family had him shipped off-planet to an asylum, I believe." Anderson paused. "But as you see we have to be very careful of what we write about."

"So sensitive topics have to be covered by your best gunmen?" Croft asked.

"No, the degree of sensitivity is not the most important factor," said Anderson. "The most important thing is who we're going to write about. If we're writing about someone who doesn't have a reputation, we'll assign that to one of our junior journalists. But if we're writing about, say, one of our Olympic marksmen, we'll only give that to a senior columnist, or perhaps even our managing editor, if the subject of the article is a silver medalist or above."

"I see," said Croft. "I guess that aggressive journalism isn't exactly the order of the day."

"Not at all! People wouldn't subscribe to our database if we weren't aggressive," said Anderson. "But we pick our fights."

"Meaning you only cover those who aren't good shots."

"I wouldn't put it as blatantly as that, but there is something to what you say," Anderson admitted.

"So, how did you cover the death of Rel Cadwalader?" Croft asked.

Anderson grimaced. "Is that what you're really here to talk about? How did you know?" He looked from Croft's face to Tane, to the Clapper, to Carper, and back to Croft again.

"Know what?" said Croft, looking puzzled.

"Then you don't know," said Anderson. "If so, it's just a funny coincidence you came here to talk to us. Though I heard that some of the other press syndicates had the same problem."

"What problem?"

"The family said they didn't mind us writing about what had happened to their son. But when we started digging for details, we got the word."

"The word?"

"Don't," said Anderson.

"So the family told you not to investigate?" said Croft. "Does Cadwalader come from a family of marksmen?"

"The request didn't come from the family," said Anderson uneasily.

"Anything you say here is strictly confidential," Croft assured him.

"Well, it doesn't really matter if you know, as long as it doesn't get around that it came from me," said Anderson.

"You have my assurance it won't," said Croft.

"It was Mo Quandry," said Anderson immediately. "You have probably heard of him."

"I've heard the name, somewhere," said Croft. "Why did this Quandry care what you wrote about Cadwalader?" said Croft. "Did Cadwalader work for him?"

"No. There was no direct connection between the two. That was one of the things we wanted to look into. Understand,

Mr. Croft, that off-planet deaths at the hands of sh-, begging your pardon, one of your kind, is pretty rare. That piqued our curiosity enough to investigate the matter. But Quandry shut us down. Said if we looked into it any more he'd send one of his Olympic marksmen after us. He has gold medalists working for him. We took him seriously."

"Huh," said Croft. "What do you think he's really up to?"

Anderson shrugged. "There's obviously something about the death he wants to keep quiet. Maybe there's some details about it that would prove embarrassing to him."

"Such as?"

"I don't know," said Anderson, shrugging. "Right now we're too busy working on other articles to investigate further. We're working on a great human interest piece right now about a former silver medalist who's gone past his prime."

"Coincidentally, the target of that article won't be someone who can shoot back at you."

"Not very effectively," Anderson grinned. "And now, my time is quite limited. I wish you well, I really do." He stood up suggestively to signify that the interview was over.

Croft thanked him and got up to go.

"Mr. Toft?"

Croft turned around.

"One last parting piece of advice. Do you plan to live a long life?"

Croft considered. "I hope to."

"Would you like some advice for staying alive?"

"If it's good advice."

"If you want to live, get off Grafton."

Croft raised an eyebrow.

"Don't get me wrong, I'm not threatening you," said Anderson. "It's Quandry. He's stirring people up. There's no telling what will happen to off-worlders when things explode."

Croft touched his blue denim. "But I'm traveling incognito."

Anderson laughed and showed him to the door.

As they drove back to their lodging, Croft said, "All right, what did we learn?"

The Clapper clapped.

"Ok, you learned a new rhythm," said Croft. "Sylvia?"

Tane said, "I don't think we learned anything about Quandry's level of support."

"But we did learn that he's hiding something about the death of Cadwalader."

"That's off-profile for our mission," said Tane. "We should be focusing on who we will interview next."

"Good! While you're doing that, I'll check in with Preston and Levi."

Croft called them the following morning. He spoke to Preston first.

"Well?"

"There's no police report," said Preston.

"No police report?" Croft frowned.

"We located the alley where the incident happened, based on the holo you sent. No one in the area claimed to witness the incident or even hear the sound of blaster fire."

"They could be lying, they probably don't want to get involved," said Croft.

"Possibly," said Preston. "But I also did a quick forensics sweep of the crime scene. There was no sign of blaster fire."

"Are you sure?"

"There's no sign of blaster fire in the area around the incident," said Preston definitively. "If the marksmen only hit Cadwalader, that would make sense. But if any stray energy bolts missed, and hit the walls around him, there should be residual scorch marks."

"A Graftonite marksman might not miss his target."

"But supposedly the ones who killed Cadwalader were ordinary people," said Preston.

"Supposedly," said Croft. He paused, then said, "What did you dig up on Cadwalader's employer?"

"Nothing," said Preston.

"Nothing?"

"Nothing I could find in a day," said Preston.

"So let me get this straight. Nobody saw anything; nobody heard anything, there's no police report, no sign even of a firefight, and no sign of Cadwalader's employer. Your conclusion?" Preston wasn't a genius of course, not even in Croft's league, but he was one of the few people level headed enough that Croft at least listened to.

"One possibility is that whoever killed him was so powerful, so connected, that they were able to cover up a murder without leaving any traces."

"But not so powerful or smart since they overlooked a holorecorder," said Croft.

"I couldn't even find any sign of a holorecorder in the area," said Preston. "Perhaps the killer taped the execution as a warning to others."

"Or perhaps Cadwalader wasn't killed," said Croft. "Perhaps Quandry staged this event to stir up the Graftonites and gain support for his agenda."

"That's the other possibility," said Preston.

"That's what I'm starting to think," said Croft slowly.

"So what do you do?" said Preston.

"I find Cadwalader."

"That sounds dangerous," said Preston. "I mean, he's a Graftonite. What happens if you find him and he's not in a friendly mood?"

"I'll tickle him," said Croft. "Thanks, Pres."

"Be careful, Croft," said Preston. "These Graftonites are really quick."

"Quick witted?" said Croft, raising an eyebrow. "I don't think so. Worry about them, not me. Croft out." He pressed a button, terminating the link, and then made another call.

All Croft saw was a big cloud of steam, making him wonder if he had connected properly. But in seconds the hissing steam cleared, showing Levi pouring something into a large pot.

"Levi," said Croft.

"Eh?" said Levi, looking up. "Why you always call when I cooking?"

"Maybe because you're... always cooking," said Croft. "What did you find out?"

"Did not tell me I would have to infiltrate private networks," said Levi.

"Private, public, what difference does it make?" said Croft.

"No public data networks on Grafton. Many private. Had to break into several of them. Only gave me one day."

"Let me guess, it took you two hours," said Croft.

Levi shook his head, as he sprinkled something into the pot. "Only one hour; what you think I am, retarded?"

Croft sighed. "Levi, what did you find out?"

"Dead man not very dead."

"I had already surmised that. But how did you find that out?"

"Still withdrawing credits from private account."

"Wouldn't that be a bit conspicuous?"

Levi gave Croft a pitying look. "First he transferred money to alias account. Then he started doing withdraws. If was doing it under real name would not have taken me one whole hour of work."

"Where is he, Levi?" said Croft.

"Wires traced to this location. Uploading," said Levi, hitting a button with a large wooden soup spoon. "Since I do work for you, will I get medal too?"

"Sure, Levi." Croft eyed the flashing indicator to one side indicating the upload was complete.

"What about meat recipes?" said Levi.

"Still working on it, Levi. I'll talk to you later," said Croft. Then, as if remembering something, he said, "Good work."

Levi grimaced.

"Out." Croft cut the connection. He sat in silence for a moment, then went into the other room where Tane and the Clapper were.

"I've been making a list of names of people I think we should talk to," said Tane. "There's the head of the bounty hunter's union, a local industrialist, an olympics official-"

"I have a name for you to add to the list," said Croft. "Rel Cadwalader."

"You want to talk to a dead man?" said Tane.

"Dead men don't withdraw money from their account several days after they've died," said Croft, showing Tane the readout.

Tane looked at it. "It could be a number of other explanations, such as someone else taking his money. But you're right, from the looks of it, it's certainly suspicious, to say the least."

"The least," said Croft.

"If he did withdraw those sums, that means he's still alive, and exposing him could unravel Quandry's plans."

"Good thinking," said Croft dryly.

"We should inform the Chief and ask for instructions."

"No," said Croft. "I'll handle this myself."

The Clapper clapped.

"Let me amend that," said Croft. "The Clapper can come too. You stay here."

"You want me to stay here?" Tane asked.

"It could be dangerous."

"Oh," said Tane. "I really think we should talk to the Chief first."

"You are absolutely forbidden to talk to the Chief first," said Croft.

"Why? She might approve of your plan," said Tane.

"She also might not," said Croft. "If she agrees to my plan, there was no need to contact her. If she disagrees, then contacting her was a bad idea. Either way, there's no useful reason for contacting her."

"But-"

"But me no buts," said Croft. "And not a word about this to our tame Graftonite guide, you understand?"

Tane nodded. "You don't trust him?"

"I don't trust anyone," said Croft.

Tane gave him a hurt look.

Croft sighed. "But, in a relative way, my level of distrust for Carper is measurably deeper than my distrust of you. Does that make you feel better?"

"Why do you distrust me?" said Tane.

"It's nothing personal," said Croft. "But I never met you before last week. You work for a different organization with different agendas."

"Stellar Intelligence and the Column both work for the League," said Tane. "You have a very suspicious nature."

"When you get back to August, check the database for the list of killed in action agents. They were the trusting ones," said Croft. He turned to the Clapper. "All right, it's showtime."

The Clapper bounced up and down with a big smile on his face.

Their destination was far enough away that they had to rent air transport and a ground car at the other end. As Croft negotiated with the owner of the transport the Clapper wandered off and muttered something, but Croft didn't pay attention; the Clapper often muttered to himself. Similarly when they arrived in the transport and Croft again negotiated to rent a ground car, the Clapper went off on his own for a few minutes. But like any obedient pet, he didn't stray far. When Croft was ready to go he found the Clapper muttering and fidgeting by the back of the groundcar.

"Let's go," said Croft simply.

Several hours of driving later they arrived at a large ranch surrounded by woods in all directions. It was very... isolated.

"Are you ready?" said Croft, turning to the Clapper.

The Clapper gave a watery smile and nodded like an eager puppy.

"I can't tell you how much confidence you give me," said Croft, getting out of the ground car.

As they moved towards the ranch somebody stepped out on to the front porch. It wasn't Cadwalader; Croft had studied his holo and this didn't look like him.

The man looked at Croft coldly. "What do you want?"

"I'd like to talk to the owner of this home," said Croft.

"About what?"

"A business proposition," said Croft.

"He's not interested. Go away," the man suggested.

"How does he know? I haven't even told him what it is yet," said Croft.

"Don't push your luck, sheep," said the man. His hand strayed down to his blaster. "Leave now while you can."

"Ok," said Croft immediately. He started back to the groundcar, still keeping an eye on the Graftonite.

A curtain of uncertainty crossed the Graftonite's face, as if he were weighing several different courses of action, and then he drew his blaster. "Just a minute," said the Graftonite, changing his mind. Croft, seeing the rapidfire motion of the man's hand, instinctively ducked behind the groundcar as a blaster bolt whined over his head.

This was it. Pressing hard against the side of his boot, Croft heard the slight hiss of the accelerant being injected into his foot.

Suddenly he felt a warm current of electricity run through his body. Casting aside all caution, he jumped over the car, pulled out his blaster, and started firing. As he fired, he couldn't help but jump and dodge in different directions. It was if he were all rubbery and bouncing around like a toy. None of his shots came near the Graftonite.

But if he was having trouble hitting the Graftonite, the Graftonite was having the same trouble hitting him. All of Croft's jumping and weaving around made him a difficult to hit target, even for a Graftonite. Still, the Graftonite's bolts were closer to Croft's bouncing form than Croft's shots were to the perfectly still Graftonite.

A shot whizzed over Croft's shoulder. "Clapper!" he shouted, still bouncing around and shaking as he fired again.

The Clapper looked out of the car window. He didn't even come out. Suddenly, the Graftonite spun around, facing away from Croft. He turned around again to face Croft, blaster firing, but then he spun away again. Soon he was spinning like a top, with blaster bolts firing aimlessly.

"Hee, hee hee hee!" cackled the Clapper.

Croft gritted his teeth and willed himself mightily not to move. For a moment, he managed to still himself so that he was only vibrating. He aimed carefully, breathing slowly, and squeezed of a discrete shot.

The Graftonite stopped spinning and fell to the ground, a smoking hole in his chest.

Croft collapsed to the ground, breathing heavily. But at least he was facing the ranch when the front door opened and out stepped not one or two but three Graftonites.

Three Graftonites! Croft felt exhausted. There was no way he could take them.

All had blasters in their hands.

"What's going on?" said their leader. He looked at the body on his porch and then to Croft.

Croft, trying to act as normally as possible, got to his feet.

"He wasn't being very friendly," he said, in a cold voice.

"Who are you?" said the Graftonite, squinting angrily at Croft.

"I'm looking for Rel Cadwalader," said Croft, trying very hard not to shake from the aftereffects of the drug. If he had the Clapper's help, could he take these three on? Probably not. His hands started vibrating. In a moment, like it or not, he would start bouncing around again.

"Wrong answer," the leader snarled, raising his blaster.

Suddenly he gave a scream. His arm holding the blaster was on fire.

Suddenly, everyone noticed a young woman with reddish blonde hair standing to one side. Faint wisps of steam rose from her hair.

"Drop your weapons if you want to live!" she yelled, grinning like a maniac.

Thus challenged, the other two Graftonites instinctively raised their blasters, but the woman was quicker, sending bursts of flame at all three Graftonites. Flames burst out in other directions as well, but it was the Graftonites who were the main targets. Their entire bodies lit on fire and they ran around screaming, until they collapsed.

Croft only got a partial view of this spectacle as he was too busy jumping and bouncing around. It was several minutes before he could still himself again. Breathing heavily, he gripped the edge of the groundcar to keep himself still and stared at the smoldering bodies. He looked up at the woman and tried, despite the drugs in his system, to speak in a level voice.

"Hello, Sally."

Red Sally, her hair bright red now under the morning sun, gave a little smile.

"I suppose it's too much of a coincidence that you just happen to be here several hundred miles from the nearest town on Grafton at the same time as we are," said Croft.

Sally gave a wider grin as she went to the groundcar and closed the trunk. The trunk. She had been in the trunk.

Croft looked at the Clapper. The Clapper cringed.

"You brought her," said Croft. "You smuggled her on the transport while I was negotiating with the pilot, and did the same with the groundcar." How could he have been so dumb to fail to keep a closer eye on the Clapper?

"Don't blame him," said Sally, walking casually up to Croft. Her body was still steaming. "I made him do it."

"I thought we left you on August," said Croft.

"Why do I never get any action?" she said, making a face.

"Do you remember what you were assigned to do on August?" Croft asked.

"I was assigned 'fire control exercises'," she said, making a face.

"Do you remember why you were assigned these exercises?" Croft asked.

"They said I couldn't control the flames," said Sally. "But they're wrong!"

"Have you looked around recently?" said Croft.

The ranch was on fire. Actually, not just the ranch, but the plants and trees around the ranch as well.

"Oh," said Sally. "A little bit of collateral damage. Sorry about that." She considered. "Wait, what am I doing apologizing? I just saved your life!" Her hair started to steam again.

"Thanks for that, but I was handling the situation well enough on my own," said Croft. He felt strong enough to stand now. He got up, took an experimental step, only felt a slight tremor. Good. He made his way over to the body of the lead Graftonite.

"Perhaps I should have stood aside and watched how well you handle those three Graftonites," said Red Sally. "It would have been very instructive."

"Instruction is what you need," said Croft. "I'm taking you back to the transport and arranging a flight back to August for you."

"I'm not leaving!" said Sally, as sparks of fire spit out of her. "You need me!"

"I could certainly use you if you could control your instincts," said Croft. "But the first time a Graftonite gives us a dirty look, you'll burst into flame. That's not very inconspicuous."

"Inconspicuous, who cares?" said Sally, taking a few steps forward to avoid the new brushfires around her.

"You may think you did well taking these three out, but what if you don't always have the advantage of surprise, or if there are five or ten of them?" said Croft. "We can't always afford to go in with guns blazing, or in your case, torches burning." He paused. "Now, are you cool enough to get into the car?"

Sally nodded.

"Are you sure? They made me put a hefty deposit on it, and I don't want any scorching on the seats."

Sally nodded again.

"All right then, let's go," said Croft.

Before leaving he looked at the ranch. There was flames everywhere. No way to investigate further. Then he turned to the bodies, which were lying blackened on the ground. Something caught his eye about the leader. He gingerly turned over the body with his boot. The face was burned, but not completely.

Croft took out a datapad and stared at an image, and then at the burned face.

"What is it?" said Sally.

"Well, I don't think we'll have to spend any more time searching for Rel Cadwalader," he sighed.

He stood up and eyed the raging fires around them. What a day.

Chapter 5: A Visit to the Quandry Ranch

"But I didn't kill him," Croft explained for the fourth time.

"His death might have been avoided if you hadn't gone off on this unauthorized mission," said the frowning holoimage of the Chief.

"It was Sally," said Croft. "Her presence on my unauthorized mission was most definitely unauthorized. So don't blame me. Besides, we found out a crucial fact: Cadwalader was alive."

"Was is the operative word," said the Chief. "And then there's the body."

"What about it?"

"Why didn't you recover the body? That would have been concrete evidence that Cadwalader hadn't died in some shootout on Whenfor."

"Well, I can't deny that," said Croft. "But while I wouldn't have flinched at the thought of carrying around a charred corpse, if we had publicized what we found, there might have been some uncomfortable questions asked."

"Such as?" the Chief asked.

"Such as how did said corpse get burned almost beyond recognition? I suppose I could have told them that a supersecret gamma operative with pyrotechnic mental powers (from a section we don't even acknowledge the existence of to the outside world), burned him to a crisp. But even if we put aside the security breach involved, I think such as disclosure would have served Quandry's purposes."

"How so?" The Chief asked.

Croft wanted to slap his head and frustration and call the Chief an idiot, but resisted the impulse. "Quandry is basing much of his campaign on the fact that Cadwalader was killed by outsiders under unfair circumstances. If we reveal that an outsider, namely big red here, burned him to death before he had a chance to fire his weapon, that wouldn't have significantly improved the situation," said Croft.

"We could attribute his death to another cause--an accidental fire, perhaps," said the Chief.

Croft made a face. "The Graftonite who rented us the transport and the Graftonite who rented us the groundcar knew we were in the area. Sooner or later the incident would be traced to off-worlders."

"Do you think that will happen now?" the Chief asked.

"I'm not concerned them that they will publicize it, if that's what you're asking," said Croft. "If they do, they will also have to answer some uncomfortable questions as well, such as how this formerly dead person was killed a second time. So I think this situation is basically a no-win for either side." Croft brightened. "A tie. That's not so bad, is it?"

"I don't see it that way at all," said the Chief. "You had the chance to discredit Quandry and failed."

"I keep telling you it was Red Sally. Don't blame me if you can't put a lock on the looney bin," said Croft.

Clap, clap! "I heard that!" came the Clapper's voice from the background.

The Chief paused, as if straining for another thought, and then she slumped, and sighed. "Well, what's done is done."

"I've found that to be true too," said Croft.

"Then continue on your original mission," said the Chief.

"Ah, can you refresh my memory....?"

The Chief glared at him. "Meet with local elites and attempt to gauge Quandry's popularity. Try to find out what he's up to and see if local leaders can be brought over to our side. I know that Tane has come up with a credible list of local leaders for you to meet with."

"Very credible, I'm sure," said Croft. "All right. Just one more thing. As I might have mentioned, it's entirely possible that this incident will be traced back to me and my cover, what little I had, will be blown. What do I do if a bunch of Graftonite gunmen come after me?"

The Chief raised an eyebrow. "You're a level one agent; I'm surprised you need to ask."

"We're not talking about your typical adversaries here," said Croft. "I think a Graftonite on life support could shoot quicker and faster than any off-worlder can."

The Chief paused, and tried to think of an answer. "Well, as a diplomatic envoy you should have diplomatic immunity," said the Chief.

"I'm not sure that will mean very much to Graftonite killers," said Croft.

"It will have to do," said the Chief. "I've spent enough time on this matter as I can. Report back at regular intervals. And one more thing, Mr. Croft." She leaned closer into the pickup for emphasis. "No more slipups." Her holoimage faded.

Croft turned to Tane, who had been standing in the background. "Simply delightful, wouldn't you agree?"

* * * * * * * * * * * * * * * * * * * *

"Dead?" said Quandry, looking stunned. "How?"

"We're not sure," said Rocco. "He and the guards we put on him were burned."

"Burned," said Quandry, looking puzzled. How had that happened? "How odd. Do you think someone is trying to tell us something? Is there any idea who did this?"

"Actually, we're fairly sure," said Rocco. "There were some sheep in the area at the time." He pressed a button, and a holoimage of Croft appeared.

"Who's that?"

"The sheep who appeared at your rally. Says his name is Toft, a League ambassador."

"Yes, I remember your mentioning him," said Quandry. "He had a lot of guts, showing up here. But surely he couldn't have killed Cadwalader."

Rocco pressed another button, and an holoimage of Carper appeared. "He's not alone."

"The sheep has hired some local muscle?" said Quandry. "Perhaps that explains things. Who is he?"

"I checked him out. Tallas Carper. Strictly small fry," said Rocco.

Quandry said nothing for a moment, staring into space.

"What do you want me to do?"

"I'm thinking," said Quandry. He stared a moment longer. Then he turned and faced Rocco. "Kill him."

"Carper?"

"The sheep."

"If he really is a diplomatic envoy, that could put us at odds with the League," said Rocco.

"One would hope," said Quandry.

"Isn't that a bit ahead of schedule?" said Rocco.

"Not any more," said Quandry.

"And what about Carper?"

"He's not a priority. But when you send someone to eliminated this sheep, make sure he's good enough to take Carper too, just in case," said Quandry.

* * * * * * * * * * * * * * * * * * *

"I think I now know what went wrong with your chimp," said Croft.

The holoimage of Levi frowned, looking sad even in his classic chef's outfit. "Not understand; jumping around everywhere?"

"And dizzy and disoriented, yes," said Croft. "Didn't you see that in your chimps?"

Levi considered. "Saw some wild behavior, yes, but thought it was… chimplike."

"Well, I guess this teaches me a lesson about volunteering to be a test subject in your lab," said Croft. "Levi, seriously, I'm desperate here; is there anything you can send me that can protect me?"

"Let me think," said Levi. He hummed softly to himself as he kneaded some dough in front of him. Croft let him work at it for a minute, then decided enough was enough.

"Levi?"

"No," said Levi. "No ideas yet."

"What about an energy shield?"

"Too bulky."

"Some kind of armor?"

"None available."

"Nothing?"

Levi considered again. "No."

"Then I guess it's up to me," said Croft, trying to keep the bitterness out of his voice.

"You master spy," said Levi. "You survive."

"Thanks," said Croft. "I can't tell you how much that means. Please don't let me interrupt your important cooking. Be sure to bake something tasty for my funeral," he added, signing off.

"Do you really think we're in danger?" Tane asked.

"I think you'd have to ask that question of the last agents who preceded us," said Croft obtusely.

"But they're all-"

Croft abruptly got up and started pacing around the room.

"What-"

"Shhh!" said Croft. He paced some more, thinking intently. Then he paced even more. Then he stopped, and smiled at Tane.

"An idea?"

"Maybe," said Croft. "If I can't outdraw them, maybe I can out think them."

"What does that mean?"

"You'll see," said Croft. "Now, about these very important meetings you're arranging-"

"I've scheduled a meeting with the head of the largest bounty hunter's union on Grafton tomorrow. I'm still working on several others-"

"Good, good," said Croft. He would need at least a day to get the electronics he needed ready anyway. "Just don't schedule anything for the day after tomorrow."

"Why?"

"I'm going on a little trip," said Croft.

The following morning Croft, Tane, the Clapper, and Carper found themselves at the office of Tendan Ribbers, the planetary head of the Union of Graftonite People Locators. They had sent Red Sally back to August, while the sullen Carper once again accompanied them.

"I'm surprised that he's agreed to see us, especially on such short notice," Croft commented, as they walked to Ribbers' office, which was in the heart of Regular.

"He seemed almost oddly eager to meet with us," said Tane. "I'm not sure why."

"Maybe because it's a trap?" said Croft.

Carper gave a dry laugh.

"Something amuses you?" Croft asks.

"If one of us wanted one of you dead, we wouldn't need anything so elaborate as a trap," said Carper. "We'd just come up to you and shoot you."

"But that wouldn't be very sporting, would it?" said Croft. "What about the Graftonite sense of fair play?"

"Oh, he'd give you a chance to draw your gun," said Carper. "It would be a fair one-on-one contest, as fair as a battle between one of you and one of us could be."

"Fair, hmm," said Croft, filing that information away. The beginning of a plan was forming.

They went inside, were announced, and very shortly was in the office of Tendan Ribbers.

A fat Graftonite. Ribbers was the first fat Graftonite they had ever seen. Of course, he had a gun strapped around his waist, but it almost looked comical on him. Still, Croft was almost certain that Ribbers could outdraw him on any day of the week.

"Come in, come in, sit down, sit down," said Ribbers, giving an automatic smile. "So good to see representatives of the League here."

"Your welcome is most... unexpected," said Croft. "I was under the impression that Quandry-"

Ribbers waved a hand dismissively. "Don't get me started on Quandry. Part of a very small band of malcontents which is trying to give Grafton a bad name." He smiled again.

"You don't like Quandry?" said Croft.

"It's no secret, Mr. Toft," said Ribbers. "May I call you Clifford?"

"By all means," said Croft.

"Clifford, Quandry's nothing but a troublemaker, a bag of hot silesium gas," said Ribbers.

"So do most of your bounty hunter members-"

"Bounty hunters?" said Ribbers, frowning.

Croft cast a look at Tane, as if wondering if he were in the right place. "I thought-"

"I'm the chief steward of the Union of Graftonite People Locators, yes," said Ribbers. "But we're no bounty hunters, Clifford."

"So... what are you?" said Croft.

"We're people locators. We locate people, and bring them to whomever pays us."

"No offense intended, but that sounds a lot like bounty hunting to me," Croft commented.

Ribbers laughed. "Bounty hunting is a crude term for unprofessionals, people who give our entire industry a bad name. Did you know that 44% of unlicensed people locators purposefully inflict pain on their bounties?"

"No."

"Did you know that 29% of unlicensed people locators allow themselves to be bribed out of completing their mission?"

"No-"

"Did you know that an astonishing 54% of unlicensed people locators break local laws to complete their missions?"

"I guess I knew it was some number, but didn't know the exact percentage," Croft admitted.

"It's amateurs like them who give our members a bad name," said Ribbers.

"So bounty... people locators in your union are more professional?"

"Of course," said Ribbers. He held up a small disc. "A code of conduct. Rules of regulations, for locating and capturing bounties and dealing with employers. Even rules for the humanitarian handling of the captured sheep in transit--begging your pardon, Clifford."

"No offense taken," said Croft. "So your members are kinder, gentler... people locators."

"There's no reason for our industry to be a cruel one. We pride ourselves on locating our targets, and acquiring them with a minimum of hassle. In fact, when our targets hear that a Graftonite has been hired to locate them, they only hope that it's one of us."

"I guess only the lucky ones get caught by you," said Croft, wondering what happened to the people who were "returned" to the employers who put out the bounties.

"Absolutely! We've made people locating a respectable, humane process," said Ribbers.

"So do most... people locators belong to your union?" said Croft.

"Nearly all the respectable ones do," said Ribbers.

"Ah.... If you included the unrespectable ones in the totals, what percentage would that be?"

Ribbers paused. "Well, that's hard to say," he said, looking uncomfortable.

"Maybe you could write it down?" Croft asked.

Ribbers sighed. "About a quarter of people in the profession work within our union." He added defensively, "In a fiercely individualistic society such as ours that's actually quite an achievement-"

"And the other 75%? Do they work with other unions?"

Ribbers shook his head. "As I just said, Clifford, we are a fiercely independent people. No, the rest are freelancers. They are so strong willed that they don't see the benefits--did I mention the benefits? Full medical, dental, and death benefits?"

"No, you didn't."

"Our locators are even insured for up to two million credits for accidental injury or dismemberment. That's why potential employers come to us. They know if an innocent third party accidentally gets shot by a people locator they hire, they're in good hands if they're working with us."

"It all sounds very... professional," said Croft. "So how do your members feel about Mr. Quandry?"

"Oh, he's so unprofessional," said Ribbers. "Did you know he was once a member of the Union?"

"Really?" said Croft.

"He tried a takeover, a number of years ago. Didn't have the votes," said Ribbers. "People saw right through him."

"What did they see?" said Croft.

"Well, he has no honor. Totally unprofessional," said Ribbers.

"I'm glad you feel that way," said Croft. "He's trying to muster support for some very dangerous and aggressive policies."

"I agree," said Ribbers.

"He could destabilize the situation and make all Graftonites look… unprofessional."

"I agree again," said Ribbers.

"That's why if you were to speak out against him-"

Ribbers held up a hand. "Mr. Toft, I don't get involved with politics."

"But we're only talking about exercising your right of free speech-"

"And then he can exercise his right to bear arms," said Ribbers.

"What do you mean?"

Ribbers shook his head. "Mr. Toft, you really need to become more familiar with our political system."

"I didn't gather that you had one," said Croft. "But if you speak up-"

"Sure, I can convene a gathering, or maybe a great gathering, and speak my mind," said Ribbers. "But if Quandry or one of his lackeys doesn't like what I have to say, they may call me out."

"Call you out," said Croft dumbly. "What about your fiercely independent streak? What about exercising the right to say whatever you want?"

"We do--if we think it's worth the consequences," said Ribbers. "Don't get me wrong, I don't agree with what Quandry is doing. But unless he's going up directly against the Union-- and he isn't--I can't take the risk of sticking my neck out without some sort of provocation."

"I see," said Croft, not trying very hard not to let his disappointment show.

"You have to understand, he has some gold medalists working for him-" Ribbers was interrupted by a buzz on his desk. He pressed a button. "Yes?"

The voice on the other end was projected directly to Ribbers. Croft could only hear Ribbers talk.

"What does he want?" Ribbers asked.

They didn't hear the response.

Ribbers looked at Croft. "I see." He considered for a moment. "Well, tell him to stay off the grounds, then."

Another response.

"If he refuses, send the groundskeeper. He's a retired bronze medalist, you know," said Ribbers. He pressed a button and ended the conversation.

"I'm afraid our time together is at an end," said Ribbers.

"What was that all about?" said Croft.

Ribbers looked away, as if debating what to say.

"Mr. Ribbers?"

"There's a gentleman waiting outside," said Ribbers.

"Waiting... for what?"

"He's waiting for you," said Ribbers.

"Who is he?" said Croft.

"I didn't catch the name," said Ribbers.

"Well, what does he want?" said Croft.

"To kill you," said Ribbers.

Croft pondered for a minute. The brashness of the act stunned him. Someone had simply walked into Ribber's establishment and announced he was here to murder someone. On any other planet he could call the police. But here there was no police, no laws, only the power of the gun.

"He's waiting, just outside your office," said Croft, his hand snaking down to his blaster. Not that that would do him much good. How could he outdraw a Graftonite?

"Oh, no," said Ribbers. "I won't tolerate a contract killing here in the building. Here at the Union we do have standards, you know."

"So you sent him away?"

"No. He's waiting for you outside our building."

"Do you have a back exit?" said Croft.

"No," said Ribbers. He stood up. "I'm sorry you have to die, but it's been nice talking with you." He left the office without shaking hands or making eye contact.

Croft, the Clapper, Tane, and Carper sat alone in Ribber's office for a long moment.

Then Tane said, "What are we going to do?"

Croft stood up. "We're going to leave."

"But you'll be killed!" said Tane.

"I'm not very killable," said Croft.

Carper laughed.

"Do you see something funny?" said Croft.

"You don't have a chance," said Carper. "There's no way you can outshoot one of us." He chuckled.

Croft pressed a button on his comm. "Then it's a good thing I just canceled your next paycheck."

Carper immediately stopped in midlaugh.

"Is there something you want me to do?" Tane asked.

"Well, I wouldn't advise you to stand right in front of me," said Croft.

"What's the plan?"

"Let's go outside and see," said Croft, as he started for the door, trying to look more casual than he felt.

"Did you really cancel my next paycheck?" Carper asked.

"Now who is the nervous one?" Croft asked.

They left the building. A man stood there expectantly. A crowd had formed around him. Obviously, the word had spread that there was going to be some action here.

Croft exited first, keeping space between him and Tane and the Clapper. He didn't care where Carper was standing.

Carper nodded slightly to the man, keeping his good arm away from his weapon as he stepped aside. The man nodded slightly to him. Carper had made his intentions clear; he wasn't getting involved.

"Hello," said Croft, slowly walking forward. He kept his hand well away from his blaster. "Can I help you?"

The man still hadn't drawn his gun, but he stood there, staring at Croft intently, waiting for Croft's slightest move towards his own gun.

"I'm here to kill you, sheep," said the man.

"May I ask why?" Croft said, still walking forward. He was only about 20 feet away now.

"Because I feel like it," the man grinned.

"If I've done something to offend you, please let me know," said Croft.

"You offend me, sheep," the man spat.

Croft was now five feet away from the man. There was no way a Graftonite, or anyone else, could miss at this distance.

"What're you doing, sheep?" said the man, eyeing Croft suspiciously.

The crowd held its breath.

Croft slowly went down on his knees in front of the Graftonite.

"Please!" he said. "Please don't kill me!"

The Graftonite looked at Croft in disgust.

"Pleeeeeease!" said Croft, starting to cry. "I'm just a humble, defenseless diplomat!"

"Get up," the Graftonite muttered.

"Pleeeeassseee…. Don't…. kill…. meeeeeeeeee…….," Croft sobbed.

"Get up," said the Graftonite. "I have a schedule to keep. You're going to make me late for my next appointment. Stop crying and draw your gun."

Croft turned to the watching crowd. Still sobbing, he wailed, "I'm simply defenseless! This isn't going to be a gunfight, this is going to be an execution!" He started crying even louder.

The Graftonite took a step back and quickly turned to eye the crowd, his attention not straying from Croft for more than a second. He didn't like what he saw even in this quick scan of the area. People were muttering and shaking their heads.

"Pleeeease, I'm helpless heeeeeere!" Croft wailed again.

The muttering in the crowd grew louder. The Graftonite hesitated. He was only slightly reluctant to kill the wailing Croft. What concerned him more was the crowd. If one of them objected to this execution, he could be called out. And someone in the crowd could be an olympic medalist.

Looking down at Croft, his expression hardened as he made a decision. Quandry had paid him to make a real kill, not to execute livestock. "Get out of my sight," said the Graftonite. "You disgust me," he said, with real revulsion in his voice.

"Yes… yes… thank you…. Thank you…," said Croft, still sobbing uncontrollably as he crawled away. He slowly got to his feet, acutely aware that the Graftonite could shoot him in the back as he slowly made his way through the crowd, around the corner.

The sobs immediately cut off as Croft turned the corner. He turned and waited for his approaching companions.

"Very clever," said Tane.

"The crybaby defense," said Carper. "You were lucky this time, sheep. Next time there may not be a crowd, or a killer who is that sensitive."

"That was no luck," said Tane. "How did you know that would work?"

"Simple psychology," said Croft. "I know the Graftonites like fair fights. So I tried to make the fight as unfair as possible--in my opponent's favor."

"Very clever," said Tane admiringly.

"Perhaps you'll put in a good word for me with the Chief," said Croft dryly.

He had done it. He had survived an encounter with a hostile Graftonite without resort to any of Levi's tricks, and he had survived.

"What do you mean, he let him walk away?" Quandry thundered. It was the following evening and only now that Quandry had learned the news. He sat in his spacious multiroom office on his ranch.

"The man made a spectacle of himself, weeping and helpless," said Rocco.

"So? Why didn't he just shoot the sheep?" Quandry raged. He abruptly got up and went into the adjoining room, opening a food storage unit. There were several of them in the room; crouched behind the side of one of them, only partially obscured from view, was Clifford Croft, dressed in black from head to toe.

Quandry carried a sandwich back to the other room, apparently not noticing the odd shape sticking out of the side of one of the cupboards.

Rocco said, "There were people around, they might not have liked it...."

"Who cares what they liked!" Quandry exploded. He looked down at his sandwich, as if something was missing, or something puzzled him.

Quandry got an odd look on his face, as if he were trying to remember something. Suddenly, he went in quick strides back to the food storage area.

Quandry looked around slowly, as if scanning for something. Then, in purposeful steps, he moved to the food storage unit that Croft had been hiding behind, went to it, opened it, pulled out a drink, nodded to himself, then closed the unit, returning to the other room.

"If there had been a silver or gold medalist in the crowd, they might've caused trouble," said Rocco.

One of the food units in the other room opened. Croft snuck out. He planted something under one of the units, then crept out of the room through another doorway.

"I don't care!" said Quandry savagely. He swept his hand across his desk, accidentally knocking his drink over. He quickly righted the bottle, but the damage was done, and several of his papers were wet. "Let's continue this in the dining room," he said.

They both entered a nearby dining room. Neither apparently noticed the dark shape under the table.

"I want you to fire him and find someone else who can do the job right," said Quandry, chewing vigorously. "Now, what's the status of our operations?"

He kicked out vigorously with his foot, just missing Croft's head by an inch. Croft leaned backwards just barely in time, still in a crouch.

"We're still working on phase two," said Rocco. He lazily stretched out his legs under the table. Suddenly, he felt something solid.

Rocco look startled. He started to look down under the table when he felt a sharp kick from the object he had just touched. "Watch where you put your clumsy legs, you just jabbed me," Quandry snapped, finishing his sandwich. He took a long drink and said, "I don't want to hear about delays. Get working on it."

He abruptly got up from the table, and looked down thoughtfully at it.

"What?" said Rocco.

"I've always thought it was too small," said Quandry. "Get a bigger table."

He and Rocco left the room.

Croft, covered in sweat, got out from under the table. He tiptoed to the doorway, waiting for the sounds of footsteps to recede.

He had planted eavesdropping devices in several rooms of the ranch. He had wanted to wire the entire ranch, but Croft sensed his luck was running out and that it was time to go. He walked silently upstairs, to the bathroom. He had entered through the second story bedroom window, and he intended to exit the same way. He had special climbing gloves on that could grip almost any surface, so climbing down would not be a problem.

But just as he got to the bedroom he heard footsteps rushing behind him. He dashed inside, hiding behind the door.

Heavy footsteps entered the bedroom. And then the footsteps stopped, just inside the door, and a voice, said, "What?"

It was Quandry.

Croft heard a faint voice in the distance say, "There's a new report you need to see."

"Hang on, I just want to change into more comfortable boots," said Quandry.

He entered the bedroom and immediately turned left to one of his closets. He cast a quick glance at the empty space on the other side of the doorway and then looked into the shoe closet. He took off his boots, picked out a new pair, and sat on the edge of the bed, humming as he put them on.

Then he walked out of the room, and his footsteps grew distant.

Croft stood up from behind the far side of the bed, where he had been lying. He reflected that this would have been a good opportunity to assassinate Quandry; he could have shot the Graftonite in the back.

Croft grimaced; he didn't feel any special need for "fair fights" like the Graftonites did, but he wasn't at all sure that killing Quandry would solve the problem. Besides, the Chief probably would want to be consulted on little things like political assassinations in advance.

There had never been so much paperwork in the olds days.

Sighing softly to himself, Croft moved to the window and made his escape.

Chapter 6: The Industrialist And The Olympics Official

"I don't think we're getting anywhere with this," said Croft. He was in another endless conference with the Chief, with Tane at his side. Croft hated these constant consultations with the Chief. It made him feel like a heavily supervised child.

"What do you think, Sylvia?" said the Chief. Croft noted the Chief's familiarity with Tane. The Chief liked Tane. Tane was her pet.

Tane glanced worriedly at Croft. She clearly didn't want to alienate Croft, but she also didn't want to get dragged down with him. She took a breath and said, "I think Ribbers could be a moderating influence, but political space in Grafton is limited."

"So limited you can get shot if you say something someone doesn't like," Croft translated.

"As a political actor, according to the Keman-Nolan political science model for a developing world with only informal governmental structures, Ribbers is behaving like the classic rational actor man-"

"Rational in that he doesn't want to get shot," said Croft, continuing to translate.

"But if we can create more political space, perhaps an enlightened dialogue in the community, we may get more prominent non-state actors to express their views."

"Are you suggesting we call the Graftonites together for a fireside chat?" said Croft.

"I think we can if we approach the proper non-state actor elites. For example, your friend the Silencer is very well respected-"

"My friend the Silencer is no one's friend, and if you called him a non-state actor elite he'd either laugh at you or shoot you, or both," said Croft. "He's not going to do anything for us unless there's something in it for him."

"But surely we can convince him that what is good for Grafton is good for him-" said Tane

"The Silencer isn't a dummy," said Croft. "If there's a civil war going on outside his house he won't get involved unless it spills over onto his front lawn."

"Well, then maybe we can use other non-state actors to enlarge the political debate," said Tane.

"Who did you have in mind?" the Chief asked.

"I've identified several other individuals who are respected Graftonites who might help," said Tane. "A prominent industrialist, a leading Olympics official, and a major weapons manufacturer."

"And what makes you think that any of those will offer to help, or even be sympathetic to our cause?" said Croft.

"You'll have to convince them," said the Chief.

"I'm a spy, not a diplomat," said Croft.

"This time you'll need to be a little of both," said the Chief.

"We have diplomats for this," said Croft. "Wait, I forget, they're afraid to come out of their embassy, right?"

"They're under a security lockdown for their own protection," said the Chief. She changed the subject. "Now listen, Croft. Quandry's demand that other worlds make 'security' payments to Grafton has caused quite a stir."

"I'll bet," said Croft. "Is the League going to let itself be blackmailed?"

"Of course not," said the Chief. "That's totally against our principals."

"Totally," said Croft.

"On the other hand, we are considering extending development assistance-"

"So you are considering paying," said Croft.

"It would not be for blackmail, it would be for local economic development," said the Chief.

"I see," said Croft. "And you think this will defuse the crisis?"

"Once the moderates see that we are ready to deal, the hardliners will have to go along or lose support," said the Chief.

"Right," said Croft. He managed to keep a straight face until the Chief signed off.

When the Chief's image faded, Tane turned to him. "Why didn't you tell her that you had planted listening devices in Quandry's home?"

"For the same reason you didn't," said Croft.

"You threatened me with bodily harm if I did," said Tane.

"Exactly," said Croft. "It was only common sense to say nothing about it."

Tane looked puzzled but plowed on. "Have you heard anything useful?"

Croft, not being able to listen to hours of tapes, was using a computer program that filtered out blank time and mundane conversation to present him with condensed highlights. So far he hadn't heard anything tremendously interesting but he had just planted the devices the day before. "Not yet."

"Then you'll have time to attend a meeting with Mr. Tagan," said Tane.

"Tagan?"

"Of Tagan Industries. It's the biggest corporation on Graftonite."

"With a population of only eight million people, how big can that be?"

By galactic sizes, not so big. But Croft soon learned that Tagan industries had a monopoly or near-monopoly on a wide range of products and services produced on Grafton, from roads to building equipment to clothing to technical tools to electronics and more. Tane had arranged a meeting with the organization's President, Til Tagan, whose offices were on a large tract of land outside the capital, Regular.

Carper led the way, driving them there in a rented ground car. Croft, looking lazily behind them as he drove, said, "I think we're being followed."

"By whom?" said Tane.

"I don't know," said Croft.

"What if it's another Graftonite killer?" said Tane.

"I don't think a second one will be taken in by tears," Carper said, chuckling nastily.

Croft looked at Carper, started to say something, stopped, and then said something other than he had first intended. "You're only working for us because we couldn't hire anyone else. You said that Graftons didn't want to work for off-worlders. And yet Ribbers didn't mention that the members of his union had any qualms about working for off-worlders."

"That's off-planet, sheep," said Carper. "Out of sight of other Graftons. It's a world of difference working for a bounty off-planet, for a real job. Being led around by sheep on Grafton like a trained seal, however, is another story."

"So you're a trained seal," Croft remarked absentmindedly. But he frowned as he said it. He sensed there was something important he was missing here, an idea that wasn't quite crystallizing, but he wasn't quite sure what it was. The more he tried to grab at it, the more it slipped away. Just what had he been thinking?

"We're arriving at our destination," said Carper, slowing the groundcar to a halt. "If they're going to shoot you, they'll probably do it now."

Croft looked behind them. The other car had slowed to a halt too, some two blocks away. Whoever it was, they weren't coming to challenge him in close combat.

Could it be a sniper with a long distance rifle? That wasn't the Grafton way. But anything was possible here. Croft took out a pair of electrobinocs and trained them on the distant car.

He found himself looking into a groundcar with two occupants, both of whom were using electrobinocs pointed at him.

"Fool, Yuri! I told you we shouldn't have followed him this closely!" said one of the occupants of the other groundcar, putting down the electrobinocs.

"We would have lost him otherwise," snarled the one called Yuri. "So he knows we are here. We are still keeping an eye on him."

"The Major will not like knowing we were discovered," said his companion. His name was Samov.

"Then the Major doesn't have to learn that inconvenient fact," said Yuri. "She is not our direct superior."

"But she is with the Bureau of Special Tasks-"

"We will answer all questions asked of us, but volunteer nothing," said Yuri. "They're going into the building now. Watch closely!"

When Croft saw that they were merely being observed, he decided to take no action and to proceed with the mission. They entered the building and announced their presence. Within a few short moments, they found themselves before Til Tagan.

Til Tagan was a tall, dark haired man like most Graftonites. He greeted Croft with a nod as he, the Clapper, Tane, and Carper took seats in his office.

"I'm very impressed what I hear about your company," said Croft. "You represent the largest company on all of Grafton-"

"Not just represent, but own," said Tagan.

"All of it?" said Croft.

"Yes, Mr. Toft."

"I thought a company this size would be publicly owned-"

"We don't place much stock in publicly owned companies," said Tagan.

"I'm amazed that your company has managed to branch out into so many areas," said Croft. "Everything from heavy construction to linens. I'm really surprised you don't have more competition."

"Well, you have to understand that Grafton is an unusual market," said Tagan. "We have the population of a province spread out over an entire planet. A small market in a large area is difficult to serve, and not many companies think it's worth the effort."

"Does that explain why prices are, ah, marked up a bit?" Tane asked, choosing her words very carefully.

"Precisely," said Tagan, not taking offense. To the contrary, he seemed to be proud of monopoly pricing. "It's the difficulty of serving such a geographically distributed market that reduces economies of scale and forces higher prices. That's why if you're poor-"

"You shouldn't come to Grafton," said Croft. "Yes, we've heard it."

"Did you know I invented it?"

"Invented what?" said Croft.

"The slogan," said Tagan. "If you're poor, don't come to Grafton. My company invented the slogan, it's used in all our marketing pieces. Graftons always think prices are too high and are always grumbling. We realized a marketing campaign was in order. So we came up with the slogan, 'If you're poor, don't come to Grafton'. Ingenious, isn't it?"

"Your slogan implies that Grafton is the home to the well-off elite who shouldn't mind paying higher prices," said Tane. "And if they do mind, then they're not in the elite."

"Precisely," said Tagan, beaming. "You have quite an analytical mind, Ms. Tane."

Tane smiled back.

"Your higher prices have nothing to do with the fact that you're a monopoly, does it?" Croft asked.

"Of course not!" Tagan assured him. "We use the most efficient monopoly market pricing models."

"Uh huh," said Croft. "Still I'm surprised you don't have any competition at all, given the wide range of products and services you sell."

"We have a little competition here and there," said Tagan. "But most weren't able to withstand the rigors of competing against us." He didn't elaborate.

And Croft didn't see any reason to ask him to. He had a pretty good idea what had happened to the competition. Not that he cared. His mission wasn't to audit Tagan industries, but to enlist Tagan's help in the fight against Quandry. They had had more than time for small talk, it was time to get to the point.

"I'm sure you've heard about Mo Quandry and his movement," said Croft.

"Yes, of course," said Tagan.

There was silence for a moment. Then, seeing that nothing more was forthcoming, Croft asked, "May I ask your feelings on the matter?"

"I support a peaceable solution to the dispute," said Tagan.

"That's a relief," said Croft. Perhaps Tagan could be an ally.

"I think the matter will be settled peacefully, once the other planets start shouldering their fair share."

"Fair share?"

"The security fees," said Tagan.

"You mean, the blackmail payments?" said Croft.

Tagan smiled. "I believe your government is publicly calling them 'economic assistance grants'. I think once the League starts paying its fair share, that the matter will be resolved."

"So… you think this is simply an economic dispute, and once Quandry gets his 'development grants', that everything will be settled?"

"Of course!" said Tagan. "Ambassador Toft, on Grafton, everything is about money. Once your League settles on a price with our people, I'm sure that amicable relations will resume."

"And it doesn't trouble you that these are essentially blackmail payments, backed up by threats to attack the League?"

"Mr. Toft, the language of politics really boils down to the language of business. One side needs something, and the other side offers a price," said Tagan.

Croft looked at him shrewdly. "Let me guess; Tagan Industries would get a share of the 'development grants' that the League would pay."

"And why should it not? We are the largest promoter of economic development on the planet. What's good for Tagan Industries is good for Grafton," said Tagan.

Croft winced. It sounded suspiciously like another slogan. But he pressed on. "But what if the League doesn't make a deal with Quandry? What if this spirals into a major war?" Croft asked.

"I'm sure that won't happen," said Tagan smoothly. "And now, my time is quite limited..."

Tagan immediately got up, and gestured to show Croft to the door. Obviously, the interview was over.

He lead them outside his office.

Meanwhile, back in the spy car...

"There's a man waiting outside the building," said Samov, peering through the electronoculars.

"Who is it?" said Yuri, sitting on the groundcar.

"Looks like a Grafton killer," said Samov.

"They are all Grafton killers," said Yuri, reclining on the hood of the groundcar.

"Having fun?" said a new voice.

Samov snapped to alertness; Yuri, fumbling, fell off of the car. "Major! You did not announce you were coming-"

"And obviously anyone can simply walk up to your observation post without being noticed," said Major Nancy Kalikov of the Slurian Special Tasks Bureau. "What is your report?"

"They have been inside for nearly half an hour," said Yuri.

"They are coming out now," said Samov, still peering through the electronoculars.

"There is a Graftonite killer waiting for them," said Yuri. "I think we may have our Croft problem solved for us."

"If you think that, you're a bigger fool than I give you credit for," said the Major coldly. "Samov?"

"Croft sees the man. The man is standing there. Croft is approaching the man slowly…."

"Don't think you're going to get away this time with a crying fit," said the man pleasantly. There was no spectator crowd this time to help Croft; unlike the last time, there were no other Graftonites around, except for Carper; and Carper had made it clear he wouldn't lift a finger to help him.

Croft slowly approached the man, his hands carefully away from his blaster. This was not the same assailant he had faced the last time. "Do I know you?"

"I'm the man who's going to shoot a hole in your head," said the man.

Croft took a few steps closer. His hands went slowly to the belt of his holster. He undid it and let it lose; his blaster, and his holster, slid to the ground. "Are you really going to shot an unarmed man?"

"Yes," the man spat.

Meanwhile, from two blocks away...

"He's dropped his weapon," said Samov. "But I don't think that trick is going to work."

"I think we may finally see the end of Croft," said Yuri happily.

The Major glared at him but said nothing

Croft took a few steps closer to the gunman.

"That's not necessary, I can hit you at any distance," said the killer.

Croft, now about ten feet away, stopped. Perfect.

"You're very confident, aren't you?" said Croft.

"Against you?" And by his tone nothing more needed to be said.

"So even if I had my weapon, you're confident that you could outdraw me, correct?"

"Correct," said the killer.

"But can you conceive of a circumstance where I could outdraw you?"

"No," said the killer, giving a slight chuckle.

"Sure you can," said Croft. "What if I shot you from behind, and you didn't even know I was there?"

"Well, sure, I suppose," said the killer, wondering where this was going.

"So you admit, if I could take you by surprise, that I can outdraw you."

"You wouldn't be outdrawing me, you would be taking me by surprise, there's a difference," said the killer. "What's this all about? You're right here in front of me."

"I am, but...." said Croft, his eyes widening as he looked over the killer's shoulder.

The killer, almost more quickly than Croft could see, jerked his back and forward again like a blur. "Nice try," the killer sneered.

"I didn't try anything," said Croft. "I just wanted to establish that if I took you by surprise, I could outdraw you."

"Enough talk," the killer snarled.

Croft could see that the gunman was about to reach for his gun. Croft did nothing visibly, only tilting his right boot up slightly. But inside the boot his big toe was pressing down, hard.

There was a slight whistle in the air and the Grafton looked startled. He reached for his gun but his arm froze as he touched it. With a giant expression of surprise, he fell backwards on the ground. Croft looked down at the body. Looking carefully, he pulled a tiny needle from the man's leg. Getting down he whispered into the man's ear. "It's only temporary. But I am grateful that its effects are almost instantaneous. Next time, don't be so sure of yourself."

Two blocks away...

"What happened?" said Samov. "He just fell down."

"You underestimated him, again," Major Kalikov snapped.

Yuri raised a sniper rifle. "Let me kill him, Major.

The Major knocked the rifle away. "That will not get us the answers we need!"

"Then what will?"

"I will," said the Major. "I will get the answers from him. Then Clifford Croft can be eliminated."

"An unfair trick," said Carper, curling his lip as he looked a the unconscious gunman.

"As unfair as a Graftonite taking on an unarmed man with slower reflexes," said Croft. He turned to Tane. "What next?"

"We have to meet with a senior Olympics official," said Tane.

"Let's go play," said Croft dismissively.

Tane glared at him.

The Clapper clapped joyously.

* * * * * * * * * * * * * * * * * *

"He escaped? Again?" said Quandry.

"He had some kind of weapon in his boot. It was concealed," said Rocco.

"I am beginning to get the idea that this is not a typical sheep diplomat. Diplomats don't typically have needle guns in their boots."

"Agreed," said Rocco.

"So he's trying to stir up opposition against me?" said Quandry. "And he thought he was going to get anywhere with Tagan?"

"Apparently so."

"He's only an annoyance, but when I say I want someone dead, they'd better be dead," said Quandry. "Send someone else, send several someones, just get it done."

"Yes sir," said Rocco.

* * * * * * * * * * * * * * * * * *

"Who cares about the Olympics?" said Croft, as they rode in the groundcar.

"Sheep," said Carper dismissively, before Tane could answer.

"Sheep care about the Olympics?" said Croft, deliberately playing dumb.

"Only a sheep would fail to understand," said Carper.

"Maybe you'll explain it then," said Croft.

"On most worlds the Olympics only celebrate sheep sports," said Carper.

"And on Grafton...."

"We find out who the best marksmen are," said Carper. "Our contests show who the best of the best are, in the only thing that matters."

"The only thing that matters being the ability to shoot a weapon," said Croft, interpreting.

Carper glared at him.

"There's more to it than that," said Tane. "It's also tied into the color war concept."

"Color war?" said Croft.

"Every two years Grafton has the Olympics, but every four years at the same time they also have color war."

"What, exactly, is color war?" Croft asked. He ignored Carper's pitying look.

"Every four years every resident of Grafton is divided into four teams-Blue, Purple, Green, and Yellow-"

"Orange," corrected Carper. "No Graftonite would be caught dead in yellow."

"Orange," said Tane nervously. "Team leaders are selected from among the most respected members of society, and they select their senior staff based on established rules. Most of the general population is assigned to a team by random lottery."

"What then?"

"Then they fight," said Tane. "For the month leading up to the Olympics, everyone drops what they're doing, spend a week in training, and then a month fighting as an organized army to beat the other forces." She paused. "Of course, no one gets hurt, not usually. Blasters are set to stun."

"Why is this such a big event?" Croft asked.

"Proving yourself as a gunman, or gunwoman, is the most important thing for a Graftonite to do," said Tane. "This gives people a chance to prove themselves and test themselves repeatedly against their neighbors."

"So the entire planet simply drops what it's doing for a month?"

"Well, it's not mandatory, I don't think they get 100% participation, but most people do," said Tane.

"How does the planet run if everyone is off at play for a month?" Croft asked.

"Run?" said Tane.

"I forget, no government, no industry, except for monopoly incorporated," said Croft, referring to Tagan Industries. "So if we're supposed to be talking to 'non-state actors' we should probably be talking to a past or current leader of one of these color wars."

"You already have," said Tane.

"Eh?"

"According to my research, your friend the Silencer was the head of Blue Army; he even won two wars in a row," said Tane. "Didn't you know?"

"The Silencer is not a sharer," said Croft.

They knew they were getting close to the Olympics practice grounds when they heard the sounds of weapons fire. They passed not one or several but dozens of different kinds of firing ranges, where Graftonites blazed away at incredible speeds. As they drove by Croft saw several objects fly into the air and one gunman, blasting away with five, precise shots, shoot them all down in little more than an instant.

At that moment he knew the reason behind peoples' fear of a "gold medalist".

Methlid Okuna was the current head of the Graftonite Olympics committee. He gave them a broad smile as he welcomed them into his office.

"A rare treat! We seldom get off-worlders here," said Okuna, smiling broadly as he gestured for them to sit. There was a window built in behind him that showed a broad view of a stadium where various gunmen were practicing.

"Are off-worlders forbidden to compete in your Olympics?" Croft asked.

Okuna looked puzzled. "Of course not! They just know that it's futile to do so. An off-worlder could never compete with a Graftonite, of course."

"Of course," said Croft.

"Mind you, there are always exceptions. We do attract some of the best gunmen in the world for our junior league Olympics."

"Junior League?"

"For lads 15 years and under. Some of the off-worlders occasionally provide reasonable competition."

"You let off-world children compete against your children?" Croft asked.

"No, that would hardly be fair, would it?" said Okuna. "We let off-world adults compete against our children. We waive the age requirement for off-worlders for obvious reasons."

"Obvious reasons," Croft repeated dully.

"They provide good competition for our children," said Okuna. "They seldom win, of course."

"Of course," said Croft. "But if all your events are shooting, how many can there be?"

"We have over 50 sporting events," said Okuna. "We have trick shooting, distance shooting, precision shooting, the triathalon-"

"Triathalon?" said Croft.

"Blaster, blaster rifle, and blaster cannon," said Okuna. "We also have gunnastics-"

"You mean gymnastics, don't you?" said Croft.

Okuna glared at him. "Gunnastics. It's mostly a women's sport-while twirling around on the bars or in midair they have to shoot moving targets."

"Interesting," said Croft.

"What else, let me see... in the winter there's downhill skiing shooting, figure skating shooting-"

"Figure skating shooting?"

"Elegant skating while shooting targets," said Okuna. "Participants get judged on form as well as accuracy." He paused. "We also have team sports, such as military soccer, and more traditional ones, such as the 200 meter sprint-"

"A running race?" said Croft. "Let me guess, the racers have to shoot targets as they run."

"That's ridiculous," said Okuna. "The contestants have to shoot the racers. Stun shots, of course."

"Of course," said Croft.

Okuna stared at Croft, wondering if he was being sarcastic. "Let's get down to business. What brings you here?"

"We're very concerned about Mo Quandry and his supporters," said Croft. "We're trying to... sound out prominent members of society to find out what level of support he has."

"Quandry. Oh," said Okuna. Abruptly his expression changed. "If you're asking whether I'm a big fan of Quandry, the answer is no."

"No?"

"He has no honor," said Okuna. "Five years ago he was a senior official in the Orange Army-that's our color war, you understand."

"So I've heard."

"Well, let's just say he engaged in a series of... questionable maneuvers that nearly got him ejected from the war."

"What kind of questionable maneuvers are we talking about?" Croft asked.

"That's not important," said Okuna. "Some folk-not me, you understand, but some-say that he cheated. Of course, to make a public accusation of cheating-"

"Can open you up to a double barreled lawsuit, I understand," said Croft. "But if Quandry has a reputation for being a cheater, why does he have such a following?"

Okuna made a dismissive sound. "I don't think he does. Oh, a certain percentage of the population may sympathize with his goals, but his hard base of support can't be more than one or two percent of the population."

"One or two percent, that doesn't sound so bad," said Croft.

Okuna stared at Croft. "There are 8 million of us, Mr. Toft. Two percent is 160,000. Do you have any idea what 160,000 can do to the League?"

"Do you think he's going to attack the League?" said Croft.

"It's not my job to speculate," said Okuna carefully.

"If you convened a great meeting, spoke out against him, you-"

"If I spoke out against him, that wouldn't be very polite," said Okuna.

"He would kill you?"

"Or have one of his men do it," said Okuna.

"That wouldn't be very polite either," said Croft.

"No, it wouldn't." Okuna gave a small smile.

"If he represents such a small percentage of the population, why does he have everyone scared?" said Croft.

Okuna sat up, looking angry. His hand dropped down behind the desk. His voice cold, he said, "Are you calling me a coward?"

"No! No, of course not," said Croft soothingly. "It just seems that… well.. people don't want to publicly criticize him."

Okuna nodded, and eased back in his chair. "You have to understand that he has gold medalists working for him. And even if people don't like him, they're not going to stand up unless they're involved. And whatever he's doing, it doesn't involve most of us."

"But if he plunges Grafton into an interplanetary war-"

"He can't plunge Grafton into anything. He doesn't represent the government because we have no government," said Okuna.

"Don't you think if he attacks the League that the response may spill over and affect your fellow Graftonites?"

Okuna shrugged. "I'll deal with that when I see it happen. But I'm not going to get involved when there's no direct danger to me or my interests--nor, do I suspect, will anyone else."

Croft nodded slowly, getting up. "Do you mind if we walk around the grounds a bit?"

"Not at all," said Okuna. He gave them a phony smile and eagerly showed them to the door.

When they got outside Tane said, "Well, it looks like he won't help us either."

"Are you really surprised?" said Carper.

They walked to a nearby target range where Graftonites were blasting away. Croft didn't say anything for a while, as he thought of what to do. He watched Graftonites decimating paper targets. If only brute force could solve their problems.

"Let's get back to the groundcar," said Croft. "I want to get back to our quarter to check, ah, things." He didn't want to mention the listening devices he had placed in Quandry's ranch in front of Carper.

But as they turned to go, they heard a voice say, "Just a moment."

They turned to see a few Graftonites staring at them, guns in hand. One of them beckoned for them to come forward. Croft, seeing little choice, slowly did.

"You're off-worlders, aren't you?" said one of them.

Croft nodded.

"See, I told you so," their leader said, grinning to his companions. "We were wondering if you could help us out."

"Help? How?" Croft asked.

"Hold this in your open hand," said the leader. He dropped a bucket of apples on the ground in front of Croft, and reached in and handed Croft an apple.

Then he took a few steps back.

"Why do I get a bad feeling about this?" said Croft.

The leader stepped back farther and raised his blaster. "Now stand very still!"

He squeezed the trigger. Croft, cringing, saw a beam of light, and felt heat in his hand. When he looked at his hand he saw the cindered remains of the apple. The blaster wasn't set on stun.

"Now pick up another apple."

Croft reluctantly complied, holding it as far as possible from his body.

One of the Graftonite's companions aimed carefully, and squeezed the trigger. The blaster flared out, incinerating the apple, as well as singing Croft's index finger.

"Oh!" said Croft, grabbing his finger.

"Sorry," said the Graftonite, laughing. "You shouldn't have moved."

"I didn't," said Croft, nursing his burn.

"Now pick up another apple, and put it on your head," said the leader.

Croft did nothing.

"Do it!" said the leader, raising his blaster.

Croft, seeing no choice, picked up the apple, and thought about his options. He didn't have many. He looked at the Clapper. There was no way the Clapper could use his power to distract so many Graftonites.

"Now put it on your head!" said the leader. "Do it!" He aimed his blaster for effect.

Was this Graftonite one of the killers sent after him? Or was he just trying to have fun at Croft's expense? He had no way of knowing, but he had to know, because a mistake would be fatal.

Croft was still paralyzed, trying to figure out whether the leader would really shoot him if he didn't comply, when a new voice said, "What's going on here?"

They turned to see another tall, dark haired Grafton standing there. He looked grim.

"I said, what's going on here?" the man said. Frowning, he said, "Don't make me ask again."

"We were just doing some target practice," said the leader, his tone markedly different now.

"With fully charged blasters? On real people?" said the man. A man who Croft thought he recognized.

"He's only a sheep. We wouldn't have hurt him," said the leader.

The newcomer just stared at him coldly.

Gulping, the leader said to his friends, "Come on, guys," and headed off.

The newcomer slowly approached Croft. "Why is it every time I see you, you're always getting shot at?"

As he came closer Croft recognized him.

It was Traker Fields.

Graftonites were killers, and they were bounty hunters, but they took on many other professions as well, and one of those were serving as mercenaries, operating in small teams. There were individual mercenary units that had legendary reputations throughout populated space. And the leader of one of the most famous units was standing before Croft. Traker Fields.

Croft had met Traker Fields before, but usually in combat situations. Their paths had crossed before, but never on

Grafton. Like most Graftonites, Traker was neither allied with or against the League, but Croft had found him to be an honorable man.

Croft extended his hand. "Usually when we meet you're the one getting shot at."

Traker took his hand, shaking it. "I seem to recall a fair share of hostile fire aimed at you." He gave a small smile. "What brings you to Grafton? No, let me guess, you're here about Quandry."

Croft nodded.

"Well, you can have him," said Traker. "If you shot a hole in his ugly head I wouldn't shed a tear."

"You don't care for him?"

"He's a cheater, a liar, a dishonorable Graftonite. We'd be better off without him," said Traker.

"That's bold words, on a planet where free speech can be fatal," said Croft.

"So what?" said Traker.

"Aren't you worried that your opinions will get back to Quandry."

"No," said Fields coldly.

"And what of your fellow mercenaries. Are they also against him?" said Croft, getting the first glimmers of an idea.

"Quite the opposite!" said Traker. "I'm just about the only mercenary who's not on his side."

"Why?"

"Who do you think led off on the invasion of Grafton IV? Hired mercenaries, of course. Most of us are hoping that a wider war will break out; it will give us more work."

"But you already have work."

"Mo pays better. He gives us a generous share of the spoils," said Traker.

"Us...?"

"Not me," said Traker impatiently. "I'm basically out of it."

"Out of it?"

"I'm taking a vacation from the profession," said Traker. "I'm trying to get in shape to compete in the next olympics."

"What areas?"

"Maybe the triathalon, or precision shooting," said Traker. "Say, the word has been going around that Quandry has put a hit out on some nosy off-worlder. That wouldn't be you, would it?"

"Anything's possible," said Croft.

"You'd better be careful. Is this your bodyguard?" he said, indicating Carper.

Carper gave a bitter laugh.

Croft shook his head. "He's just along for comic relief."

Carper glared at Croft but, after a quick glance at Traker, decided not to react.

"Still, you'd better watch your step," said Traker, turning to go.

"Maybe you can help us," said Croft. "We're looking for people to speak out against Quandry."

"Speak out against him? Why would I do that?" Traker asked.

"He may plunge all of Grafton into war," said Croft.

"Hm…." said Traker.

"Hmm... what? What does that mean?" said Croft.

"I'm trying to decide if that's good or bad," said Traker. "A good war might shake people up. They're getting pretty complacent lately, even for Graftonites."

Croft sighed. "It's been great talking to you, Traker."

"Try to stay out of trouble, Croft."

For once there wasn't an assassin waiting for them as they returned to the groundcar. Croft said nothing for much of the journey back. Once they reached their rented quarters, Tane asked, "What are we going to do?"

"I'm going back to my room to think," said Croft. "I want to spend a few solitary hours without being shot at or threatened, and then I want a good night's sleep. We'll talk further in the morning."

Without saying another word he entered his room and closed the door behind him. As he turned around to walk further into the room, a woman stepped out of the shadows, a blaster pointed straight at Croft's chest. "I've come to kill you, Clifford Croft."

Chapter 7: Exploding Tempers

Major Nancy Kalikov of the Slurian Special Tasks Bureau stepped out of the shadows. The Slurians were the sworn enemy of the League, which Croft worked for, and Special Tasks was one of their elite espionage bureaus. Their specialty was high tech theft... and assassination.

Croft looked at the determined woman as she glared at him, her gun held rigidly in her right hand, pointing straight at him.

"Do I get to make a statement before you shoot me?" Croft said. He took a step forward. The blaster didn't waiver.

"Maybe," said Kalikov. "What kind of statement?"

Croft took another step forward. "A request."

"That's far enough!" said the Major, raising her blaster slightly. Then, "What request?"

Despite the order to halt, Croft took another step forward, so that his face was only inches from hers. "A kiss," he said.

He hesitated for only a moment, judging her expression, and then reached out and kissed her on the lips. He pulled back, staring at her. Then he reached forward and kissed her again.

This time she moaned slightly. "Oh Clifford," as she lowered the blaster.

"I've missed you," Croft said softly.

"We don't have much time," said Kalikov.

"Then let's make the best use of it, shall we?" said Croft.

Later, Croft was lying in bed with his arm around Kalikov.

"So what are you doing here, Clifford?" said Kalikov.

"Isn't it obvious?" said Croft.

"There's some thought that you might be trying to forge an alliance with the Graftons."

"Is this your thought, or your superiors?" said Croft.

She reached over and kiss him. "Come on Clifford, you can trust me."

He kissed her back. "Yes, I know. For the record, I'm not here to establish an alliance. The most obvious explanation is also the correct one. I'm here to stop Quandry."

Her eyes widened.

"You have an objection?" said Croft.

"You can't kill him, Clifford. He's one of their best gunfighters."

"Who said anything about killing him?" said Croft. "And in case you haven't noticed, I've been handling Grafton killers quite well lately."

"You spotted our lookouts," said Kalikov, making a face.

"Of course," said Croft. "Special Tasks doesn't make them like they used to."

"They are amateurs, NGB, not even attached to Special Tasks," said Kalikov. She abruptly got up and started to get dressed.

"You have to go?"

Kalikov nodded. "I must report."

Croft admired her slim form as she dressed. "You know, you don't have to report. You could defect."

Kalikov struggled into her pants. "You know that's not possible, Clifford."

"The reagent."

"The reagent."

Agents in Special Tasks were drugged with a slow acting poison to ensure their fidelity; unless they periodically received the antidote, they would die.

"We could try to synthesize an antidote," said Croft.

"Others have tried," said Kalikov bluntly. She put on her shirt and looked at Croft. They stared at each other for a long moment. Then she reached forward and gingerly kissed him.

"Take care of yourself, Clifford," she said.

In a moment, she was gone.

Yuri watched curiously as the Major finished buttoning her blouse as she sat down in the ground car. She glared at him.

"Do you have something to comment?"

"No, Major," he said.

"I have the information we need," said Kalikov. "If you wish, you may kill him now."

Yuri allowed himself to look surprised.

"At least you may try. I neither official endorse or disapprove of such action," said Kalikov. "Unofficially, I will offer some advice, if you request it."

Yuri, gulping, nodded.

"Do not attempt to kill Croft at a close distance. I would mount two snipers on the roof of the building opposite the apartment he is staying at. When he comes out in the morning, they can kill him even before he sees it coming."

"Thank you, Major!"

"Do not thank me," she said. "Success or failure will be on your own head. Now arrange for someone to take me to the spaceport. I have to report back."

"I will report on Croft's death to you in the next hyperwave."

"Very good," she said, without any emotion.

* *

The next morning, two Slurian NGB snipers perched on the top of a nearby building. They had their scopes trained on the door of Croft's apartment. There was no other exit.

"This should be easy," said one of them, named Victor.

"If it would be easy, the Croft pest would be dead long ago," said the other, named Tyusha.

"He will not even see it coming," said Victor.

* * * * * * * * * * * * * * * * * * * *

The Clapper heard a buzzing sound in his apartment. He grinned at the comm unit. It continued buzzing. After a few more seconds of grinning blankly at it, he pressed a button on it. Croft's image appeared on the screen.

"Where have you been?" said Croft. "I've been calling you for a while."

"I've been here," the Clapper grinned.

"Never mind. Get over to my apartment."

"Huh?"

"Leave your apartment, and come to mine," said Croft. "Would you like me to draw a map?"

The Clapper clapped. "That would be great!"

"Just get over here," Croft sighed, terminating the connection.

The Clapper nodded and headed to the door of the apartment. He didn't wonder why Croft had called him over the comm unit when previously Croft usually came for him personally. He opened the door to the outside. Brilliant sunlight streamed in.

* * * * * * * * * * * * * * * * * * *

"There!" said Victor, seeing someone come outside the residence.

"That's not Croft," said Tyusha. "That's the mental deficient."

"Why does Croft bring it with him?"

"I do not know," said Tyusha. "Nor do I care."

They both watched the Clapper, grinning like a maniac, as he stumbled his way to Croft's apartment. When he got there he pressed the buzzer at the door.

"This is our chance!" said Victor. "Aim carefully!"

They watched through their scopes as the door opened. Their fingers tightened on the trigger as they scanned inside the open door.

But there was no one there.

After a pause, the Clapper stepped in. He stood there for a moment before looking puzzled, and then he closed the door behind him.

"What is going on?" said Tyusha.

"Patience," said Victor. "They will have to come out sooner or later."

Actually, it was sooner. After only a moment's pause the door opened again. Once again they took up firing position, waiting for the first sign of Croft.

"Wait until he is out in the open," said Victor. "We must get a clear shot."

But only the Clapper stepped out of the door.

"It is the deficient again!"

But the door remained open behind him.

"Croft will be coming any second!" said Victor.

They were so focused on the door that they didn't at first notice what the Clapper was doing. He was looking up and around, squinting his eyes in the morning sunlight.

"What is the deficient doing?" said Victor.

Tyusha didn't have a chance to answer, because all of a sudden she felt an enormous tug and with a scream was pulled over the edge of the roof. Victor barely had time to look over and see her fall before he, too, felt an invisible force pull at him, jerking him over the edge of the rooftop.

"Is that the last of them?" came a voice from inside the apartment.

The Clapper grinned. "I think so."

"How reassuring," said Croft dryly, exiting the apartment.

"How did you know?" said the Clapper.

"What?" said Croft.

"I could barely see the peoples on the roof, and then only when you told me where to look," said the Clapper. "How did you know they were there?"

"A lucky guess," said Croft. "Come on."

They once again conferenced with the Chief over a secure holotransmission.

"So Tagan wasn't receptive to our arguments," said Croft.

"But why?" said the Chief.

"I think we can understand this better from the perspective of an appropriate economics model," said Tane. "According to the Hanlin model of monopolistic and ogopolistic actors, profit maximization is a senior priority of economic actors. Conflict can be seen as a way to surge the demand curve upwards, shifting both price and quantities-"

"He thinks he can clean up if there's a war," Croft translated.

"Ah, yes," said Tane. "I was getting to that."

"Didn't you try to tell him that a war could disrupt his business?" said the Chief.

"We tried," said Tane, "But he wasn't receptive,"

"Probably because he's a typical Hamline monopolistic actor," said Croft.

"Hanlin," said Tane, glaring at Croft.

"What about your meeting with the Olympics official?" said the Chief.

"He was sympathetic, but not willing to get involved in the body politic-"

"For fear someone would shoot his political body," said Croft.

"Has everyone been cowed into silence by Mo Quandry?" the Chief asked.

"Many of them have," said Croft. "But for most of them, they take a very narrow view of their self-interest. If it's not directly affecting their bottom line at that very moment, they're not interested."

"Hm…" said the Chief. She turned to look at something outside the range of the holographic imprinter.

"Chief?"

"Quandry has called a meeting with local diplomatic representatives next week to try to iron out differences," said the Chief.

"You mean, to present his demands," said Croft.

"Probably," said the Chief. She paused again, and then made a decision. "I want you to keep trying. Meet with more local   elites-"

"MORE local elites?" said Croft. "I think we've met them all!"

"As well as a local psychologist," said the Chief.

"Respectfully, Chief, I'm feeling fine-"

"Not for you, Mr. Croft," said the Chief. "We need a better understanding of the Graftonite psyche so we can best learn how to deal with Quandry. Consult a local expert and see what insights you can gleam."

Croft said, "Actually, Chief, before I start gleaming, I think there's a better use that my time can be put to."

"Really, Mr. Croft? And what would that be?" Her voice was as cold as a stone.

"Checking out a warehouse on the outskirts of Regular," said Croft. "I have a feeling that there might be something interesting to find there."

"What is the basis of that feeling?" the Chief asked.

"It's just a feeling," said Croft.

"Croft!"

"All right," said Croft. "I put several listening devices in Quandry's ranch. I was listening to excerpts last night and he mentioned something about receiving an important shipment yesterday."

"You conducted a covert operation without consulting me?" said the Chief.

"I also had dinner last night without consulting you, and extracted useful information from a Slurian agent without consulting you," said Croft. "Do you manage the affairs of the other seven Level One operatives this closely?"

The Chief restrained her rage to digest this latest news. "The Slurians? What are they doing here?"

"Watching me, mostly," said Croft. "They're also trying to find out what Quandry is up to."

"And how exactly did you find this out?"

"I, ah, interrogated one of their agents," said Croft.

The Chief glared at him. "What did you learn about this shipment?"

"Not much. They only referred to the fact that it was important," said Croft. "So rather than go in search of mental help, I'd like to check this out."

"You'll do both," the Chief decided.

"That's a very bold compromise," said Croft generously.

"I may not be impressed by your attitude, Mr. Croft, but you do get results," said the Chief. "But if you no longer get results, I will no longer feel the need to endure your attitude. Am I clear?"

"As clear as transparent steel," said Croft.

After the Chief signed off, Tane said, "Why do you purposefully and repeatedly antagonize her?"

"She's micromanaging me," said Croft. "And more importantly, she's also wrong."

"Wrong?"

"This business of talking to elites is a waste of time," said Croft.

"It's a useful method of gathering information," said Tane.

"For a researcher, perhaps," said Croft. "But I'm an operative. That's a derivative of the word "operations". If I wanted to be a reference librarian, I'd work in the dictionary department at the Grand August Database."

Tane ignored the slight. "Are you going to this warehouse today?"

"No, tonight."

"Then you have time to meet some more elites."

"As long as no one accuses me of being an elitist," said Croft. "Whatever happened to the idea of talking to the common man?"

"We have encountered several of those," said Tane. "Most of them tried to kill you."

"The elite it is, then," said Croft.

"This is crazy," Croft said, as Carper drove them to a suburb of Regular.

"Bigree Industries is the largest weapons manufacturer on Grafton," said Tane. "That certainly makes Bigree a powerbroker."

"I'm not denying that," said Croft. "But he's very likely to be sympathetic to Quandry. Arms dealers like wars. Quandry is trying to start a war. Why are we wasting our time here?"

"You never know," said Tane. "True, according to a rational economic actor model, you might think that Bigree would be a supporter of Quandry's efforts. But I took a chance and established holocontact with the company. Very quickly I found myself speaking to Mr. Bigree himself. And I have to say, I found him very sympathetic to our cause."

"How so?" said Croft.

"That's what we have to find out," said Tane. "But perhaps he thinks he can get larger weapons contracts with the League than he can with Quandry. Maybe he knows that doing business with Quandry is bad for business."

"Did he say that?"

"No," said Tane. "But he was very friendly. I have a feeling we can pick up an ally here."

Carper snorted.

"Hm," said Croft. "We'll see."

When they arrived, Croft, Tane, and the Clapper were quickly escorted to Bigree's office. Carper waited for them in the groundcar.

Salmon Bigree was a friendly man with a strong handshake.

"Thank you for coming," said Bigree, giving a big smile to each of them.

Croft and his companions started to sit down.

"Oh, I wouldn't bother sitting down," said Bigree.

Croft froze. "What do you mean?"

"You won't be here long enough," said Bigree. He pressed a button on his desk and a gunman entered through a side door. "You've been on the move so frequently that it's been difficult to track you down. I appreciate you coming to us."

"You're on Quandry's side," said Croft.

"Or he's on my side, it's all a matter of perspective," said Bigree. "Of course I support his efforts! Once the war gets going, just think of all the arms contracts my company will get! We don't merely manufacture hand lasers, you know; we also produce the heavy stuff—shipboard weapons systems, missiles, the works. This conflict will be very, very profitable to us, and you're not going to be allowed to interfere."

Croft looked at the gunman who was standing alertly in the room. Suddenly, he noticed something odd; the gunman had no holster! He didn't even seem to have a gun in his hand.

Bigree noticed Croft's stare. "I see you're confused. Can it be that you've never seen a zipgun before?"

And then the gunman flexed his wrist Croft saw, on the other side of the gunman's palm, a small box that was glued or attached to his hand.

"What is that?" said Croft.

"A zipgun," said Bigree. He turned to the gunman. "Perhaps you'd care to demonstrate."

The gunman nodded. He merely pointed with his hand, and a beam of light stabbed out, streaking a mere inch above Croft's right shoulder, leaving a small but smoking hole in the wall.

"I didn't say to shoot a hole in my wall," said Bigree, looking noticeably annoyed. "That will come out of your pay. Take this outside." He looked down, already absorbed in his own work again.

"If you're busy, perhaps we'll talk again another time," said Croft.

"I don't think we will meet again," said Bigree. "Goodbye, Mr. Croft."

The gunman gestured, and Croft, Tane, and the Clapper walked single file out of the office.

"I told you we shouldn't have come," Croft hissed to Tane. "But nooooo, you said he could be an ally."

"So what are we going to do?" Tane whispered.

"Get shot, probably," said Croft.

The gunman marched them outside the building, and then said, "That's far enough."

Croft turned around to face the gunman. "Are you simply going to shoot me?"

"If you like, you're welcome to try and outdraw me," said the gunman, looking amused.

"Not very sporting, considering you don't have to reach for a gun," said Croft. And at that moment he pressed down hard with his right boot. An anesthetic needle shot out and buried itself in the gunman's lower leg.

The gunman's smile didn't waver a fraction of an inch. It was only a few seconds later when he didn't fall down that they realized something was wrong. Reaching down, the gunman casually pulled out the needle and pulled up his right trouser leg. It was encased in a layer of white plastic.

"That wasn't very sporting either," said the gunman, standing tall again. "Your mistake was not killing your last opponent so he couldn't live to tell what trick you used on him. Did you really think that would work twice?"

"Maybe not," said Croft. He wet his lips, thinking quickly. "But do you still intend to offer me a fair fight?"

"A fair fight?" said the gunman, still amused. "How can a fight with a sheep be fair?"

"I think the only reason you're so confident is that you have one of those cheat guns," said Croft.

"I'm sure I could outdraw you with a regular blaster," said the gunman.

"Why don't you go and get one?"

"You're not getting away that easy," said the gunman. "This is boring me. Draw!"

"Wait!" said Croft. "What if I could arrange a fair test, here and now?"

"Test?"

"You say you're a better gunman than I am, correct?"

"There's no doubt about it," said the gunman.

"Well, there's no doubt you can outdraw me with that thing," said Croft. "But how are you for accuracy?"

"Accuracy?"

"Sure," said Croft. "I mean, it's easy to shoot a person, a person is a big target, especially at this distance. But what about a smaller target?" Holding up a restraining hand, Croft very slowly moved inside his jacket and pulled something out.

An apple. Actually, an apple he had saved from the Olympics the other day when he had first considered this idea.

"What are you proposing?"

"I'll toss this apple into the air. We both wait until it reaches its maximum height. The first one of us who can shoot the apple after it reaches its maximum height is the better marksman."

"I know I'm the better marksman," said the gunman. "What do I have to gain from this?"

"If you're afraid, of course, I can't force you to do it," said Croft. "But if you simply kill me, you'll always know that you let an off-worlder, a sheep, make you back down from a challenge-"

"Throw the apple," said the gunman, his voice cold. "Go ahead! Then I have to kill you and go about my business."

"Whatever you say," said Croft. "Just remember, it doesn't count if you fire before it reaches its maximum height."

"Whatever," said the gunman. "Just do it."

With one hand Croft tossed the apple into the air with as much force as he could. With his other hand he simultaneously drew his blaster...

The gunman waited until it reached its maximum height and then casually aimed with his finger and shot the apple out of the air. He looked down again to make a caustic remark to Croft when suddenly he saw Croft's blaster discharge and he felt a very painful explosion in his chest.

Looking very shocked and surprised, the gunman, openmouthed, dropped to the ground wordlessly.

"The quicker they make them, the dumber they make them," said Croft.

"Especially if you don't fight fair," said Carper, who walked up to them.

"You were watching the whole thing?" said Croft.

"I have nothing else to do," said Carper.

"You wouldn't have helped out, would you?" said Croft.

"I don't interfere with fair fights," said Carper.

"Even one with these," said Croft, pointing to the zip guns.

Carper knelt down and examined it. "I've heard about these but never seen one." He looked up at Croft. "I don't think they're very fair in duels; but then, I don't think what you did was very fair either."

Croft turned to Tane. "We've finally found a job for him; he can referee!"

That night there was extra security on warehouse 44 in the industrial district. Graftonite guards patrolled along an electrified fence; electric monitors and sensors ringed the perimeter.

Clifford Croft restrained a laugh as he observed this from the roof of the warehouse, inside the perimeter. These security measures would have deterred most ordinary people, even many agents. But for him? Hah! It was so pedestrian that it wasn't even worth describing his entry.

Croft opened a hatch on the roof and slid down onto a catwalk. He saw Graftonites roaming among large stacks of crates of all sizes. The mark of Bigree Industries was prominently stamped on all of them.

Taking out a small scanner, he cast it in front of the nearest boxes, and moved from one stack to another.

Weapons, weapons, and more weapons... There was enough here for a small army. But these were merely handguns. Quandry had talked about receiving a special shipment. What was so special to be found here?

Croft's attention was fixed on some very large crates, each two stories tall, that were sitting under a spotlight. Two Graftonites were roaming around it. He would have to time things precisely to get between the two without being seen by either.

Croft crept between them and got close to the crates. He looked down at his scanner briefly, while still looking about in all directions. What he saw made him frown. He crept along the side of the crate, careful to keep some distance of the Graftonite ahead of him. The other Graftonite behind him would be turning the corner and would see Croft in a few seconds....

A few seconds later, the Graftonite behind Croft turned the corner. He looked ahead of him and continued walking. A few steps took him to a large hole in the crate. The Graftonite passed by without even looking.

Inside the crate, Croft waited until the footsteps receded and then quickly risked a bit of light from a handflash. What he saw made him gasp.

The crate was filled with large anti-ship missiles. Mo Quandry must have something bigger in mind than gunfighting.

But Croft recognized that these were surface to air missiles, primarily defensive in purpose. Did Quandry fear an attack? That didn't make sense. Quandry was the one doing the attacking.

Shutting down the light, Croft considered his options. Sabotage? He didn't have the right equipment.

But that shouldn't stop a truly capable infiltrator. Croft risked a brief flash of light again. He saw an inspection hatch for one of the primary warheads....

He narrowed the scope of his handflash to a tight beam and opened it up. He started manipulating wires... the

activation mechanism was there, the timing mechanism there….
Good….

Several minutes later Croft worked his way out of the crate, and then the warehouse, and then over the fence. The guards inside the fence didn't even notice him leaving.

He had only walked a few feet from the fence when he heard a voice say, "You certainly took your time."

On any other planet Croft would have whirled around, his blaster drawn or firing. But here Croft merely froze, and then turned around slowly.

A gunman stood outlined in the dim starlight.

"You didn't detect me entering," said Croft.

"No," said the gunman. "I followed you here. I was debating whether to raise the alarm, but feared you might escape. I decided it was safest to wait until you came out. I see my assessment was correct."

"Are you here to kill me?" said Croft.

"Correct," said the gunman.

"May I ask why?"

"For a very important reason," said the gunman.

"Which is?" Croft asked.

"Because I'm paid to," the gunman said. "I'm aware how you tricked previous operatives, so I don't think I'm going to give you any more time to-"

"Wait!" said Croft. "I'm working for Quandry!"

"What?" said the gunman. "Impossible. Quandry sent me to kill you."

"When?" said Croft. "When did you get the order?"

"Two days ago," said the gunman."

"Things have changed," said Croft. "I've reached an accommodating with Quandry." He tried to conceal his nervousness. That warehouse would explode at any minute. And he was still too close.

"An accommodation," said the gunman skeptically. "Does this accommodation include sneaking into Mr. Quandry's private warehouse?"

"I'm an infiltrator," said Croft. "I've reached an arrangement with Mr. Quandry where I'm to test his security. That's what I was doing tonight."

"You can't seriously ask me to believe this," said the gunman. But there was a bit of doubt in his voice.

"I have proof," said Croft. "If you'll allow me to reach into my jacket, I have a copy of the contract, with Quandry's signature."

The gunman paused, and with each passing moment Croft expected to be blown up by the warehouse just a few dozen feet away. But he said, "All right, take it out. But slowly."

Croft gingerly reached into his jacket. He pulled out a folder paper, carefully holding it by the lower right hand corner. Still holding it by that very corner, he handed it to the gunman.

The gunman took the paper and unfolded it, peering at it in the dim starlight. "There aren't even any words here!"

"I know," said Croft.

The gunman gurgled something, and then collapsed to the ground.

Croft quickly walked over to the gunman, who was lying rigid on the ground but still conscious. "While the paralysis isn't lethal, I'm afraid you won't be around to tell anyone else about this particular trick."

He started running for the trees. A few second later, the warehouse exploded.

The whole area was engulfed in flame. The explosions continued for several minutes, as other munitions ignited, creating a cascading effect.

"What do you mean, it blew up!" Quandry roared. "What was the cause?"

"We're not sure, sir, but the body of the assassin we sent after Toft was found on the grounds," said Rocco.

"Toft, Toft, and again Toft!" said Quandry. "Who is this man?"

Two men were escorted into Quandry's office.

"I can tell you who he is," said one of them. "His name isn't Toft, it's Clifford Croft, and he's an agent with the Column."

"The Column? I thought we eliminated their stationpost on Grafton," said Grafton.

"He's not a local operative," said the newcomer. "He's one of the eight."

"A Column Eight operative," said Quandry. "That would explain a lot." He looked hard at the newcomers. "And you are telling me this because…."

"Sluria only wants peace and friendship with you," said Samov, one of the newcomers.

"Peace and friendship," said Quandry.

"Yes, an alliance," said Samov.

"But we do not want an alliance with you," said Quandry.

"What do you want, then?" said Samov.

"Tribute," said Quandry. "A billion credits a year, for starters."

"A billion!"

"For starters," said Quandry. "The Slurians can afford it."

"We will never pay blackmail payments," said Samov.

"Then take a message back to your people-" Quandry broke off in mid-sentence. "No, I have a better idea. Instead of taking a message back to your people, I think you will be the message. Take them away."

"What? What?" said Samov.

Samov and his companion were pulled out of their seats by Graftonite guards.

"Leave their bodies in a public place, where they will be found relatively quickly," said Quandry.

"Wait, you can't just kill us-"

"Actually, I can." Faster than they could see, Quandry raised his right hand and pointed at each of the Slurians in rapid succession. A thin beam of light struck their foreheads, and they collapsed to the ground.

Rocco looked at the fallen Slurians in disgust. "Now we have to carry them out."

"Be glad that's all you have to do," said Quandry. "I want this Croft taken care of. I don't care how you do it. Send bronze medalists, silver medalists, whatever you need. Even multiple operatives."

"Multiple operatives?" said Rocco.

"You heard me. Move!" Quandry barked.

Chapter 8: A Meeting With Mo

"Surface to air missiles?" said the Chief. "What on August would they use those for?"

"You mean, what would they have used them for?" said Croft, grinning, accentuating the fact that he had destroyed them.

The holo of the Chief nodded, grinning slightly. "Very well, Mr. Croft, you have earned a bit of praise. But what was their purpose?"

"I don't know," said Croft.

"Have you gleaned anything else from your listening devices?"

"Not really," said Croft. Most of the conversations he had monitored were mundane. Either Quandry held his important conversations somewhere else, or he had figured out that his ranch was being monitored.

"Then continue with your primary mission. Talk to more elites."

"Chief, every time I talk to elites I get attacked by gunmen."

"You seem able to handle yourself well."

"There's a limit to the number of tricks even I can pull," said Croft.

"All right," said the Chief. "Spend one more day at it and then we'll regroup and consider our options. Agreed?"

Croft mumbled something.

"Very good." Her holographic image faded.

"She seemed almost pleased with you today," said Tane.

"Yes, very nice," said Croft, distracted. "So, where are we going today so someone can shoot me?"

"I've set up a meeting with one of the foremost psychiatrists on Grafton," said Tane.

"Good, I feel I need to have my head examined," said Croft.

The Clapper clapped.

"And make sure you book some time for the Clapper as well," Croft added.

"-I'm not a psychiatrist, Mr. Croft," said Arn Arco.

Croft, having monitored the grisly conversation where Quandry had learned of his identity, realized there was no longer any reason to operate under his alias.

"Not a psychiatrist?" said Croft, casting a glance at Tane.

"Well, perhaps I am the closest thing to a psychiatrist on Grafton," said Arco. "You have to understand, there are no mentally ill people on Grafton."

"Let me guess; 'If you're mentally ill, don't come to Grafton'," said Croft wryly.

"Yes, well, if by that you mean that there aren't a lot of social services here for the mentally ill, you're correct. In fact, the mentally ill don't survive very long here," said Arco.

"And why is that?" Croft asked, although he already guessed the answer.

"The mentally ill tend to be ill-mannered in public; and on Grafton, if you're ill-mannered, it's best if you be a good gunfighter; unfortunately, the mentally ill rarely are," said Arco.

"So if I were a paranoid schizophrenic with a gold medal from your shooting Olympics, I'd do just fine here?"

"I wouldn't phrase it that way, but... well, actually, the way you phrase it works too," said Arco. "But getting back to what I am, I am a culturist."

"Culturist?"

"Ah... sociologist, you might call it. I study the culture of Grafton, our dynamics, what makes us what we are on a societal level."

"I see," said Croft. "I'm curious; how much demand is there for... your kind of work here?"

"None," said Arco promptly, with a smile. "I mostly publish my papers in off-planet journals. I have to supplement my meager income by hiring myself out to kill people."

Croft raised an eyebrow. He felt his body temperature rise slightly, and he shifted in his seat.

Arco smiled again. "Oh, I have a code of ethics, Mr. Croft. I only kill those who have killed others. It's so unfortunately rare for people in my profession to have such ethics, wouldn't you say?"

Croft thought it was time to tactfully change the subject. "Ah, getting back to the purpose of our visit-"

"Ah, yes, you want to learn more about the culture of my people. But that would take years, Mr. Croft. Can you be more specific?" Arco asked.

"For years the Graftonites have been content to hire themselves out as bounty hunters and bodyguards and the like," said Croft. "Now all of a sudden they're all stirred up and talking about war. Can you tell me why the sudden change?"

Arco nodded. "The answer is simple, Mr. Croft. It resolves around fairness."

"Fairness?"

"You are probably familiar with the death of Rel Cadwalader, yes?"

Croft nodded.

"It really enraged people," said Arco. "Not because he was killed (because a number of people are killed every day on Grafton), but in the way he was killed. A sneak attack by multiple opponents."

"But I have seen Graftons attack in groups before, or launch surprise attacks," said Croft.

"Were they one on one encounters?" Arco asked. "Or was the Grafton vastly outnumbered, or part of a group attacking another group? The rules for war are different, you see. But one on one encounters are supposed to be fair. The rule of law has been replaced by the rule of ability. If one cheats the rules, one risks societal disapproval."

"Which can be quite lethal, I see," said Croft. "But you were explaining how this ties in with the current situation."

"Well, the unfairness of his death enraged the population. It cast sheep—begging your pardon, off-worlders in quite a bad light. Previously, off-worlders hadn't been held in the highest of regards, but they were never as intensely disliked as they are now."

"Because they don't kill by the rules?" Croft asked. "Because they don't play right?"

"Play right? Yes, that's one way of putting it," said Arco. "There is another strand to it, of course, the fight for civil rights."

"So Quandry is invading other planets to fight for all of your civil rights?" said Croft.

"Precisely!" said Arco. "We on Grafton believe that one should be rewarded based on one's ability. For centuries we've taken jobs as bounty hunters, killers, item locators, and other high risk positions. While our pay has been higher than what you would think of as traditional professions, it has still only been a fraction of the reward."

"How do you mean?"

"For example, an associate of mine recently was hired to terminate a business rival on Selekaris," said Arco. "This rival ran a multimillion credit business which was a competitor to the client who hired my associate. My associate was paid 75,000 credits to eliminate the rival. But the elimination of the rival led to the collapse of the rival's company, leading to gains of millions of credits for the client. Imagine that! A gain of millions of credits, and my associate was only paid in five figures."

"I almost feel sorry for the killer," said Croft ironically.

Arco frowned. "I note your sarcasm, Mr. Croft. But consider that the rival had bodyguards. It was a dangerous mission. With the reward so high, my associate should have had a greater share of the rewards, because it was his superior ability that made it possible to eliminate the rival."

"Then why not do something more peaceful, such as going on strike," Croft suggested.

"In our culture, invading other planets is the equivalent of going on strike," said Arco. "It's our way of getting noticed."

"It certainly works," said Croft.

"Thank you."

"I'm surprised that a scholarly 'culturist' such as yourself would endorse such violent means," said Croft.

"But I don't," said Arco.

Croft looked surprise.

"I merely said I understand the cultural imperative. I didn't say I agree with it."

"Do you?"

"No. No offense, but off-worlders can't help being inferior to us, they should be pitied, I think, rather than punished."

"A most enlightened perspective." Croft commented.

"I support a more moderate solution," said Arco.

"Which is?"

"Quandry is promoting a conference next week to work out a solution involving the payment of transfer fees to cement galactic unity."

"You mean the blackmail payments."

"I prefer to think of them as economic exchanges which will promote greater harmony," said Arco.

"What if the League doesn't pay up?"

"Then the results could be most tragic, for the League," said Arco.

"Do you really want to see a wider war?"

"As I've stated, I do not."

"Then what can we do to stop it?"

"I'm not sure you can," said Arco. "Quandry has done an extraordinary thing, uniting our people."

"Uniting? I thought he only has one or two percent of the population who actively supported him."

"For one or two percent of Graftons to agree on anything is considered unification," said Arco. "And a much greater proportion of the pollution sympathizes with him."

"Is there any way he can be discredited? What if he publicly showed fear or cowardice?" said Croft.

"Mo Quandry? That's highly unlikely, Mr. Croft," said Arco.

"Well, is there any way we can change cultural norms, then?"

"Certainly," said Arco. "Become a Graftonite, win some gold medals, hold a large number of great gatherings, face down your opponents in combat, and persuade people to believe in your cause."

"I'm not sure we have the time for that," said Croft.

"Then your government had better be prepared to pay," said Arco.

They went outside Arco's suburban office. It was a hot day on August, and Croft felt an unusual amount of perspiration.

Tane looked at him oddly.

"Something wrong?" said Croft.

"You look… different," said Tane.

"Different how?" said Croft.

"I don't know, but ever since we left this morning to go to Arco, you've looked somehow different," said Tane.

"Do I look like myself?" said Croft reasonably.

"Yes, basically," said Tane.

"Then that's sufficient," said Croft.

They walked to the groundcar. Standing there waiting for them was a gunman.

"Don't tell me, we're in a no parking zone," said Croft.

The Gunman stood very still, watching Croft, waiting for him to draw.

"Before you shoot, will you at least tell me who you're here to kill?" said Croft reasonably.

"Croft," the gunman spat.

"Well, then you can't shoot me."

"Can't I?" the gunman leered. He looked at Carper. Carper looked shocked.

Croft noticed that. "What's wrong?"

"It's Alat Bates," said Carper.

"Is that supposed to mean something?" said Croft.

"He's a quick shooting silver medalist," said Carper. "You don't stand a chance."

Croft turned to face the now grinning gunman, who was undoubtedly pleased to have been recognized.

"I don't need any special chances," said Croft. "Because you've got the wrong guy. For you see, I'm not Clifford Croft."

"Nice try," said the gunman. He looked amused, enough so that he took out a small datapad which had a picture of Croft's face on it. Bates held it up.

Croft nodded. "Yes, that's Croft, but as you can see, I'm not him."

The gunman was about to ask what he was talking about, when Croft casually reached up and carefully pulled on his own face. Pieces of his forehead, nose, and cheeks started to come off, revealing a face underneath that was very different.

The gunman gasped.

"As you can see, you fell for the decoy," said Croft.

"Maybe I should just kill you anyway," said the gunman angrily.

"Why? Have you been paid to kill a decoy?"

"No."

"Then why reward your boss with something more than you were paid for? If you were paid to kill me, I could understand that. But are you really going to give your boss a free kill?" said Croft reasonably.

The gunman snorted and stalked off.

When a moment had passed and there was no sign of his returning, Tane allowed herself to exhale and looked at Croft.

"What…. How….?"

"I believe your real question is, 'who'?" said Croft. He pulled at his face again, and another layer of plastiform came off, revealing his real face. "It was getting hot in here. I'm glad we're done with these interviews, because I'm all out of tricks."

Putting on (and taking off) two layers of disguises is not something for an amateur; but no one had accused Croft of being an amateur in hundreds of years.

When Croft got back to their apartment he checked his listening devices. Quandry had already heard the news and was raging about it.

"Of course it was Croft, you idiot," came Quandry's voice.

"But boss-" came Bates' voice.

"Don't 'but boss' me," said Quandry. "I'm going to give you one more chance. Don't fail me again."

"Yes boss," said Bates.

"Now get out of my sight."

His footsteps receded, while a new set took their place.

"Has the latest shipment arrived?" said Quandry.

"Yes," came a voice that Croft recognized as Rocco's.

"Did it all arrive?"

"Yes, the bombs are all there."

"Good," said Quandry. "Where are you storing them?"

"In Regular. We're temporarily storing them at 1572 Uantra street," said Rocco.

"I don't want them in an office building, I want them here!" said Quandry. "That Croft pest is still on the loose! I want them moved here first thing tomorrow!"

"Yes, Mo."

The footsteps receded.

"What kind of bombs?" asked the Chief.

"He wasn't specific."

"First surface to air missiles and now bombs," said the Chief. "While at the same time he is convening a peace conference."

"Maybe he's trying to keep his options open, in case the peace conference fails."

"Or perhaps he intends to blow up the peace conference," said Croft.

"What would he have to gain from that?" said the Chief. "That wouldn't help him make more money. And where would the surface to air missiles fit in? No, we don't have the whole story."

"Perhaps he ordered the weapons to shore up his flank among the hardliner faction in his organization," said Tane. "Perhaps that show of force will give him the political room to open negotiations."

"Do you actually believe the things you say?" Croft marveled.

"It's a possibility," said Tane. "There are bound to be differing elites with different ideas for strategy even within Quandry's own group. If we negotiate with him in good faith and strengthen the moderates-"

"Chief, the League can't seriously be considering making blackmail payments to Quandry, can they?" said Croft.

"Blackmail payments? Never," the Chief assured him. "However, as I've already said, we might be willing to contribute to an economic development fund, to cement a bond between our two people and reduce tensions-"

"I think it will be very dangerous to go forward with this conference," said Croft.

"It's not my decision to make," said the Chief. "I share your concerns, Mr. Croft. That's why you need to investigate further. Go to this warehouse and find out what these bombs are. Then we will talk more. The conference is in two days, and we don't have much time."

"Right," said Croft, signing off. He turned to Tane, "Well, at least we didn't waste any time talking about our meeting with Arco."

"That wouldn't have been a waste of time," said Tane. "He provided some useful insight into the culture of this planet."

"What useful insight?" said Croft. "Name one useful thing he said that could be of any use to us."

"He told us that Graftonites have a certain angst about off-worlders that may be appeased by an economic development fund," said Tane.

"Yes, they want money, a lot of it," said Croft. "I already knew that."

"Do you always rush to conclusions, Mr. Croft?"

"Pretty much," said Croft.

That night Croft drove to the office building where the bombs were supposed to be hidden. He brought Carper along with him, but had mixed feelings about doing so.

Last time he had gotten caught as he had left the warehouse containing the missiles. He wanted to be able to get away quickly if needed and having Carper at the controls of the groundcar waiting for him would help shave precious seconds off their escape.

But he didn't know how Carper would feel about his breaking and entering; Carper knew he was going to break into the building, though Croft hadn't told him about the bombs. If Carper had any qualms about it, he didn't say so.

Croft bypassed automated security measures and slipped into the building. It was a modest three story building. It appeared deserted. It should only take him a few minutes to run through each floor. But he was not expecting what he saw inside.

The building was empty. Completely empty—no office equipment, furniture, or anything, just a giant empty building.

This meant trouble. Croft immediately got out of there, and ran for the ground car-

Only to find four Graftonites waiting for him.

All had their blasters raised.

Carper was leaning against the groundcar, with an odd expression on his face. The four Graftonites had him in their line of sight, but they were primarily facing Croft. Bates was among them.

Bates made eye contact with Croft. "If you reach for anything, we'll shoot you. If you try anything, we'll shoot you."

"We?" said Carper, frowning. "All of you against him?"

Bates turned to Carper. "You're Carper. Do you know who I am?"

Carper nodded. He knew that Bates was a silver medalist.

"Then don't get involved," said Bates. He gave Carper a smug grin.

Bates and his men tensed up, looking carefully at Carper for any sign of reaction. At the slightest hint that he might reach for his blaster, they would draw.

Carper hesitated for a moment, and held his breath. Then he nodded, and some of the tension dissipated.

"What are you doing working for this off-worlder anyway?" said Bates.

"Money," said Carper simply.

"Do you really care what happens to this one?" said Bates, indicating Croft.

Carper shook his head. "In fact, I dislike him rather intensely."

"Then why don't you join us?" said Bates. He studied Carper appraisingly. "Why don't you come back and talk with us?"

Carper considered for a moment, then nodded.

Bates walked over to Croft, his gun pointed straight at him. "You're very lucky, you know."

"Lucky?" said Croft. "How does getting caught make me lucky?"

"Mr. Quandry wants to see you," said Bates. "That means you get to live for at least a few more hours."

"It's nice to be wanted," said Croft, as Bates plucked his blaster out of his holster. One of his men came forward and patted Croft down.

"Off with your boots," said Bates.

Croft opened his mouth to protest.

"If he tries anything, kill him," said Bates.

After Croft had removed his boots, Bates turned and gave him a smug smile. "This way, please."

The ride back to Quandry's ranch was quiet and uneventful. Croft tried to think happy thoughts, but wasn't having very much success. Finally, they arrived at Quandry's ranch and Croft was taken to his office.

"So we finally meet," said Quandry.

Croft shrugged, as if it was inconsequential to him.

Quandry motioned with his head. "Sit down, Mr. Croft," said Quandry, grinning at Croft hesitated, then sat down. Behind him he was flanked by two Graftonite killers.

"You've led us through quite a chase," said Quandry.

"I hope it was entertaining," said Croft.

"Not really," said Quandry, his face going stone cold.

"So what brings me here?" said Croft. "Have you decided to give up?"

Quandry laughed. "I don't think so, Mr. Croft. No, I brought you here to get some information."

"Information?"

"You are one of the most senior agents of the Column. I want to know what your people know about our plans and what you reported to them before we discovered... these....," he said, holding up one of Croft's listening devices.

"Your discussion about bombs was all a setup to capture me," Croft realized.

"If you've only realized this now, you're not quite as clever as your reputation suggests," said Quandry. "Yes, once we discovered the devices, I thought of the plan to capture you."

"I'm surprised."

"Surprised?"

"I didn't think you were that bright," said Croft.

Quandry's face was hard with rage, and he pointed a finger at Croft. Croft could see a zap gun box mounted on the back of his hand. "Take care, Mr. Croft. I have only to twist my finger slightly upwards to burn a pretty hole in your forehead."

"I wouldn't be able to give you very much information with a pretty hole in my forehead, would I?" Croft asked. "But I'm not very good at talking about me; what about you? What do you hope to gain by this peace conference of yours? Surely you can't believe the League will give into your blackmail demands."

Quandry leaned back and grinned again. "On the contrary; there has been active discussion of funding development projects on Grafton."

"But surely not on the scale you're looking for," said Croft. "Do you really think they're going to negotiate and give you everything you want?"

"Who said anything about a negotiation?" said Quandry, his grin shrinking into a small smile.

"Well, if you're not there to negotiate… wait, I see, you're going to take them hostage," said Croft. "But that won't work. The League still won't pay billions to free a bunch of low level diplomats."

"Who said anything about taking them hostage?" said Quandry, that odd small smile still on his face.

Croft looked at Quandry, generally puzzled for a minute. Then, with a tone of disbelief, he said, "You're simply going to kill them?"

"Not simply," said Quandry. "They will indeed be taken hostage for a short period, while we wait for your League to accede to our demands."

"Purposefully unreasonable demands," said Croft, suddenly understanding.

"At which time they'll be regrettably executed."

"You never intended for the League to accept your terms," Croft realized.

"I admit I was worried when I received feelers from the League saying they might pay several hundred million credits a year. That was when I had to increase my demand to several billion," said Quandry.

"But why are you turning down easy money?" said Croft.

Quandry just looked at him and continued to smile.

"If you accept the money the crisis will ease and you won't have a rallying point," said Croft. "This whole exercise is an attempt to rally support for your cause. You're going to provoke the League into attacking Grafton, so you can increase your base of support."

"Very good, Mr. Croft," said Quandry.

"But this makes no sense. Do you really want a full scale invasion of Grafton?"

"There will be no invasion," said Quandry bluntly. "But I will get what I need. How much of what you've said does your League know?"

"All of it," said Croft.

"I think not," said Quandry. "Your diplomats have agreed to attend our meeting, which is set to start in the next two hours. I hardly think they would agree to simply show up for their own execution, do you?"

Croft said nothing.

"But your League must have some suspicions, which is why they sent you. I want to know what they know, and how they will react to our plan."

Croft said nothing.

"I could kill you in an instant," said Quandry, half flexing his finger at Croft. Croft forced himself not to stare at the finger.

"But threats of death are probably wasted on you," said Quandry. "Anticipating this, I have called in a specialist."

"A specialist?"

"One who specializes in pain," said Quandry. "I think you'll find him most instructive. Unfortunately, you'll have little time to appreciate it as his subjects rarely survive for very long." Quandry checked his chronometer. "He will be here in a short time. In the meantime, we'll find a nice place to put you." He nodded slightly and the Graftons around him gestured for Croft to get up.

"Goodbye, Mr. Croft," said Quandry.

"That has a ring of finality to it," said Croft.

"So it does," said Quandry. "Take him away."

Croft sat glumly behind a force field in an underground level of Quandry's ranch for several hours. He was rather depressed. He didn't have any great love for diplomats but even they didn't deserve to be slaughtered. At least Tane and the Clapper were free.

But what could they do? Tane was an analyst, and the Clapper had the mind of a child. They were both good in what they did, but were not operatives.

And what of Carper? Croft had hardly been surprised when the Graftonite had switched sides. Still, there had been something odd about Carper's conversation with Bates... even though he didn't like Croft, Carper hadn't seemed happy to see Croft captured.

Well, maybe his unhappiness would be assuaged when he got his first paycheck from Quandry. That's all Graftonites cared about, their money.

Croft heard a door open in the room outside the forcefield, and a guard said something to the newcomer. The newcomer said something back. There was silence for a moment, and nobody moved or said anything.

Croft wondered what was going on when he heard blaster fire outside of his view, and then a crumping sound as someone fell to the ground. His eyebrows went up as Carper, holding a smoking blaster, stepped into view.

"I knew they had visiting hours here but I didn't think you'd be the first to sign up," said Croft.

Carper stared at Croft expressionlessly, as if he were considering something. Then, making a decision, he reached out and deactivated the forcefield.

Croft gingerly stepped out, seeing for the first time the smoking body of the guard on the ground. He looked inquiringly at Carper.

"I still don't like you," said Carper.

Croft continued to look inquiringly.

"Maybe I liked what they did, but not how they did it," said Carper. "Maybe there was something about them that annoyed me. Maybe I didn't like the fact that there was four of them against one. Maybe there was something in Bates' smile I didn't like. Maybe when he, an accomplished silver medalist, challenged me, a guy with a busted arm, to stand down, I found something unfair."

"And now?" said Croft.

Carper raised his blaster, pointing it at Croft. "The only way you'll get out of here is if you're under armed escort."

"And what about you?" said Croft.

"I think I'm going to leave Grafton for a while," said Carper. "Until things settle down. My arm is almost healed. I can find work to keep me busy."

"I'm sure you can," said Croft. He paused. "Would it mean anything if I thanked you?"

"Not really."

"That's what I thought."

Chapter 9: Attack On The Conference

League   Ambassador Don Miller sampled some refreshments as he eyed the crowd. The entire diplomatic corps was here, not just senior diplomats but midlevel staff as well from all the major embassies. The League was there in full force, of course, but also there were the diplomats from the Directorate, the Slurians, the Kalaspians, the Tensorites, and all the other major interplanetary governments.

Quandry had wanted it this way, extending broad invitations to all the embassies, to bring their entire staff. After being cooped up for weeks in their embassies because of the hostility of the local population, most of the embassy staffs had accepted, even if they were a bit wary. Quandry had capitalized on the weariness and especially the gullibility of the diplomats, which, as it turned out, was not very difficult to do.

Grafton was a difficult planet under the best of circumstances. It had no government to speak of, so there were no unified authorities to deal with. The planet didn't recognize the concept of diplomatic immunity, which meant that embassies were not considered sovereign territory and diplomats could be shot or even killed without due process. Not that that had happened, even during this current period of ugliness. The local Graftons took a patronizing view towards them, referring to them as 'sheep', and as long as the diplomatic corpse took pains not to offend anyone there were no problems.

As least until several weeks ago. Several embassy staffs were threatened by hostile mobs, and they fled to their embassies, and soon no off-worlder was leaving any embassy for any reason.

But Quandry had given them his personal assurances of safe-conduct to and from the meeting hall and Miller was pleased that he had delivered. There were Graftonite guards around the building who were unfailingly polite, and the hall was well stocked with excellent food, which Miller thought was a good sign. Quandry was taking pains to treat them well. That meant only one thing: he was prepared to deal.

Miller approached the Slurian ambassador, a man named Stod Rukanan. He was Miller's counterpart on Grafton, as much as any Slurian could be. Of course, all members of the Slurian foreign service were almost automatically also members of various branches of the Slurian Secret Police, usually the NGB, but that didn't mean that they couldn't be civil with each other.

Rukanan eyed him coming warily, rapidly gobbling down food from a tray, like an animal fearing that it would be taken away at any moment. Slurians were like that.

"Ambassador," said Miller, by way of greeting.

"Um," grunted Rukanan, as he eyed Miller warily. He continued to eat, only stopping when the tray was empty. Miller wondered if there was enough to eat in the Slurian embassy.

"This is an auspicious beginning, don't you think?" said Miller.

"What makes you say that?" said Rukanan, looking about for something else to eat.

"The banquet hall is very well provided for. Perhaps Quandry is prepared to be reasonable."

"You are very foolish if you trust Quandry," said Rukanan.

"It's my understanding that Slurians never trust anyone," said Miller.

"That's why we always win," said Rukanan.

"Do you?" said a new voice.

They turned to see Ambassador Steve Yardin of the Directorate. "It seems to me that the Slurian Union has had some reverses of late."

"All lies and enemy propaganda," said Rukanan, waiving a hand dismissively.

"The industrial accident that blew up your largest powerplant on Sluria, reports of low harvests and food shortages on Ufranda Prime, further reports of unrest-"

"As I said, all lies and propaganda," said Rukanan. And then, as an afterthought "But even if they were not all lies, they would be exaggerations, not under my jurisdiction, and caused by bad weather."

"Well, I suppose that covers all the bases, then," said Yardin. "I wonder when our host will make an appearance?"

They didn't have to wait long. Part of the room darkened and a hologram of Mo Quandry appeared.

"A hologram?" said Miller. "Why doesn't he appear in person?"

"Greetings, noble diplomats," said the hologram. "As most of you know, I am Mo Quandry. I want to thank you for taking the time to come to our conference."

"How are we supposed to have a conference when their main negotiator won't appear in person?" Yardin wondered.

"Perhaps appearing in person might anger hardliners in his faction," Miller theorized.

"We've had a lot of discussion and argument over the past few weeks regarding our proposal to have your governments make economic development grants to our planet. While most of your governments have accepted the idea in principal, the amounts they've offered have been insultingly small," said Quandry. "Take the League, the biggest and richest federation of planets. They offer a meager 500 million credits in aid a year, when we requested 20 billion. They might as well not have bothered to respond."

"We've gone back and forth for some time but the numbers have not moved markedly in our direction. That's why we've called this conference, to resolve our outstanding issues," said Quandry. "After analyzing the problem in depth with a blue ribbon panel of political scientists, we realize the problem is that we aren't getting the attention of sufficiently senior government officials on your homeworlds. With your cooperation, we have figured out an efficient way to deal with this problem."

He paused, and if by signal, Graftonite gunmen streamed into the room. The crowd started to murmur with trepidation.

"You will be held at this facility for the next 50 hours. Your governments will be told that if they do not agree to pay, you will be executed."

The murmur grew into a roar.

Quandry raised the volume of his broadcast. "Naturally, I'm sure it will not come to that. We are all civilized people, aren't we? You will be kept comfortable and safe during this period, but you will not be allowed to contact your governments." He paused. "One last thing: I ask, for your own safety, that you do not attempt to leave or interfere with my diplomatic representatives. I would not want to needlessly create a diplomatic incident."

Graftonite gunmen fanned through the room, carrying weapons detectors. Their detectors flashed when they scanned two Slurian diplomatic representatives. The Slurians moved to draw their weapons—and were shot dead before they could get their hands on their blasters.

"If you want to live, drop your weapons now," said Rocco, speaking loudly. After a moment's hesitation, there was a clatter as weapons were dropped to the ground. The gunmen fanned out and picked them up. Once they were done scanning the crowd, they took up positions along all the exits.

"This is not good," said Miller. "I'm not sure if my government will pay."

"I'm certain my government won't," said Yardin.

Yardin turned to Rukanan, who before Yardin had a chance to ask the question, bitterly said, "What do you think?"

"Well, then perhaps we will be rescued," said Miller.

"We don't have more than a handful of military guards at our embassy," said Yardin. "And none of them would have a chance against Graftonites."

"Our situation is the same," said Miller.

Rukanan said nothing.

"We're changing the scramble code every half second, but even that is no guarantee," said Croft, eyeing the hologram.

"Elements of the Eighth Fleet are already on their way to Grafton," said the image of the Chief. "But it's unclear if they're going to make it in time or not."

"Is negotiation not an option?" said Tane.

"You're wasting your time," snapped Croft. "He wants to execute the captives, but he needs an excuse to do so. He's not going to negotiate."

"You've got a point," said the Chief. "What, then, are our options?"

"I could attempt a rescue," said Croft.

"The nearest Column team is more than four days away," said the Chief.

"When I said I, I meant 'I' as in 'I' singular," said Croft.

"That compound is ringed with Graftonite guards. How do you propose to rescue the ambassadors while holding off all of the Graftonites on your own?"

"I don't know... yet," said Croft.

"I'm leery about a haphazard rescue attempt," said the Chief.

"What alternative do you have?" said Croft.

The Chief was silent for a moment. Then she said, "You do have a reputation for achieving the very difficult."

"I have a good publicist," said Croft.

"All right," the Chief said finally. "We have no other choice. What is your plan?"

"I'm afraid you can't micromanage me this time, because even I don't know all the details of my plan yet and I can't tell you what I don't know," said Croft. "I'm not even certain it will be possible to rescue them all safely. I may only be able to rescue a handful of people. I'll try to do what I can." Before the Chief could respond further, he said, "Croft out." And cut the connection.

"I rather like that," said Croft.

"I know you did," said Tane. "What can I do to help?"

"You see that spot?" Croft asked, pointing to the ground.

"Where I'm standing?"

"Yes," said Tane.

"I need you to man that position," said Croft.

"Why? For how long?"

"Until further notice," said Croft.

"How can that help?" Tane asked.

"You're an analyst, not an operative," said Croft. "No, this work is only for the operations guys." He reached out and put a brotherly arm around the Clapper.

The Clapper squealed and pulled away. "Not to touch!" he said, trembling.

"Let's go and have a look at that building," said Croft. He turned to go, but saw something out of the corner of his eye. He turned back to the Clapper.

"Is there something you want to tell me?" Croft asked.

The Clapper looked nervous, avoiding eye contact. "...noooo...."

"Are you sure?"

The Clapper nodded.

"Then can I ask a question?" said Croft. "Just a little one?"

The Clapper, considered, then nodded.

"Why is there a fire coming out of the bathroom?"

Red Sally stepped out of the bathroom, a small flame coming out of her fingers. "I got bored," She complained.

"You came back to Grafton against orders because you got bored, or you lit a fire because you got bored?" Croft asked.

Sally thought about that one for a moment. "Both."

"I thought I told you to return to August," said Croft.

"I followed your orders," said Sally, making a face. "I did return to August. But then I got bored again. I'm tried of training exercises. All they do is try to do is to keep me from starting fires."

"They're such villains, I know," said Croft.

"Please don't send me back," said Sally.

Croft started to say something, stopped, and started again. "All right. Maybe we can use you."

Sally smiled and actually jumped into the air for joy.

"On one condition!"

"What?" said Sally.

"You must not ignite any Graftonite without my permission."

Sally considered, looking crestfallen. "You drive a hard bargain."

"Don't pout," Croft advised.

Croft parked the ground car outside a familiar home. Although time was of the essence, he needed to recruit some more help for what was sure to be a tough job. He got out of the car and looked at the Silencer's home. He had commed Annie and found out that the Silencer had returned from his latest mission. If he could persuade the Silencer, perhaps the best gunman of all the Graftonites, to help, it would be much easier to rescue the hostages.

Annie met him at the door. "Clifford! Good to see you again." She was wearing her trademark old-style cowboy hat and brown leather skins.

"I wish the circumstances were better," said Croft grimly.

"Yes, I heard the news," said Annie.

"Is John in?" said Croft, knowing he was.

"Let me take you to him," said Annie.

She led him into another room where the Silencer could be seen packing up items into a backpack.

"Shouldn't you be unpacking?" said Croft.

"I did that last night," said the Silencer. "I just got another job, I'm heading out again."

"There's a lot of demand for your services," said Croft.

"There usually is for the best," said the Silencer.

"I was hoping I could hire you," said Croft.

"I'll be happy to talk about it when I get back," said the Silencer.

"I kind of need your help now," said Croft.

The Silencer stopped packing for a moment and looked Croft in the face for the first time. "To rescue the diplomats."

"I'd pay double your fee."

"It's suicide. That building is ringed with gunmen," said the Silencer.

"Meaning you couldn't do it?" said Croft.

"Well, I didn't say that," said the Silencer. "But you have to understand, it wouldn't be me going up against ten or twenty people; I would be going up against ten or twenty Graftonites. And some of them probably know how to shoot. What you need is a commando team."

Croft knew that. He had already tried flashing Traker Fields by comm, but had been quickly turned down.

"I'd love it if I could get one," said Croft. He noticed that the Silencer had started packing again. "John, I really need your help. Do you know what will happen if they're not stopped?"

The Silencer shrugged.

"It could mean war," said Croft.

The Silencer shrugged again. "It won't affect my work."

"John, maybe we should listen to him," said Annie.

"Annie, I love you, but you have to restrain your philanthropic impulses," said the Silencer. "Charity work is nice, but doesn't pay the bills."

"John, we have more than enough credits, and you know it," said Annie.

"It's the principle," said the Silencer. "I'm not going to risk my life unless there's something in it for me."

"There is something in it," said Croft. "I'll double your normal fee."

No change in expression.

"I'll quadruple it," said Croft desperately.

The Silencer hesitated, then said, "Tempting though it might be, I've already committed to another employer. To be honest, I think your mission is too crazy for one person to take on. So what if a few paper pushers get shot? There are always more to take their place."

"Yes, that may be true," said Croft. "But the League will take particular offense to having its paper pusher shot. I happen to know there's a League fleet on the way here."

The Silencer said nothing.

"What happens when the League fleet start bombing the planet?"

The Silencer shrugged. "As long as they don't bomb my house, that's fine." He resumed packing.

"I'm sorry, Clifford," said Annie.

"So am I," said Croft, grimly. He started to turn away.

"You're a fool if you try to free them by yourself," said the Silencer. "These aren't Slurians, or Happy Worlders. These are Graftonites you're going up against. You'll get yourself killed."

"It looks like I have no choice," said Croft.

He walked to the front door and stepped out on the porch. Two men stood outside waiting for him.

Croft matched stares with them for a moment.

"Are you here to kill me, or just delivering the mail?" said Croft, tensing up.

"We're here to kill you," said one of the men.

"Wait a minute," said a new voice.

Annie Oakley stepped out onto the porch. Her pearl handled pistols gleamed in the brilliant daytime sun.

"Two against one?" said Oakley.

"We have our orders," said the first gunman who had spoken.

"It's not enough that you have to challenge an off-worlder, but you need two against one to do it," said Oakley. "Shame on you."

"He's eluded us before," said the gunman. "If I were you, I'd stand out of the way."

They waited for her to move. Annie considered for a moment. Then she said, "I don't think so."

All was almost completely silent as everyone tensed up. Croft and Annie stared at the gunmen. The gunmen stared back. There was a slight sound of the morning wind.

Croft readied himself. There was no way he could outdraw those two. His only chance was if Annie could take both of them. He knew she was good, but good enough to take on two Graftonites?

He wasn't going to be the one to draw first. He was so slow in comparison to the other Graftonites, that drawing would be an invitation to shoot him.

Something clicked in the lead gunman's expression. His muscles tensed, he reached for his gun almost faster than Croft could see-

There was a brilliant exchange of blaster fire, one shot whizzing right by Croft's face. Before Croft's gun was halfway out of its holster, it was over. Both gunmen were still standing there. So was Annie.

And then slowly one gunman dropped to the ground, and then so did the other.

Croft cautiously felt himself over. He wasn't hit. He turned to Annie. She gave him a small smile.

"Thank you," said Croft sincerely.

"I'm not the only one you have to thank," said Annie.

"What do you mean?" Croft asked.

She turned back to the house. There was a small hole in one of the windows.

Annie looked up with a small smile on her lips. "I know what you did. You can come out now."

The Silencer stepped out of the door. "There were two of them. I didn't want you to get hurt," he said.

"You shot them?" said Croft.

"One of them," said the Silencer. "I couldn't let anything happen to Annie."

"There were only two of them," said Annie simply.

The Silencer turned to her. "What did I tell you about killing people at home? I thought we always agreed to consult with each other first."

"They were about to kill Clifford, your friend," said Annie. "It's rude to let a guest get shot in our home."

"Hm," said the Silencer. He went back inside without a word.

Annie suddenly saw something that made her eyes widen. "Look at this!" She said, pointing to a scorch mark on the porch. She wet her fingers in her mouth and tried to rub off the mark. She looked worried. "I'll have to get that repainted."

Croft turned to eye the two bodies on the front lawn. Vultures circled above.

It was starting to be one of those days.

"How do we reason with them? Let them know we're not a threat?" said Miller.

"I think they already know that," said Ambassador Yardin grimly.

"You don't really think they're going to execute us, do you?" said Miller.

"No, not for another four hours," said Yardin. He turned to Ambassador Rukanan, who was eyeing the food on the table but eating nothing.

"Lost your appetite?" said Yardin.

"How can I be hungry at a time like this?" said Rukanan.

"Unless our governments come up with billions of credits, this could be our last chance to eat," said Yardin. "Unless…"

"Unless what?" said Rukanan.

"You must have agents here," said Yardin.

"Agents?" said Rukanan, looking innocent.

"Every member of your foreign service is an agent," said Yardin.

"I resent that implication!" said Rukanan. "In any event, they were all disarmed."

"But not all your agents are here," said Yardin. "Spies are your number one export. You must have some operational teams in the field here."

Rukanan said nothing. Slurian Security had a number of operational teams on Grafton. He had actually expected rescue several hours ago. Each passing minute made him more nervous. If he were going to get out of this alive, he would have to do so on his own.

The gunmen were concentrated largely near the exit, on one end of the grand ballroom. Rukanan went over them, but was stopped by an armed sentry.

"Get back to your flock, sheep," said the guard, pointing the muzzle of his blaster at Rukanan's nose.

"I want to speak to the man in charge," said Rukanan.

The man said, "I'm only going to say this one more time-"

"Wait," said Rocco, stepping forward. "What do you want?"

"My name is Stod Rukanan, I'm the Slurian-"

"I know who you are, sheep," Rocco snapped. "What do you want?"

"I have a proposal for you," said Rocco.

"The only proposal we're interested in is several billion credits from your bosses," said Rocco. He checked his watch. "And it doesn't look like they're going to deliver."

"We can get the money to you, but it will take more time," said Rukanan.

"Unfortunately, you don't have much more time," said Rocco. He gestured for Rukanan to be taken away.

"Wait!" said Rukanan. "I have personal funds. Kill the others—the Leaguers, even my own staff. But spare me and I can make it worth your while."

"You don't have anything I want," said Rocco contemptuously.

Rukanan was given a friendly shove to indicate that the conversation was over.

"I wonder what that was all about," said Miller, eyeing the exchange.

"He was probably trying to sell us out to the Graftonites," said Yardin nonchalantly.

"But we're all in this together!" said Miller.

"You know the Slurians," said Yardin philosophically.

Croft lay on the ground outside the building where the hostages were being held.

He studied the building with his electronoculars set to infrared. There were entrances in the front and back that were tightly guarded. But there was also an open terrace on the third floor. Unfortunately, the were no other nearby buildings they could gain access to it from. Quandry had been careful to pick an isolated building to hold the hostages in.

Hm…

Croft panned the electronoculars in other directions. A glint caught his eye…

"What do you see, Ostrav?" Yuri asked.

"Several guards, patrolling around the building," said Ostrav, looking through his electronoculars. "We could take them out with long-distance sniping-"

"Correction," said a new voice.

They both turned, guns raised, to see Clifford Croft standing behind them. His blaster was pointed squarely at them.

"You might get one, or two, but the minute the light from the first target shot out of your barrel the Graftonites would have your position pinpointed and you'd be dead," said Croft.

"We must rescue our ambassador," said Yuri.

"And the rest of your staff too, of course."

Yuri waved his hand dismissively. "Yes, I suppose."

"Only the big bosses matter, eh? I'm surprised, given how egalitarian Slurian society is reputed to be," said Croft.

"What are you doing here?" saidYuri.

"I'm here to tell you not to throw away your lives. Your plan won't work."

"And you have a plan?" Yuri asked.

"Maybe," said Croft.

"You really think you can rescue everyone?"

"I didn't mention rescuing everyone," said Croft. "My focus is on League personnel."

"What about Slurians?"

"What about them?"

"If you're going to rescue your people, why not also rescue ours?"

"Let me get this straight," said Croft. "A few days ago you tried to have me killed. And now you're asking me for a favor?"

"That was not us!" said Yuri.

"No," said Ostrav.

"Oh no, not you, that must have been some other Slurian agents," said Croft.

"It wasn't us," said Yuri. "But even if it were, we were acting under orders and had no choice."

"Are you a lawyer?" Croft asked, recognizing arguments in the alternative when he saw one.

"What will it take to get you to rescue our ambassador as well?" Yuri asked.

Croft pretended to consider for a moment. "Well, since you ask so nicely, there is one small thing you can do."

"Yes?"

"We need a getaway vehicle."

"Getaway vehicle?"

"One that can fit about, oh, 200 captive diplomats."

"200?" said Yuri. "What did you have in mind?"

Croft told him.

"And where would we bring it?"

Croft told him.

Yuri looked at the building. "Impossible!"

"Quite possible," said Croft. "But, if you'd rather I just rescue my own people...."

"We'll do it," said Yuri. Then, looking suspiciously at Croft, he said, "Why are you trusting us?"

"I'm trusting you because if you don't show up, I'll kill your ambassador myself. Before I launch this mission I intend to record delay a personal message to your security services detailing your role in this mission. If I don't return in time to cancel it, your people will know that it was your incompetence, or treachery, that led to your ambassador's death."

Yuri looked relieved. "You are prepared for betrayal. Your actions make sense."

"I'm glad we can all feel good about it," said Croft. "I want you to be there in exactly... two hours from now."

"Two hours! We have no time-"

"In two hours and 4 minutes the ambassadors will be killed. I suggest you get moving," said Croft.

Yuri looked at Ostrav, who nodded, and they both headed off.

Croft made his way back to Red Sally and the Clapper.

"Talking to friends?" said the Clapper, grinning moronically.

"Ahhh... no," said Croft, rapidly thinking how he would classify the Slurian NGB agents.

"Do I have to wear this?" said Red Sally, looking distastefully at the formal dress she was wearing.

"It's quite nice," said Croft, offering no further comment.

He picked up the electronoculars again and studied the movements of the guards. He felt confidence that there was a gap big enough for him to get through them, but not enough time to climb up the side of the building to the third floor terrace without being seen. He'd have to get up there almost immediately, like with an external lift, or...

Croft turned to the Clapper. "Can you lift people?" he asked.

"What?" said the Clapper, repeating his most commonly used word.

"Can you lift me into the air?" said Croft.

"I... I think so," said the Clapper. He tried to clap his hands together but Croft held them shut.

"Can you lift me three stories into the air, onto that terrace, over there?"

The Clapper looked at the terrace. It looked like a nice terrace.

"Can you?"

"What?" said the Clapper.

"Lift me up there, and then Sally?"

"I don't know," said the Clapper.

"Well, we're all about to find out," said Croft.

Croft studied the situation for some time, waiting until the guards were in the optimal position, and then ran to the building and waved his arm, giving the signal.

The Clapper waved back. Like an idiot.

This was not according to plan. A Graftonite guard was going to be coming around the corner any second now.

In the gloom Croft saw Red Sally punch the Clapper in the arm and say something while pointing at Croft.

Suddenly he felt himself jerkily lifted into the air, first a few inches, then a few feet, then he started to float higher, and higher…

A guard came around the corner. Croft was only seven feet above him. If he even looked slightly up…

There was no shout, or blaster bolt, and the guard simply continued walking. But Croft started to sink. Terror gripped him.

Then, just as suddenly, he started to climb again. Climbing… climbing… his rate of ascent slowed. By the time he almost reached the third floor terrace he was ascending at a crawl. Finally, he stopped.

He was still several feet short of the terrace. Reaching up, he was barely able to grab the edge. Laboriously, he pulled himself up and over the edge.

Croft reached out and activated his comm.

"That was close," he whispered, putting the receiver in his ear.

"It drained him. It's going to take a few minutes for him to send me," came Red Sally's voice.

"We don't have much time."

"Want me to just go in and flame them?"

"No," said Croft.

They waited a few minutes. Time was passing.

"It doesn't look like they're going to pay, Mo," said Rocco, speaking to a holo of Quandry in the privacy of a small room.

"I should hope not," said Quandry. "Sensors are detecting a fleet approaching Grafton."

"League?"

"Looks like it," said Rocco.

"Will they get here in time to interfere?"

"Doesn't look like it. They won't get here for another two hours, and it will take them another hour to send down troops," said Quandry. He checked his chrono. "And there are only 47 minutes left before our deadline. Are all the holorecorders in place and in good working order?"

"Yes. I checked them myself."

"Good," said Quandry. "We'll only get one take at this. I want holos of this massacre to be broadcast throughout League space. Make it look good."

"We will," said Rocco grimly.

"One last thing," said Quandry. "Any sign of that Croft pest?"

"None," said Rocco.

"He may still try something. Be on your guard."

"He's only one sheep," said Rocco.

"He's one of the Column Eight," said Quandry. "Don't underestimate him."

Red Sally gave a small gasp as she plonked down on the third floor terrace.

"Come on, let's go," said Croft, before she could catch her breath. "And don't ignite anything until I tell you to."

"You always say that," she grumbled.

They silently climbed down a small stairwell. As they got to the bottom they started to hear noise from the captives. They also saw two Graftonites, their backs to Croft and Red Sally, standing guard. Croft silently gestured Sally back up the stairs.

"What now?" said Sally.

"Plan B," said Croft. He went back up to the second floor and entered a small room, which was empty, and walked carefully, measuring his footsteps. Then he took out a small cutting torch…

"There's less than 20 minutes left," said Ambassador Miller, standing by a refreshment table next to a wall.

"It doesn't look good," said Ambassador Yardin grimly.

"Do you really think they'll execute us?" said Miller.

"They're Graftonites," said Yardin simply. "They do this kind of thing all the time."

"Oh, I wish I had never been posted here!" said Miller. "It's all my wife's fault. She-"

"Shhsh!" said Yardin. "Do you hear something?"

"What?" said Miller.

They stood still for a moment. "I thought it was a small hissing sound. But it stopped," said Yardin.

"I don't hear anything," said Miller. "But I do smell something… like a burning smell, maybe."

Suddenly they heard a rustle under the table. They started to look down when a voice whispered, "Act normally!"

They immediately stood straight.

"I'm here to rescue you," came the soft voice.

"You are?" said Miller. "Are you with the League?"

"Yes," said the voice.

It was Croft, of course. "Now both of you stand so that guards on either end of the room can't see between you."

Miller and Yardin did so.

Using their bodies to shield him, Croft came out from hiding through the hole in the wall he had cut beneath the table. He had cut his way down from the second floor to a small room next to the ballroom and cut his way horizontally across from there. In a moment Red Sally emerged with him. Both were dressed in formal diplomatic clothing.

"I still hate this dress," Red Sally hissed.

"Keep your voice down," said Croft, through gritted teeth as he checked to make sure that none of the guards had seen him coming out from underneath the table. None did, but one of the ambassadors, eyeing him curiously, was slowly approaching.

"How many commandos are there?" said Miller.

"None," said Croft.

"None?" said Miller. "Not even you?"

"No."

"Well, then, how many soldiers?"

"None," said Croft.

"Is there anyone else besides you and this young lady?"

"Not really," said Croft.

Miller looked stunned. "I hope this is not a joke. We are scheduled to be shot in less than 15 minutes!"

Ambassador Rukanan approached, with an odd expression on his face. "I don't think I've seen either of you before."

"Stod, he's here to rescue us," said Miller, before Croft could say anything.

"You? How many soldiers do you have with you?" Rukanan asked.

Croft sighed. "None. But we don't have time for this. I need you guys to create a distraction, just for a few seconds, by one of the exits-"

"There's absolutely no way I'm going to help you," said Rukanan. "A rescue team of one? You'll surely get us all killed!"

"It doesn't seem like you have a lot of options," said Croft. "Now, this distraction I need-"

An idea suddenly occurred to Rukanan. If he informed the Graftonites of the plot, they might spare his life. After all, one man had no chance of rescuing him. This, then, was his only chance of survival.

His mind made up, he started running for the group of guards guarding the exit. "Help!" he cried.

Miller stood paralyzed with fear, as he watched their only hope of escape go to pieces.

But not everyone stood still; Yardin snarled something and ran after Rukanan.

"Help, help!" Rukanan cried, as he approached the guards.

They all looked at Rukanan, their weapons raised, as Yardin tackled him from behind.

"You dirty Slurian!" he cried, landing a fist into Rukanan's face.

The Graftonites laughed, enjoying the spectacle.

"Well, that's a diversion," said Croft philosophically. He turned to Sally. "Get going. And whatever you do, don't let them see you starting the fire. Remember, we want it to look natural."

Sally edged closer to the side of the room where the guards were watching Yardin wrestle with Rukanan. Rukanan kept trying to say something but Yardin kept punching him in the face.

While the guards were not so distracted that anyone could have slipped out, their attention was definitely not on Red Sally.

Her hair started to smoke, and flames reached out and hugged the walls.

It was a few seconds before someone started screaming, "Fire! Fire!"

The Graftonites turned to see the area around the exit covered with flames. The Graftonites looked around to see what they could use to fight the flames but there were no fire extinguishers. The crowd started screaming and fleeing to the other side of the room. The guards at the exit looked startled and alarmed.

Rocco took in the situation. The fire was getting close to the exit doors. If they stayed inside they would be trapped. But if they all went outside…

That was it. This was a rescue attempt. Their goal was to get the hostages outside.

Rocco considered his options. Mo wanted a holorecording of the diplomats being shot. But maybe being burned to death would suffice. The holorecording equipment might survive long enough to record that.

"Out, out, everyone out," said Rocco, speaking to his fellow gunmen. They cleared out; when the last one was outside, he said, "Is that everyone? Seal the doors!"

They used their blasters at a lower setting to seal the doors.

Inside the ballroom the fire was spreading throughout the room. Diplomats were screaming and running around in panic.

Croft fired a blaster into the air.

"Quiet!" he yelled.

The noise level temporarily subsided.

"If you want to live, follow me," he said.

Croft started running for the internal stairwell….

Rocco tried to tap into the internal holorecorders from his wrist comm, but he was having trouble. He wanted to see the end live, as it happened. But all he was getting was static. Finally he pressed the right combination and an image of the ballroom appeared, burning in flames.

A ballroom that was substantially empty.

Completely empty of people, in fact, as far as he could tell.

Had they escaped? How could they have escaped? Where?

And then Rocco heard a roar and looked up, as a small transport slowly descended on the building, and everything became clear in an instant.

The transport touched down on the rooftop; there was barely enough room for it and the burgeoning crowd, most of which Croft had forced to stay in the stairwell.

Once it touched down and the hatch popped open they ran for it. Croft was among the first to reach the transport's cockpit.

"Do you realize this building is on fire?" said Yuri. "It could collapse at any minute!"

Even from the rooftop view in the cockpit Croft could see flames licking at the upper sides of the building. The interior support beams must be getting very hot about now….

"We should leave!" said Ostrav. Blaster fire was intermittently hitting the ship around them. It must be the Graftonites. Fortunately, they couldn't get a very good angle of attack from the ground.

Croft eyed the side scanner. People were still streaming into the scanner.

"Not yet," said Croft.

The ship trembled as something shifted inside the building. They waited a long second before it settled again.

"We are leaving!" said Ostrav, reaching for the controls.

The cold muzzle of a blaster touched the back of his neck.

"When I say so," said Croft calmly.

They waited another few seconds that seemed to pass very slowly.

The ship shifted again, just as Croft saw the last of the stragglers board the ship.

"Now!" said Croft.

Ostrav grabbed for the controls. The ship lifted off to a hail of blaster gunfire from the ground. It hovered for a minute, jolted downwards as a stabilizer was hit. The ship pitched down slightly, until the other stabilizers compensated, and then the ship took off.

"That was close," said Yuri.

"Where should I set course?" said Ostrav.

"There are League ships in orbit," said Croft. "We'll rendezvous with them."

"The League?" said Yuri. "I don't think so. Set course for Sluria. All non-Slurians will be interned and eventually returned to their place of origin."

Croft was about to say something when he felt a blaster against his gut. "Correction," said Yuri. "All non-Slurians except for state enemies will be returned to their place of origin."

Yuri gave a grin and Ostrav chuckled. They both looked very happy until Yuri's blaster suddenly grew so hot that he yelped, dropping it on the ground.

Croft easily pointed his at the other two. "Thanks, Red," he said, not looking behind him.

"That was good," said Red Sally. "Can we go back and do it again?"

Chapter 10: The Fleet Steps In

The transport landed in the main landing bay of the Battleship Majestic, and a large number of very shaken diplomats slowly emerged. Medical and support personnel were waiting to take them away. On Croft's say-so the Slurians were put under guard.

"I'm looking for Clifford Croft," said a officer.

The Clapper came forward and gave a moronic grin. The officer looked at him. "Are you Croft?"

"What do you think?" said Croft, stepping forward.

"Admiral Lillard wants to see you," said the officer.

"I'm used to being in high demand," said Croft dryly.

The officer made a deprecating face, but led Croft to the bridge. Before they got there, however, they felt something and the ship shook slightly.

"What was that?" Croft asked.

"I don't know," said the officer.

They hurried to the bridge.

A middle aged admiral sat in the battle chair. Admiral Lillian Lillard was one of the few women Admiral in the League fleet. She was often compared to a crusty, weather beaten boot. And that was one of nice things people said about her.

The officer led Croft to the Admiral, and saluted.

Admiral Lillard looked Croft up and down. "This is Clifford Croft?"

Croft looked Admiral Lillard up and down, and turned to the junior officer. "This is Admiral Lillard?"

"Your levity is ill-timed," said Lillard.

"Admiral, they're launching a second wave," said one of the bridge officers.

"A second wave of what?" said Croft. But he only had to check the holoviewer to see what was going on. The Graftonites were lobbing anti-ship missiles from the planet at the fleet.

Anti-ship missiles. Either Croft hadn't destroyed them all, or Quandry had procured another shipment.

Croft eyed the trail of the ten or so slow moving missiles. Surely Quandry didn't think he could destroy the fleet with a relatively small number of missiles.

"Anti-aircraft batteries on full," said the Admiral. "Target their launching points."

"Admiral," said Croft.

'We're a little busy now, Mr. Croft,' said the Admiral.

A holoimage of the launching points appeared in the air. They were all clustered at one point on the eastern seaboard.

"They're launching from a very narrowly confined area," said Admiral Lillard. "Not very smart. Set main lasers."

A narrowly confined area? Croft eyed the image closely. That was Regular! All the launchers were in Regular.

Why, with so much open space over a nearly completely empty planet, were all the launchers clustered in Regular, the only real city on the entire planet?

It didn't take Croft more than half a second to figure out the answer.

"Admiral-" said Croft.

Suddenly they felt a small explosion, and then another, and then another.

"Damage?" said Lillard

"All ten offensive missiles destroyed," said an officer. "The destroyer Janson reports minor damage from a close interception."

"Prepare to fire," said Lillard.

"Admiral, you have to withdraw," said Croft.

Lillard turned to Croft. "We are under attack, Mr. Croft. What kind of message would we be sending the Graftonites by running? That would only encourage their aggression."

"Normally I would agree," said Croft. "But Quandry wants you to fire back! That's part of his plan!"

Lillard cocked an eyebrow. "Then the warmonger will get what he wants."

"Lasers targeted," said the weapons officer.

"Fire!" said Lillard.

Brilliant stabs of light shot out from the Majestic. On Regular, deadly beams thundered from above, incinerating launchers, but also nearby streets and buildings. The explosions started fires which spread. In moments, a third of Regular was on fire.

On the Majestic, a magnified holoimage of the city could be seen.

"Launchers destroyed," reported the weapons officer.

"Cease fire," said Lillard. "We'll keep our response proportional."

"Believe me, you've done more than enough," said Croft.

Lillard glared at him.

"See what the offworlders have done to us," said Quandry. He was speaking at a great gathering, where a holoimage of Regular displayed above him. The fires were largely out, but wisps of smoke could still be seen rising here and there. Blackened and partially destroyed buildings could also be seen.

"What did you expect?" said one Graftonite, standing up. "You lobbed anti-ship missiles at them."

"Yes, that's true," said Quandry. There was a murmur in the audience. "But I only did so after I was attacked. I was willing to reach an honest parley with the offworlder diplomats; what I found instead was a commando team sent in to assassinate me."

The murmuring rose to a roar as the image of the burned out building where the diplomats had been held came on the screen. Then an earlier image of a transport hovering above the building appeared.

"They landed a commando team from the roof and tried to assassinate me; when that failed, they tried to set the building afire," said Quandry. "Should I have sit still for this?"

"No!" some cried.

"Should we sit still for this?"

"No!" more cried.

"Then join me, and help us teach the Leaguers a lesson they won't soon forget!" said Quandry.

The crowd was chanting his name now. Quandry allowed himself a small smile.

Croft was on a transport headed back to August with Red Sally, the Clapper, and Tane when he heard the news. The Chief broadcasted on a secure holo.

"The Graftonites have invaded Karis," said the Chief. She didn't have to wait long for this to sink in. Unlike Grafton IV, the previous planet to be invaded, Karis was a full-fledged member of the League. This was nothing less than a direct attack on the League itself.

"I'm not surprised," said Croft cooly. "Not after what that idiot Lillard did."

"Explain."

"Quandry wanted to provoke an attack. That was why he was going to slaughter those diplomats," said Croft. "Only since I rescued them, he had to work a little harder at it. By getting us to attack Regular, he helped unite the Graftonites behind him."

"But his attack was unprovoked," said the Chief.

"Have you checked the latest newsfeed from Grafton? That's not how he's portraying it," said Croft.

"Will the entire population believe it?" said the Chief.

"The entire population doesn't need to believe it," said Croft. "All Quandry needs is to convince a minority of the population to carry his war to us. And that's what he's done now."

"Well, we certainly have to resist him now," said the Chief.

"Certainly," said Croft. "Or, at the very least, stop the next invasion."

"The next one?"

"It's not going to stop with Karis," said Croft.

"I'll talk with the President about deploying the fleet," said the Chief.

"Good," said Croft. "If we have any chance of stopping them, it's in space. Just make sure you get an admiral with a little bit of brains."

Admiral Lillard watched as reinforcements arrived to help enforce the blockage off of Grafton II. There was now a similar blockage off of Grafton IV and Karis. Nothing was getting in or out.

If the intel could be believed, the Graftonites had invaded Karis with little more than space fighters and a handful of transports. Lillard's capital ships could handle the transports, but fighters required a different tactic.

Lillard eyed the Command Carrier Glory, which had been detached from regular duty and assigned to her. She established communications with the ship. In seconds a holoimage appeared on the bridge.

"Admiral," said the grizzled looking officer staring at them.

"Captain Harkness," said Lillard.

"I've heard things are quite a mess," said Harkness. Harkness wasn't the regular Captain of the Glory; he had been pressed into service at the last minute when the assigned captain had fallen ill. Harkness had protested that he didn't have the experience to command a Battle Carrier, but evidently his superiors thought that his skill in commanding battleships would carry him through. Either that, or they didn't have any other carrier captains available on very short notice.

Lillard glared at him, interpreting his remark as criticism. "You only have to be worried about the present, Captain. I want an airtight cordon around Grafton II. I want two squadrons in continuous CAP around the planet at all times, and the other four squadrons on active duty ready to launch."

"Continual active duty?" said Harkness. "Admiral, how long is this going to be for?"

"Until further notice."

"Admiral, I'm no genius, but having six squadrons on active duty will wear down our resources very quickly. It's only meant to be done-"

"When ordered," said Lillard. "And it is an order, Captain."

Harkness grunted something.

"Did you say something, Captain?" said Lillard.

"Just that this isn't the kind of working vacation I planned," said Harkness. "Glory out."

Battle Lieutenant Idaho J. Took sat in the cockpit of his Wildcat 98-J looking very annoyed. As the commander of Wildcat "C" it was now his squadron's turn to sit on "active ready" status. That meant the pilots had to sit in their cockpits of their very still and unmoving ships in the Glory's landing bay. In eight hours, maybe, his squadron and Wildcat "D" would get a chance to replace Wildcat "A" and "B" on patrol. Took flicked on his comm switch.

"Obe, you there?"

"No, I transferred to the seventh fleet two weeks ago," came back Ensign Obe's voice.

"I think my sense of humor is rubbing off on you," said Took.

"Or rubbing against me, in the wrong way," Obe suggested.

"I can see you're testy too," said Took.

"It's all this waiting," said Obe.

"Are you sure it wouldn't be anything else?" said Took.

"Such as...?"

"Well, I don't know, let's see," said Took. "The Captain is gone. Our new Captain knows nothing about fighter combat. We're about to face the fastest gunslingers in the galaxy."

"Being fast with a blaster doesn't automatically mean they're fast in a cockpit," said Obe.

"Don't you know anything about Grafton?" said Took. "Everyone has a starfighter. That's how they get around. I hear they have fewer miles of electric road on the planet then they do in all of Sarney Sarittenden."

"Don't believe everything you hear, Iday," said Obe.

"I don't," said Took. "But the problem is, I tend to believe most everything I say."

"A convoy is launching; forty fighters, eight long range transports."

"It looks like another invasion force," said Lillard. She reflected. "Just how do they take over an entire planet with such small forces? Never mind. Launch fighters."

"Wildcat "C", rendezvous with Wildcat "A" at the following coordinates," came the voice over Took's helmet. He eyed the coordinates which were pouring onto his screen.

"Understood," said Took. "Launching." He pressed the launch button, and was pushed back into his chair. He had just cleared the Glory launch tubes when he heard the cries for help over his comm. It was Wildcat "A". They were in trouble.

"Squadron C, full thrusters," said Took immediately. It would cut down on their fuel available for combat maneuvers, but time was of the essence. His Wildcat 98 J accelerated to the max. It was a pity they didn't have the new Wildcat 110's like Wildcat "A" and "B" did, but now wasn't the time to worry about that. He had to make do with the resources at hand.

Took checked his sensors. He could see the rapid images of ships darting around each other. There must be quite an active dogfight. He should be close enough to see it visually...

Took saw nothing. Then, suddenly, he saw a piece of debris whip by him. Then another, then another. His trained eye knew the obvious immediately. It was all Wildcat hulls. Took tried to raise the squadron leader from Wildcat "A". There was no response. Then he broadened his message to anyone from Wildcat "A".

"What's happening?" said Admiral Lillard. She had Captain Harkness on holo.

"Just a moment," Harkness growled. He was talking to another officer whose voice couldn't be heard.

"Captain!" said Lillard. She demanded his attention.

"We've lost contact with Wildcat "A"," said Harkness bluntly.

"If you can't contact the squadron commander, try one of his subordinates-"

"You don't understand," said Harkness. "The entire squadron. It's been destroyed. Just a minute." They saw him receive another battle report. He conferred with another officer.

"There are four survivors from Wildcat B. They're trying to link up with "E" and "F". Wildcats "C" and "D" are engaged in heavy combat right now."

"Blow the enemy out of the sky!" said Lillard. "Have them target the transports."

"But Admiral-"

"Carry out my orders!" she said.

"Target the transports, sure," said Took, as he received the order. He was having a hard enough time just dodging the fighter that was on his tail. The only thing that had saved him so far was that the pursuing fighter periodically diverted momentarily to destroy "easier" targets, but the fighter always returned to his tail. "Obe, need help here!"

"I can't help you," said Obe. "Every time I try to turn and acquire one, they simply flit out of the way. I've got one on my tail now."

"Time to go on the offensive," said Took. He did an inverse corkscrew maneuver, twisting the ship violently. He watched with satisfaction as his pursuer overshot him... only to return to his tail seconds later.

"Well, that bought me a good five seconds," said Took. Suddenly there was a blinding flash as one of his wingmen was blasted out of existence. The other pilots started to call for help.

On the bridge of the Glory, Harkness watched without expression as a holoimage of the battle played above him. Every few seconds one of the lights indicating one of the ships would wink out.

"What's the situation, Captain?" came the holoimage of Admiral Lillard. "How many transports have been destroyed?"

"None," said Harkness. "Our fighters are getting slaughtered."

"Slaughtered? With two to one superiority?" Lillard asked. How could this be?

"Our pilots can't keep up with them," said Harkness. "More than thirty ships have been lost already."

"Thirty? How many of those are Graftonite?" Lillard demanded to know.

"None," said Harkness. He signaled for his fighter officer. "Withdraw the fighters."

"What?" said Lillard. "I gave no such order. I order you to pursue and engage!"

"Withdraw them now," said Harkness, ignoring her, speaking directly to his comm officer.

The comm officer looked hesitant.

"I take full responsibility," said Harkness. Another light winked out on the screen. "Do it."

"Harkness, you'll be court martialed for this," said Lillard, her face a mask of rage.

Harkness snapped, "It wouldn't be the first time."

"That coward," Lillard fumed. She opened another comm line. "Fleet Battle, this is Admiral Lillard. All capital ships are to pursue those transports. I want them disabled or destroyed, immediately."

The Grafton fighters broke off from the Wildcats almost immediately after they stopped pursuing the transports and turned back towards the Glory. Took gave a sigh of relief . If the Graftonites had wanted to, they could have blasted many more of them out of space before they had reached the Glory.

The battleship Majestic, supported by a quartet of heavy cruisers, bore down on the transports. The fighters turned their attention to these capital ships. Racing across their hulls, they blasted away at sensors, gun emplacements, and engines.

Admiral Lillard felt the Majestic give another shudder. "Why haven't the anti-aircraft lasers disposed of them?"

"Admiral, they're too fast for our AA lasers," said the weapons officer.

"Then forget about them," said Lillard. "Target those transports!"

But the Majestic was losing gun emplacements almost as fast as it could target them. The situation was the same with the other cruisers. One of the weapons emplacements managed to get online, however, firing at a transport. The shot scored a near miss, and they could see the transport sputter with damage.

"Good," said Lillard. "Keep going."

The fighters as if on cue changed tactics after that, targeting their engines. In a few minutes the capital ships were either defenseless or without engines.

Lillard watched on the screen as the image of the fleeing ships faded away, and her career along with it. How would she explain it? A numerically inferior force had disabled an entire fleet, killing dozens and injuring hundreds.

For a moment Lillard thought of the Glory. It was a command carrier with capital weapons of its own. The Glory was undamaged; if she replaced Harkness and took command… the results would be the same. Lillard was enough of a realist to realize that. What, then, would she say to fleet command?

It was called the Complex. It was the command and control center for the combined armed forces of the League. Located in the heart of Sarney Sarittenden, it was a large bunker complex that extended beneath the city. In one especially secure room, deep underground, a group of senior admirals sat, watching reports.

One of them, a man in a War Admiral's uniform, sat back in his chair, scowling.

"I told you she wasn't ready," he said. His name was War Admiral Adam Lafferty.

"What was your solution to the problem?" said another, Battle Admiral Kenna.

"North," said Lafferty simply.

"That's always your answer," said Kenna. "But sending Admiral North in breeds a certain resentment in the ranks. It makes the military look impotent, as if only he can solve our problems. The resentment-"

"Obviously extends to some of those in this room," said War Admiral Lafferty calmly.

"Gentlemen," said a new voice. It was War Admiral Carnaby, the Chief of Staff. He expected a certain code of conduct in this room. "I've just briefed the Chief of Staff. He wants to know why the engagement went so poorly. We outnumbered and outgunned them by every method we can measure."

"Except that they're much faster than us," said Lafferty. "I think we've now learned that their exceptional speed isn't limited only to gunfighting."

"Gentlemen, I need options," said Carnaby. "What should I tell the Chief of Staff?"

They were silent for a moment. No one seemed to have any ideas.

"Well?" said Carnaby.

"I don't know the answer," said Lafferty. "But I suggest I know who does."

"There you go again," said Kenna.

"This is a serious crisis," said Lafferty. "Two planets have been invaded in two weeks. How long do you think it will take for them to launch another invasion?"

"How do they capture planets so quickly?" another admiral asked. "From the intel I've seen, they only invade with a few hundred soldiers."

"That's an issue for the army and the intelligence community to find out," said Carnaby. He had to keep the group focused. "Right now my issue is space defense. What am I to tell the Chief of Staff?"

"Tell them you're sending Norman North in," said Lafferty.

"Any other suggestions?" Carnaby looked around. He wasn't against using Admiral North; but he liked to have other options to consider. But the other admirals were silent. They had no other ideas. Much as they were jealous of Norman North, they knew that he was their best chance to fight the Graftonites.

Carnaby turned to an aide. "I'm going to meet with the Chief of Staff now. I want you to set up a holomeeting with Battle Admiral Norman North in sixty minutes."

The image of Battle Admiral Norman North appeared in the Complex conference room, broadcast in scrambled code from his private office on the battleship Westwind. Although he was "only" a three star Battle Admiral (only a four star War Admiral or five star Victory Admiral ranked higher), his previous string of successes on the battlefield inspired awe among both military and civilian alike. He was the best military mind the League ever had. He could analyze a situation almost instantly, predict possible and probably results, and plot the best countermeasures while others were still debating the first step to take. But while his ability inspired a great deal of support, it also created a great deal of jealousy too, causing him to sometimes be sidelined when great events were taking place.

"Battle Admiral," said War Admiral Carnaby, by way of greeting.

"Admirals," said North cautiously.

"You are of course familiar with the Graftonite situation," said Carnaby informally.

"I've been reading the intel," said the Battle Admiral guardedly, not wanting to admit too much familiarity with the situation.

"There are indications that the Graftons are gearing up to launch another invasion, this time using Karis as a springboard." said Carnaby. "We want you to take a fleet to stop it."

The Battle Admiral nodded. "My resources?"

"You can use whatever's in the area," said Carnaby.

"I want the Glory back," said the Battle Admiral promptly.

"That's doable," said Carnaby. He knew that the Battle Admiral was sentimental about his old ship. "But the Glory has lost about forty percent of its fighters, and thirty percent of its pilots. It will take at least two weeks to get new fighters-"

"We don't have two weeks," said the Battle Admiral. "Just give me the Glory, and as many battleships and heavy capital ships you can muster."

"Most of the Graftonites are in small fighters," said Carnaby. "They move so fast that your AA lasers won't be able to intercept them."

"Understood," said the Battle Admiral. "But get me those ships." And then he added, almost as an afterthought, "I'll contact Captain Harkness directly regarding the rendezvous."

"That will be impossible," said Carnaby. "Captain Harkness is under arrest for insubordination and mutiny."

"That won't work. He won't be able to command the Glory very well in a cell," said the Battle Admiral, being deliberately obtuse. "You told me I could use whatever was in the area."

Carnaby considered. If it were any other officer, he could simply order North to drop the matter. But this was Battle Admiral Norman North. Still, Harkness had disobeyed orders.

"Norm, he disobeyed the direct order of a superior."

"A stupid order," said North. Only an officer with his stature would risk being this blunt with the Chief of Staff. "Battle analysis shows that not a single enemy fighter was taken out, while we lost 39 of our own. Our fighters had no business being there. By ordering the retreat, he saved lives. If Harkness is to be at a court martial, it should be as a witness, testifying at Admiral Lillard's court martial."

Carnaby hung his head. "All right. But I'll have to clear it with the Chief of Staff."

"Do so," said the Battle Admiral. "And one last thing." He transmitted a data stream, a list of munitions. A number of eyebrows went up.

Carnaby nodded, "We'll get these to you quickly." Signing off, North's image faded.

"How did he have that list of munitions ready made?" Kenna said. "He must have known we were going to contact him."

"Be glad he's able to anticipate," said Lafferty. "That's one of his greatest strengths."

"Good to see you again, sir," said Harkness, as Battle Admiral Norman North entered the bridge of the Glory.

"Myster," the Battle Admiral smiled. He spent the next moment greeting the other senior officers on the bridge.

"Battle Admiral." "Good to see you, sir." "Welcome back," they said.

"It's good to be back," said the Battle Admiral. He turned to Harkness. "What's the situation?"

"The Majestic and the heavy cruisers are still out of action," said Harkness. "We've been joined by three battleships, and two battlecruisers should be here within four hours."

"And my special cargo?" The Battle Admiral asked.

"The cargo landed just before you did," said Captain Harkness. "The tech teams have already started work on them. But I still don't understand-"

"Later," said the Battle Admiral. "According to the latest intel, their next invasion could launch as soon as tomorrow. I want to see the chief engineer, the weapons officer, and the starfighter commander in my quarters in fifteen minute intervals, starting in thirty minutes."

"Sir. Yes sir," said Harkness. He looked at the others. They didn't know what the Battle Admiral had in mind either. But they trusted him; that was all that mattered.

The starfighter commander entered the Battle Admiral's quarters. He had been so busy that he hadn't had the time to look up his name. So when the Battle Admiral looked up he was very surprised.

"Lieutenant Took?" said the Battle Admiral.

"Battle Admiral," Took saluted.

"You're the starfighter commander?" said the Battle Admiral. "I thought you were in Command of Wildcat "C" or "D"." The senior starfighter commander was always in Command of the alpha squadron, and was almost always a captain or major.

"Now I am," said Took.

The Battle Admiral took it in immediately. "The starfighter commanders of A and B...."

"A and B went in first," said Took. "Everyone was lost in A; four pilots from B survived, but not the squadron commander."

"It must have been awful," said the Battle Admiral grimly.

"That's an understatement," said Took, equally grimly. "I can't say that morale is very good."

"That's understandable," said the Battle Admiral.

"When are we getting reinforcements?" Took asked.

The Battle Admiral held his hands out wide, to indicate the ships on a holodisplay . "This is it."

"A couple of capital ships?" said Took. "What about fighters?"

The Battle Admiral shook his head. "Intel says they won't reach us in time. Not before the next invasion fleet heads out."

"We'll be cut to ribbons again," said Took.

"Not if I have any say about it," said the Battle Admiral.

"Sir, they're simply faster than we are. We can't match their reflexes."

The Battle Admiral sighed, coming around his desk. He put an arm around Took. "Do you think your pilots can hold out against the Graftonites for two minutes?"

"Two minutes?" Took said.

"Or maybe three," said the Battle Admiral. "Not more than that."

"What are you talking about?" said Took.

"They won't have to fire a shot," the Battle Admiral assured him.

"We're going to win without firing a shot?" said Took.

The Battle Admiral explained his plan.

"That's quite a plan," said Took, after he had heard it. "Is the technology tested?"

"It's never been used quite like this before," said the Battle Admiral. "I have a full tech team working on the retrofitting. But you'd better go down to landing bay two to supervise the installations."

"Yes sir," said Took. He turned to go. "You really think we can beat them?"

"With luck," said the Battle Admiral.

"And you on our side," Took added.

The next day Captain Harkness gave the Battle Admiral a status report. "The retrofitting on the Wildcats is almost complete."

"Good, good," said the Battle Admiral. "I noticed a resupply ship arrived a few hours ago."

"Yes," said Harkness. "They're carrying D-34's, our largest ship killing missiles. But Admiral, those are only for use against other capital ships. Do you intend to use them against small fighters?"

The Battle Admiral gave an enigmatic smile.

"That's a bit of overkill, isn't it?" said Harkness. "It won't work anyway."

"Why not?" said the Battle Admiral.

"The D-34 are huge, lumbering missiles. With their super reflexes, the Graftonites will shoot down the D-34's before they get close."

"Under normal circumstances, I expect so," said the Battle Admiral.

Harkness cocked an eyebrow, but said nothing.

The intelligence reports were right on the mark; a small fleet of starfighters and transports could be seen leaving the orbit of Grafton II.

"Sir, sensors detect forty nine fighters and eight transports!" said the sensor officer excitedly.

"I see them," said the Battle Admiral calmly. "Launch all Wildcat squadrons."

"Wildcats launching," said the starfighter commander.

The War Admiral turned to Captain Harkness and pointed to a holomap. "Captain, have the following ships redeploy here, here, here, and here," he said, pointing to positions on the map with an electropointer. Coordinates immediately sprang up at those positions.

"That will cast a pretty big circle around those fighters," said Harkness. "But we don't have enough ships to prevent them from slipping through the gaps."

"Understood," the Battle Admiral said. Though Harkness was puzzled by his strategy, he knew better than to question it, and he quickly gave the orders to the other capital ships.

Battle Lieutenant Idaho J. Took commanded the squadrons going into battle. He couldn't help feeling a wave of fear as he noticed the rapidly approaching sensor blips.

The Battle Admiral's voice came over the comm. "Remember, Iday, I want you to deploy the special cargo within two minutes after you make contact. I want as many enemy fighters in the zone as possible, while minimizing the risk to you and your crew as much as possible."

"Understood," said Took. He issued orders to the other squadrons.

The Battle Admiral eyed the scene on the holomap. When the fighters had closed to a certain distance from the Graftonite invasion fleet, the Battle Admiral opened the interfleet comm. "Now," he said. "Launch all D-34 missiles."

Giant shipkiller missiles spat out from launch tubes throughout the fleet. As the fleet was encircling the Graftonite force, the giant missiles came from every direction, slowly roaring towards the enemy fighters. There was only one problem; the Wildcats were between the Graftonites and the missiles.

The Graftonite commander, a silver medalist named Tron Uorlo, saw what was coming, of course.

"They must think their fighters can tie us down sufficiently so their missiles can close with us," said his wingman. "But I can't believe that they would sacrifice their fighters to get to us."

"The sheep have become desperate," Uorlo sneered. "Those fighters are no threat; we can safely ignore them." He set his comm to interfleet. "Attention escort force: ignore enemy fighters. Target shipkillers with antiship missiles. Once those are wiped out, we'll take out the sheep fighters at our leisure. Just like last time."

The Wildcat 98-J's closed to visual range, and then they were on top of the first wave of Graftonite fighters. Almost immediately Uorlo noticed something was wrong; the Wildcats weren't trying to fire on them. Not a single one had opened fire. Instead, the Wildcats were maneuvering to get closer to the rest of the fighters.

"Wildcats... release!" said Took. He pressed a button, and a small munitions package dropped off from the weapons rack of his ship. Seconds later, similar munitions dropped off the other Wildcats.

Uorlo, busy targeting the shipkillers, didn't focus his attention on the Wildcats until his proximity alarm blared.

Suddenly, his short range sensors were filled with blips. There was a sudden explosion near him as his wingman was blown apart.

Uorlo sheered to the right to narrowly avoid a homing mine. "Incoming!" he shouted over the comm, and then he was too busy dodging munitions to say anything else."

Each Wildcat had deployed four homing mines, each programmed to home in on any target without the proper FOF (friend or foe) code. Several Grafton fighters were taken by surprise, and destroyed; the rest caught on quickly, and suddenly had to divert attention to avoid being hit. Slowly, one by one, they were blasting the mines out of the sky.

But they were so focused on the mines that they didn't notice the rapidly fleeing sensor images of the Wildcats. And they certainly didn't have time to focus on the incoming shipkillers.

The fighters were still engaged with nearly a half of the homing mines when the first of the shipkillers got into range. The first one detonated a quarter mile out from the nearest Grafton fighter, but that was enough to send several Grafton fighters spinning out of control. Others scored more direct hits, vaporizing fighters.

Captain Harkness watched the battle unfold on the Glory. "Never have so few blown up so much to destroy so few."

But the Battle Admiral had a smile on his face. The mission had been a complete and total success. He also noticed that all the Wildcats had gotten away. No casualties.

When the last missile had detonated and the last explosions had faded, they did an intensive scan of the area. The region was filled with debris.

And nothing else.

They had destroyed 100% of the Grafton invasion fleet.

250 Graftons had been killed. Zero League soldiers had been killed or wounded.

For the League fleet, a loss of 250 soldiers would be bad; for the Graftonites, with their much smaller population, the psychological impact was catastrophic.

"They're not going to take this well, Mo," said Rocco.

"I didn't ask your opinion!" Quandry screamed. He paced in his office back and forth, clutching a blaster. His aides kept very very still.

Finally he calmed down a bit and said, "All right. What are our options?"

"People are going to want to know how the sheep killed 250 of us," said Rocco.

"Then we don't talk about it," said Quandry.

"The League surely will," Rocco pointed out.

"Maybe," said Quandry. "They don't know how many we lost. We can say it's all lies, sheep propaganda."

"And what about the families of those who are lost?" Rocco asked.

"We'll buy their silence one by one," said Quandry.

"That could be expensive," said Rocco worriedly. "The families would undoubtedly demand a large amount of credits for their silence. If they would be content with any amount."

Quandry looked at him. "We have the resources. I'll talk with our backers."

"Do you think they'll want to pay?" Rocco asked timidly.

"I'll make them see the wisdom in it," said Quandry grimly.

"Congratulations, Battle Admiral!" came the holo of War Admiral Carnaby. The other admirals in the Complex also rushed to offer their congratulations.

When the cheering had died down, North nodded fractionally. "Thank you, sirs. Very kind of you. But now is not the time to celebrate."

"What do you mean?" War Admiral Carnaby asked.

"We've dealt them a severe blow, but it's just one battle," said North. "We also had the complete advantage of surprise. They were overconfident, and bunched up their fleet together. If anyone has half a brain on their side, they'll disperse their next attack fleet. That won't make the use of D-34 missiles very practical."

"But you can still use the homing mines mounted on your fighters," said Battle Admiral Kenna.

"Now that they know what to expect, they will shoot down those mines," said Battle Admiral North. He pressed a button, and a holoimage of the battle appeared to the side. "I have reviewed the telemetry. We knocked out eight of their fighters immediately with the mines in the first 30 seconds. But after they figured out what was happening, our mines didn't knock out a single enemy fighter. They avoided the mines, and shot them down. The only purpose they served was to distract the Graftonites until the shipkillers arrived."

"So what do you recommend?"

"This," said the Battle Admiral, and another holo appeared on the screen. "Smaller concussion missiles that can detonate around the area of the Graftonite fighters and disorient them long enough for our fighters to move in and take them out."

"Won't the enemy be able to shoot them down?" War Admiral Carnaby asked.

"Not as easily as the shipkiller missiles," said the Battle Admiral. "And not as easily if there are many concussion missiles. Now that we've forced the Graftons to operate in smaller groups, they will have a harder time protecting themselves. Conversely, however, we will have a harder time tracking them down."

"But you feel this strategy will be successful?" War Admiral Carnaby inquired.

"Presuming we have an adequate supply of these missiles, and presuming an invasion fleet the size of the one we just encountered, I estimate we could stop a quarter to a third of the next invasion force," the Battle Admiral estimated.

"A third!" The murmuring in the Complex was audible to the Battle Admiral.

"Perhaps a quarter," said the Battle Admiral. It was important to be honest about their chances.

"Surely you can devise a strategy with a higher chance of success," said War Admiral Carnaby. This was Battle Admiral North he was talking to; surely he could come up with a better solution!

"No," said the Battle Admiral. "Not unless we had new technology."

"New technology? What kind of technology?" War Admiral Carnaby asked.

"I have theorized that a giant forcefield or focused energy draining device might work," said the Battle Admiral.

War Admiral Carnaby looked at the other admirals, who looked puzzled. "We have no such technology."

"Precisely," said the Battle Admiral. "Gentlemen, this war will not be won in space. If it is to be won, it will need to be won on the ground."

The other admirals looked uncomfortably at each other. Never before had the Battle Admiral admitted that an enemy couldn't be beaten.

Carnaby saw the confusion and indecision on the others' faces and turned to the Battle Admiral. "Battle Admiral, we'll get back to you."

The image faded.

"They don't believe you," said Captain Harkness, stepping out of the background.

The Battle Admiral squinted, as if he were looking into the future. "They'll spend a few hours trying to think of alternatives. When they fail to think of any, they'll realize I'm right."

"Then how will we stop them?" Harkness asked.

"That's a problem for the army," said the Battle Admiral. Then, looking thoughtful, he said, "Or the Column."

The Chief listened dispassionately as the Chief of Staff and War Admiral Carnaby argued back and forth. Other senior League officials and officers jumped in.

"If the military can't stop them, why don't we just blow up the planet?" said an undersecretary for defense.

"Isn't that a little extreme?" said one of the admirals.

"They've invaded the League!"

"One planet," the admiral corrected. "Besides, this may come as a surprise to you, but we don't even have the ability to blow up a planet."

"You can bombard it from orbit, can you not?" asked the undersecretary. "Pound it until you destroy everything down there." He made it sound simple.

"It's not that easy," said War Admiral Carnaby.

"It is that easy," said the undersecretary. "They have almost no ground to orbit defense, so what's the problem?"

"The problem is several thousand spacefighters," said Carnaby. "We've only been fighting the small fraction of the population which is against us. Imagine if the entire population were united. No fleet could hold off thousands of spacefighters.

In any event, what would we bomb? There are only two small cities on the entire planet. The entire population is spread out over the countryside. Each citizen's starfighter can be parked or hidden almost anywhere—in a field, in a cave, under a tarp. We could bomb the whole planet for years and not get ten percent of them."

"We have to do something," the undersecretary persisted.

"I agree," said the Chief, speaking for the first time. "Speaking for the Column, I think we need to find some other area of vulnerability."

"Your super agent was on the planet and he didn't find any vulnerability," said the undersecretary of defense. He couldn't resist sticking the bureaucratic knife in and twisting a bit.

"Clifford Croft gathered important information," said the Chief sharply. "And in case it escaped your notice, he rescued the entire diplomatic delegation to Grafton almost single handedly."

The undersecretary said nothing.

"What do you suggest?" the Chief of Staff asked.

"The Graftonites are able to take over entire planets with only a few hundred of their fighters," said the Chief. "Many of these planets have tens of thousands of soldiers to defend them that were somehow nullified. If we can find out how the Graftonites do it, we may be able to put a stop to it on the ground."

"That sounds like a good idea," said the Chief of Staff. He started to say more, but was interrupted by an aide, who whispered something in his ear.

He looked grave.

"What is it?" said Admiral Carnaby.

"An invasion fleet launched from Karis evaded the blockading fleet, and is even now attacking Greenfields," said Carnaby.

"You are to divert immediately to Greenfields," said the Chief. The quarter sized holo flickered in the small cabin of the transport.

"I got your preliminary message," said Croft. "You want me to find out how they're conquering these planets so easily."

"That's your secondary objective," said the Chief. "Your primary goal is to prevent the capture of the Greenfields fleet. Battle Admiral North believes that the fleet will be seized and used in future invasions."

"Chief, I'm not a battalion of marines," said Croft. "Isn't this a bit outside my line of work—even you can't expect me to capture an entire fleet single-handedly."

"But sabotage is in your line of work," said the Chief coldly.

"Oh," said Croft. "How do I get there? If they control the spacelanes-"

"Battle Admiral North's fleet has been relieved at Grafton II at his own request; his fleet will arrive in orbit just a few hours before you do. He will supply any assistance you need."

Croft nodded.

"Mr. Croft, I can't overstate the importance of this mission. It is vital you uncover how the Graftonites are successfully invading these planets. Our efforts to interdict them in space has had only limited success at best."

"I'll do my best," said Croft.

The holoimage faded.

Croft turned to Tane. "Why is it I never get the easy ones?"

Chapter 11: Getting Answers on Greenfields

The small transport maneuvered into its final landing approach to the Command Carrier Glory.

"That's a big ship," said Tane, eyeing the large turrets on top.

"I hope you'll enjoy their fine dining and dancing facilities," said Croft, as he maneuvered the transport into the landing bay. Suddenly walls, floors, and ceiling rushed into the space around him.

"What does that mean?" said Tane.

"It means you're going to stay here while I check out the situation on Greenfields," said Croft.

She objected immediately. "But I don't-"

"But you do," Croft corrected her.

Suddenly, he felt rather than saw the heat of a flame behind him.

"You can spontaneously combust all you like, but you're not going either," said Croft. The craft started to slow to a halt. "And I appreciate your not starting a fire while I'm landing the transport."

"You always leave us behind," came Red Sally's voice. "Why?"

"Maybe because this time I really need to travel undercover, and undercover is not your specialty," said Croft.

"What about you?" said Sally. "You tried to pass for a Graftonite and they spotted you a mile away."

The transport was at a stop now. Croft turned to Sally and said simply, "That was because I was stuck with you and Tane. There was no reason to even try. You've never seen me in action for real."

"Good to see you again, Clifford," said Battle Admiral Norman North, shaking his hand vigorously.

"Same here, Battle Admiral," said Croft. "I just missed you on Grafton; I hear you replaced Admiral Lillard right after I left."

"Yes," said North. He sighed. "It's a very difficult situation we're in. The Graftonites are very tough fighters." He gestured behind Croft. "I think you know Lieutenant Took."

Idaho Took nodded. Croft nodded fractionally. He wondered what Took was doing here. Maybe he was here to help the Battle Admiral brief him on the situation.

The Battle Admiral pressed a button and a holoimage of the Greenfields spaceport appeared. "As you may know, Greenfields has fallen to the Graftonites."

"Fallen?" said Croft, his mouth dropping open. Greenfields was a medium sized industrial planet. It had only been invaded a little less than four days ago.

The Battle Admiral nodded. "Our primary concern is to disable or destroy the Greenfields fleet."

"If it's still on the ground, why not just blast it from orbit?" Croft asked.

"That's what we did on Karis," said the Battle Admiral. "But they've learned from that mistake." He pressed a button and the image zoomed in. They could see several ships; and surrounding them were groups of people.

"Hostages," said Croft glumly.

The Battle Admiral nodded. "If we take out the ships, the hostages will be killed by our own fire. We need to disable those ships without blowing them up, in such a way that they will not be easy to repair."

"Is there such a way?" Croft asked.

The Battle Admiral nodded. "You'll need to knock out each ship's virtual integrator. That's in engineering. Lieutenant Took will be able to show you where they are."

"I appreciate the thought, but I'm working alone," said Croft. "I need to be able to convince people I'm a Graftonite, and I can't do that if I have to babysit—no offense, Lieutenant."

"None taken," said Took, rolling his eyes.

"How will you know where to find the integrator?" said the Battle Admiral.

"How does he know?" said Croft. "He's not an engineer; if you can tell him where to find it, you can tell me."

"Hey, I'm in the same room with you, there's no need to talk to me like I'm not here," said Took.

"You're right that you can be instructed as easily as Took," said the Battle Admiral. "But how will you carry the explosives?"

"In a briefcase," said Croft.

"Even using miniaturized explosives, it will take more than one case to carry enough explosives for 27 ships," said the Battle Admiral. "You need him."

"Took," said Took. "The name is Took."

"I can carry two cases," said Croft, purposely trying to be difficult.

"That will make you even more conspicuous," said the Battle Admiral.

"Or I can hide the second briefcase until I empty the first one," said Croft.

"And how do you suppose to plant the explosives?" said the Battle Admiral. "If they have guards or technicians in engineering, how do you propose to distract them while planting the explosives at the same time? Remember, you need to avoid raising suspicions until you have planted all the explosives."

"Oh," said Croft. He seemed to pause for a moment, thinking of alternatives. Then he turned and looked over Took critically.

"Why do I suddenly feel like someone's retarded younger brother?" Took asked.

Slowly, Croft turned back to the Battle Admiral and nodded, ever so slightly.

"All you have to do is be silent, can you manage that?" Croft said. He and Took were alone in a storage room.

"Silence? No problem. I majored in silence at the academy," said Took.

"Then all we have to do is work on your look," said Croft.

"My look?" said Took. "I thought we were going to go down in typical Grafton clothes."

"We are but that's not what I was referring to. Stand straight."

Took stood straight.

"No, perfectly straight."

Took stood straighter.

"Now, walk across the room."

Took started to walk, but Croft stopped him halfway.

"No, no," said Croft. "You're walking like a starfighter pilot. You need to walk like a Graftonite."

Took frowned. "And that means…."

"Watch me." Croft walked across the room. "Notice the relaxed way I'm walking, but with calm, wide strides."

"Are they going to spot me from the way I walk?"

"You bet," said Croft. "Now practice it."

Took spent the next half hour walking back and forth, receiving a steady stream of comments and criticisms from Croft. Finally Croft stopped him.

"Did I do it right?" Took asked.

Croft made a face but said, "It will have to do. Now, the last thing we have to work on is your expression."

"My expression?" Took said.

"You have to do something about that goofy look," said Croft.

Took looked hurt.

"I don't mean to offend you, but arching your eyebrows and giving a wide grin is the quickest route to getting us shot as spies," said Croft. "I want you to practice looking serious."

Took scrunched up his face.

"No, not in pain, merely serious," said Croft.

Took tried again.

"Not so intensely," said Croft. "We're looking for a bored kind of serious."

"Bored serious?" Took said.

"Watch me, and try."

Took worked with Croft for much of the next hour. They were interrupted, however, by a crewman who entered the storage room. He looked at Took, who had a deadly serious expression on his face.

"Sorry sir, I was just... I'll come back later," said the crewman, hastily leaving the way he had come.

Took turned to Croft, giving a wide grin.

"Now if you can just get the same reaction from the Graftonites, you'll be ready," said Croft.

The two seater Graftonite starfighter zoomed through the atmosphere towards the capitol, which was also named Greenfields. Took was piloting while Croft sat in the back. The League had specially procured a Graftonite starfighter. They had also obtained the trademark blue denim clothes that Took and Croft now wore.

"So let me get this straight," said Took. "I'm told you tried to impersonate a Graftonite on Grafton and failed. So what makes you think it will work here?"

"I didn't really try on Grafton," said Croft. "I had a lot of extra baggage with me that made an undercover role impractical."

"And what about me?"

"You're a smaller amount of baggage," said Croft.

"Very nice," said Took. Then, after a pause, "You know, if we're caught, they will probably do not very nice things to us."

"Probably," said Croft.

"Isn't it tough being an infiltrator, knowing that can happen to you at any time?"

Croft shrugged. "You try not to think about it; and if you're any good, it doesn't happen. I've been on so many missions, I've just stopped thinking about it."

"That's not very comforting."

"I don't work in the comfort department," said Croft.

They reduced altitude rapidly; it was only several minutes later when they could make out ground features, that Croft directed Took to land on a small road near the spaceport.

"Isn't this kind of conspicuous, landing on a road?" said Took.

"Graftonites land anywhere they want to," said Croft. "And today we're Graftonites."

They got out of the starfighter, making sure to carry their briefcases filled with explosives. If they were searched, they would quickly be discovered.

"For such a thin thing, this is pretty heavy," Took complained.

"Pretty combustible, too," said Croft.

"You mean… it can be detonated by blaster fire?" Took asked.

"I wouldn't worry about that," said Croft. "If the Graftonites are shooting at you, they're unlikely to miss you and hit your briefcase."

"How reassuring," said Took.

The streets seemed almost empty. They could see a few people on the street, but they quickly turned away when they saw Croft and Took.

"Something's got them scared," said Took.

"Perhaps it's the invasion," said Croft dryly.

"I still don't believe that a handful of Graftonites could conquer an entire planet," said Took.

"Believe what you like," said Croft.

They walked to the edge of the spaceport, and then Croft turned abruptly away and headed in the opposite direction.

"What's going on?" Took asked.

"We need to get some information first," said Croft. He saw a single Grafton standing on guard at a street corner. Perfect

"Where are we going to get this information from?"

"Don't ask any more stupid questions," said Croft. "Be absolutely quiet now and remember the facial expression I taught you."

"Yes sir," said Took. But his heart raced wildly. Croft had never before been successful in fooling the Graftonites. Would his act work now? Croft was supposed to be one of the best infiltrators. But could he pull this off?

The Graftonite saw them coming. He was armed not only with a blaster but a laser rifle as well.

He stared coldly at Croft. When they got close he said, "That's far enough. What are you doing here?"

"Special assignment," said Croft bluntly, speaking in a very matter-of-factly voice.

"What special assignment?" said the Graftonite skeptically.

Croft looked coldly at him for a moment, but gave no answer. Then he turned to Took, saying only two words. "Come on."

His attention shifted momentarily to Took, who hoped that he looked and walked like a Graftonite.

"Halt," said the Graftonite.

Croft stopped, and turned to face the Grafton again.

"You don't have clearance to be here. I'll have to check with the Captain," he said, reaching for his comm unit.

"Halt," said Croft, in an identical tone to the Graftonite. "We're on special assignment, direct from Mo Quandry himself. No one is to be notified." he said, nodding to a building in front of them.

"I'm going to need more than that," said the guard, his face etched with suspicion. He lowered his laser rifle, and quicker than Croft could see, drew his blaster. "Where's your authorization?"

Croft glanced at Took, and nodded. Took took a datapad out of his denim jacket, and slowly handed it over to the Graftonite.

"What's this?" said the Graftonite, looking down at the datapad with one hand while holding the blaster in the other.

At that moment Croft arched his foot upwards and pushed down hard with his heel. A needle shot out of the tip, catching the guard in the foot. He yelled and fell to the ground, firing his blaster.

The shot flew only inches above Took's right shoulder.

"That was too close!" said Took.

Croft paid him no attention; instead, he went rifling through the Graftonite's clothes until he found another datapad.

"All right," said Croft. "Get the body out of sight while I go through this." Even as he spoke he rapidly sifted through the information. It contained an organizational list of the invaders, a list of commanders…. Good. That should be enough.

After a short walk, Croft and Took approached the main gate to the Greenfields Spaceport.

"Let me do all the talking," said Croft calmly.

There were four guards at the main gate.

"Halt. Identify."

"Major Tan Zoo, Captain Philmert Roh, Zarias Company.."

One of the Graftonites looked suspiciously at Croft. "I'm in Zarias Company, and I don't know you."

Croft looked bored but maintained the calm detachment. "I'm part of a special team of internal security that's just been attached to your unit."

"What is your purpose here?" said the Graftonite.

"You don't have the clearance to know that," said Croft coldly. He started to walk past the Graftonite.

"Halt!" cried the guard.

Croft slowly halted and turned around. "You're starting to irritate me," he said in a deadly voice.

The sentry paused, considering. "I'll have to clear this with the Captain first," he finally said. He was apprehensive of Croft, but at the same time, he had his orders, too.

Croft slowly walked up to the guard, and now there was clear irritation in his features. "You will do no such thing. My orders are to check on security first, and then report to the Captain. If you alert him first, I'm not going to see how your security is organized. If I don't get a real picture of what's going on here I'll report it to my boss, and I report directly to Mr. Quandry."

The sentry paused, looking indecisive. "But my orders-"

"Son, let me give you a word of advice," said Croft. "Are you a gold medalist?"

"No," said the sentry.

"Silver?"

The sentry shook his head.

"Then I don't think you want to mess with me," said Croft. He turned to Took. "Come along."

Without waiting for a further answer, they started walking.

"What if they shoot us in the back?" said Took, as they walked.

"Shut up," Croft hissed.

"What if they alert their Captain?" Took wondered.

"Shut up," Croft said again. He didn't need this kind of doubt.

They made their way to the landing pads. They could see hostages under guard surrounding each ship. The hostages looked miserable. Croft didn't risk any eye contact with them. Croft made his way to the first ship, did the required bullying/intimidation, and got them on board. They headed directly to the engine room.

The first engine room was completely empty. Croft planted the first explosives.

So was the second. Croft worked quickly.

But there were two Graftonite techs in the third, and they were suspicious.

"I didn't hear anything about an inspection," said one of the techs.

Croft just gave him a cold glare. He started to move among the columns of machinery.

"What are you doing back there?" said the unhelpful technician, straining to see what Croft was doing.

Took suddenly spoke up. "I need your assistance," he said, pointing to one of the panels. "Why did you set the configuration this way?"

"Rogga can explain it to you," said the first technician, indicating the second technician, as he attempted to peer after Croft.

"Perhaps you weren't listening," said Took coldly. "I want you to explain it. Don't make me ask again."

The technician turned around to face Took. He was a technician, but he was also a Graftonite, and this was clearly a challenge. He seemed to consider his next move, eyeing Took as if measuring him up. Then he took a few steps towards Took.

Took tried hard to appear impassive.

The technician said, in a low voice. "What is your question?"

Croft safely planted the bomb while Took kept the technicians occupied.

When they got outside the ship, Croft muttered, "Good work."

"I think I'm going to collapse," said Took.

"Not until we get back to the Glory," said Croft as they walked.

"That man might have shot me."

"Very possibly," said Croft. "Now be quiet."

He hurried his step. They didn't have that much time.

The bombs couldn't be set off by remote control since there was too much metal for a signal to reach inside the engine rooms of those ships. Therefore they had to be set using timers. There were 29 ships on the field; figuring 15 minutes per ship, Croft had set the first bomb to go off in eight hours, and the second in 7 hours 45 minutes, reducing the timer for each bomb.

But although they moved quickly, sometimes they fell behind schedule. Once they were held up by an officious Graftonite as they tried to board a cruiser; another time it took several minutes to sufficiently distract an engineering officer so they could plant the bomb; a third time they simply got lost searching for engineering.

So with only twenty minutes left they still had five ships left to do.

"What do we do?" Took asked, well aware of the time limitation.

Croft looked at the five remaining ships. The largest was a heavy cruiser. "We go for that one," he said, still walking calmly.

"And the others?" Took wondered.

"Nothing we can do," said Croft.

"The War Admiral won't like it," said Took.

"Then he can come down here and plant the rest of the explosives himself," said Croft. Personally, he thought knocking out 25 out of 29 ships would be an amazing job, given the circumstances.

They entered the cruiser, went to engineering, and planted what was to be their last bomb. Then they started walking quickly to the exit.

"We have maybe seven or eight minutes before the first bomb goes off," said Croft. "We have to get off this base before then."

"Will that be enough time?" said Took. By the tone of his voice he didn't think so.

"Just barely enough, I think," said Croft, who thought so but wasn't certain.

But when they reached the ship's exit ramp, they found two Graftonites waiting for them. One of them wore a Captain's insignia.

"Who are you?" said the Captain bluntly.

"Identify yourself," Croft responded frigidly.

"I am Captain Ult Garrison, Commander, Zarias Company," said the Captain.

Croft responded with their cover names. Then, without further word, he started walking away.

"Just a moment, Major Zoo," said the Captain. "I've recently learned from my sentries that you've been attached to my company."

Croft stopped in his tracks.

"Rather odd that I wasn't notified, don't you think?" said Garrison.

Croft turned to face Garrison. "You were to be notified once I finished my inspection," he said, his face mottled with anger.

"And why is that, Major?" said Garrison. "And just what is it that caused you to inspect every ship?"

"I don't have to answer questions from a lower ranking officer," said Croft coldly.

"And I've never heard of a higher ranking officer being put under the command of a lower ranking one," said Garrison. "Why don't we walk back to my administrative building and verify your credentials?"

Croft peered harshly at Garrison. "Certainly. Once I've completed my inspection."

"NOW, Major," said Garrison.

A small smile appeared on Croft's lips. "Are you challenging me?"

Garrison paused, and gave a small nod.

"Very well," said Croft. "Please permit me a minute's delay while I hand my notes over to my subordinate." He indicated his briefcase, and motioned for Took to come over. Casually, and very slowly, Croft handed the briefcase to him and whispered, "Get ready to shoot them."

"They're Graftonites," Took whispered. "We don't have a chance!"

Croft glanced at his watch. "In eight seconds….."

"What's going on there?" said Captain Garrison.

"Nothing," said Croft, turning to face Garrison. Took stood to the side, both briefcases by his feet, leaving his hands free.

Garrison faced him, ready to draw.

"I'll count to five," said Croft. "Will that suffice?"

"Fine," said Garrison.

"One… two… three…."

Where was the explosion? Why wasn't it going off?

Garrison stood, watching expectantly. "Shouldn't four come next?"

"Quite right," said Croft. "But I seem to have lost my momentum." If those explosions didn't go off, he wouldn't have any chance of distracting the Graftonites, and they would shoot him dead.

"One...."

Garrison waited expectantly.

"Two..." said Croft, waiting as long as he dared.

Garrison waited again.

"Three...."

Finally, as the pauses got longer, Garrison lost patience. "Enough of this-"

Suddenly, the ground shook all around them; Garrison and his aide stumbled, momentarily losing their balance.

But Took and Croft had been expecting this. They drew their blasters and fired. Even though they were off balance, Garrison and his aide drew their blasters, and they fired too.

Croft hit Garrison with the first shot, just as a shot whizzed by him; and then his aide, already having fired once, turned to orient on Croft. But the aide was slowed by his attempt to maintain his balance, and his second shot went wild; Croft squeezed off a second shot, hitting the aide, who fell to the ground.

What had happened to Took? Croft looked around to find Took on the ground, bleeding.

"I'm hit," said Took, grabbing his side. Croft quickly went to his side and saw where he was hit. It looked bad.

The sounds of explosions could be heard all throughout the spaceport. Graftonites were running around looking confused. But that wouldn't last long.

"Leave me," said Took. "There's no way you're going to get out of here with me."

"Shut up," said Croft. "Can you walk?"

"No," said Took.

"I'll take that for a yes," said Croft. "Get on your feet!" He pulled Took up. Slowly they hobbled away. Took gritted his teeth against the pain.

"We're not going to the front gate," Took gasped.

"No we're not."

"I'm too weak to get over the fence," said Took.

"We're not going that way either," said Croft.

They hobbled painstakingly to one of the few remaining ships they hadn't sabotaged, a medium sized transport. But as they got to the ramp a Graftonite came running up to them. "Everyone is to report to their duty post," said the Graftonite. He looked at Took. "You have wounded?"

"Yes," said Croft. "Get a medic."

"Will do," said the Graftonite. Suddenly he paused. "Why were you trying to get into the ship?"

"Medical kit," said Croft, still dragging Took.

"All right," said the Graftonite, suddenly understanding. He took off at a run.

"We'd better get out of here now," said Croft. He closed the airlock, dropped Took on the deck, and ran for the cockpit.

Croft had the ship in space in several moments. There was no ground fire; the only question was whether there would be any airborne pursuit. He checked the sensors as the ship gained altitude... and then heaved a sigh of relief. Only when he had set a course for the orbiting Glory and made contact with the fleet did he go back to Took.

Took was bleeding away, and unconscious. Croft bandaged him up as best he could.

"Hold on, hold on," he muttered.

He ran back to the control room and signaled the Glory. "We need medics to meet us on arrival, we have a medical emergency."

Croft landed the small ship in one of the Glory's landing bays as quickly as he could. A medical team rushed into the ship as soon as he landed. He watched with concern as Took was taken out on a hoverbed; they were pumping new blood into him even as he was being transported.

"Will he make it?" Croft asked one of the medics.

The medic shook his head. "He lost a lot of blood. It's too soon to tell."

Croft made his way to the bridge, where the Battle Admiral awaited him.

"25 out of 29 ships," said the Battle Admiral. "You did a good job."

"Tell that to Lieutenant Took," said Croft.

"He knew the risks when he volunteered for the mission," said the Battle Admiral.

Croft looked surprised.

"That's right; he was a volunteer. Didn't you know?" the Battle Admiral asked.

Croft shook his head.

"That Took, he's a real adventurous one. He'll be a real fine starfighter commander when he makes captain, one of these days," said the Battle Admiral.

"Assuming he survives the night," said Croft.

The Battle Admiral pressed a button. "Doctor Farb? This is Admiral North. What's the situation on Iday?"

"He's lost a lot of blood," said Farb.

"Is he going to make it?" the Battle Admiral asked, keeping his tone neutral.

"I think so," said Farb. "We've given him a transfusion and are sealing his wounds now. His condition is starting to stabilize, but I'll know more in a few hours."

"Keep me posted," said the Battle Admiral. He closed the comm, and turned back to Croft. "Get some rest, Clifford."

"A short rest," Croft said. "I have to go back down there again."

"So soon?" the Battle Admiral looked surprised.

"The Chief wants to know how they conquer planets so easily."

"But they'll be doubly alert after this attack," said the Battle Admiral. "They may even have holos of your face."

"I'm used to fame," said Croft, lifting his chin.

But as it turned out, Croft didn't have to go back to Greenfields the next day. The orders came from the Chief herself, in a secure line in the War Admiral's office.

"I have been ordered to delay your mission," said the Chief. She looked irritated, as if she didn't like getting orders from others.

"I thought you wanted me to find out how the armed forces of Greenfields were conquered so quickly," said Croft.

"We do," said the Chief. "But an expeditionary force of five thousand League marines arrived in orbit around Greenfields a few hours ago, and the President wants to send them down to retake Greenfields. I can't expect you to go down in the middle of a shooting war."

"I just got the notification an hour ago," the Battle Admiral confirmed.

"Just a moment," said Croft. "According to the intel I received, Greenfields had an armed forces of some 40,000 troops, not counting another 40,000 reservists. And they were conquered by the Graftonites."

"Apparently so," said the Chief.

"So can you explain to me how 5,000 marines are going to succeed where 80,000 troops failed?" Croft asked. He didn't understand the logic behind it.

"It is believed that there are only a few hundred Graftonites on Greenfields," said the Chief. "Since we have total air and space superiority, as well as ten to one odds, it is believed that the marines can retake the planet."

"All very nice... but you didn't answer my question," said Croft. "Wouldn't it be nice to find out what happened to the other troops before we send in more?" He turned to the Battle Admiral. Wasn't he talking sense? Could the others understand him?

The Battle Admiral nodded. "That's just the argument I made to the joint chiefs."

"And?"

"They decided otherwise," said the Battle Admiral simply.

"The Graftonites have just launched an invasion of Mezzanine," said the Chief. "At this rate, they'll conquer the League in two months. It was decided that we can't afford to wait."

"All right," said Croft, throwing up his hands. He turned to the Battle Admiral. "I'll simply enjoy your fine dining and dancing facilities until I'm needed again."

General Morgan Pottan listened to the reports of the first landings on Greenfields. He had sent in an expeditionary battalion to secure a landing area. What he got was a surprise, even to him.

"Report," he said, speaking to the major in charge via holocom.

"Area secure," said the Major.

"Casualties?" General Pottan asked.

"None."

"Resistance?" Pottan asked.

"None."

General Pottan thought this extremely unlikely. They had landed near the capital, where the concentration of Graftons was said to be greatest. So the Graftons hadn't resisted their landing at all? They must be planning to ambush them on the ground. Well, he wasn't going to play into their hands.

"Your orders, sir?" the Major asked.

"Hold and wait," said Pottan. "I'm bringing down the entire division. When we're all down, we'll move together." After all, there was safety in numbers.

Unfortunately, that's exactly what the Graftonites wanted. They wanted all the troops on the ground. Or rather, to be more specific, General Pottan; he was the key to their victory.

Once the division had grounded, Pottan ordered company sized units to branch out. He monitored the situation from a command post in the center of their landing area, a field a few miles south of the capital.

"I hear you're recovering," said Croft, eyeing the bandages wrapped around Took's side.

"Rumors of my recovery are vastly exaggerated," Took groaned. "What happened?"

"We got them."

"You mean, you got them," said Took. "I think he hit me and I missed, even though I knew what was coming and he didn't."

"Don't be too hard on yourself," said Croft. "You faced off two Graftonites and lived to tell about it."

"How did you know we would be able to take on those two Graftons when the ordinance exploded?" said Took. "It only threw them off balance for a second or two."

"I didn't know we could take them," said Croft.

"Really?"

"Really," said Croft. "But we didn't have a lot of choices at that moment."

"Oh," said Took, absorbing that information. Suddenly he felt glad just to be alive. "What's going on now?" he asked.

"A League force has landed on Greenfields to try and retake the planet," Croft said.

"What do you think will happen?" Took asked.

Croft shrugged. "They'll die, probably."

Battle Admiral Norman North monitored the battle from his ready room, just off the main bridge of the Glory. His face looked tense as he sat silently. Captain Harkness sat at his side.

Technically the Glory was supposed to be in position to lend air support to the marines, but so far, they needed none of it. All they could do was sit and wait.

A squad of marines circumnavigated a city block. It all seemed empty. Too empty. Then, all of a sudden, two figures approached them. The marines relaxed when they saw that the newcomers were also marines, in the same uniforms they wore.

"Where did you come from?" the squad leader asked.

"Delta company," said one of the newcomers. "We have to deliver a message to your captain."

"Why not use the comms?"

"They could be monitored; this message has to be delivered personally," said the newcomer. "Can you detail one of your men to take us there?"

"Sure," said the squad leader.

Croft entered the Battle Admiral's office. "Any news yet?"

The Battle Admiral shook his head. "We're still waiting."

Croft sighed. "I've never been good at waiting."

"Me neither," said Captain Harkness.

"Why don't we spend the time trying to figure out how a few hundred Graftonites conquered an army of 80,000 soldiers?" Croft said.

"Just a moment," said the company commander, a Captain, as the three men entered his tent. He was busy studying a datapad so he didn't look up until he heard a thunk and saw one of the three men drop to the ground. "What is this?" said the Captain..

The two men drew blasters. "Don't move unless you want a big hole in your ugly chest."

"What do you want?" the Captain asked.

"Take us to see your colonel," said one of the men.

"I mean, a few hundred Graftonites can't physically kill 80,000 men, can they?" Croft said.

"Not unless they have some kind of super weapon," said the Battle Admiral.

"Super weapons have never been the Graftonite style," said Croft.

"Still, if they have invented a weapon that can immobilize large numbers of soldiers-"

"Then why haven't we heard of this weapon before?" said Croft. He shook his head. "No, I've got a gut feeling that this is something decidedly low tech."

The two men guarding the Captain entered the Colonel's headquarters. There were four men in the room, including the Colonel; in seconds, only the Colonel was conscious.

"Who are you? What do you want?" the Colonel sputtered.

"We have a special message for General Pottan," said one of the men.

"I mean, even Graftonites can't beat 80,000 men in open combat," said Croft.

"Perhaps they did it stealthily," said the Battle Admiral. "Using ambushes."

"That would take a long time," said Croft.

"Keep in mind that that 80,000 figure includes reserves," said Harkness. "If you give the Graftonites the advantage of surprise, perhaps the Greenfielders couldn't mobilize their reserves. That reduces their base numbers to 40,000."

"Which still gives them something like 80 to one odds," said Croft.

The two Graftonites escorting the Captain and the Colonel had been joined by three other Graftonites leading a pair of majors, so by the time they entered the General's headquarters there were nine of them.

"What is this?" said Pottan, as his men were quickly disarmed.

"It's very simple," said the Grafton leader. He stood close to Pottan. "This war is over."

"What do you mean?" Pottan said.

"You are going to order your men to surrender," said the Graftonite.

Pottan gave a bitter laugh. "You must be joking."

The Graftonite casually aimed and shot a hole in the captain's chest.

General Pottan froze.

"And that was just the Captain," said the Graftonite. "We have a few majors and a colonel in this room. How much do you value them?"

"I don't know either," said the Battle Admiral. "We have too little information." He checked his chrono and frowned. "We should have heard back from General Pottan by now." He activated the comm. "General? This is the Battle Admiral."

There was silence for a moment.

The Battle Admiral spoke again. "General Pottan?" He pressed another button. "This is the Battle Admiral. I'm having trouble contacting the surface. Check the comm."

The Battle Admiral looked up.

"Not a troubling sign, one would hope," said Croft.

"One would hope," said the Battle Admiral grimly. They waited a minute before the report came back.

"Sir, there's nothing wrong with the comm. They're just not answering."

"A comm failure?" said Captain Harkness.

The Battle Admiral looked cynically at Harkness.

"Don't look at me," said Harkness. "It's just my job to present dopey alternatives." He paused. "We could send a recon squad down to investigate."

The Battle Admiral pressed another button. "Sensors. I want a real-time sensor image of the marine landing area."

The holoimage came in a few minutes later.

The encampment was empty.

Completely empty.

"All gone," said the Battle Admiral.

"Maybe they used some kind of weapon that vaporized our troops," said Harkness.

Croft eyed the holoimage closely. "No battle."

"What?" said Harkness.

"There's no sign of a battle. No bodies, no damage to any of the equipment or tents or buildings. It's simply as if everyone walked away."

"It must be some kind of new weapon," said Harkness. "Maybe something that disorients the troops."

The Battle Admiral studied the image. Then he said, "Nothing's changed. We still don't know what's going on down there."

"We could send a team of our own," said Harkness.

"So far there's only been one person who's gone down there and come back to tell about it," said the Battle Admiral.

"Is this the part where I volunteer?" Croft asked. "All right, all right. But first we need to do a little contingency planning. I have a feeling that this time getting in will be a lot easier than getting out."

The Battle Admiral raised his eyebrows.

"Take us with you!" said Red Sally. Tane looked pensive. The Clapper was jumping up and down.

"This isn't going to be a picnic," said Croft. "While Grafton nominally wasn't hostile territory, this planet is a war zone. We'll be shot on sight."

"That's only if they get the chance," said Sally. She had been cooped up on the Glory for several days, and was frustrated.

"All right," said Croft. "You can come."

"Can I (clap) come too (clap)?" the Clapper eagerly asked.

"Yes, of course, the more the merrier," said Croft. He looked at Tane. "But you'd better stay here."

"For once, I agree with you," said Tane. She didn't want to go into a war zone.

"Good," said Croft. He turned to the Clapper. "But before we go, there's a small routine we need to work out. Are you any good at jabbing?"

They took a small transport down to the planet. As they landed, the Clapper said, "Hee hee! Your face looks funny, Croft!"

"Thanks," said Croft, trying hard not to sweat under the plastiform that remolded his face. "Your analytical comments and opinions are always appreciated."

Red Sally had a thought. "After your first bit of espionage, and the subsequent marine landing, how do you know the Graftonites won't track our landing and arrange a hostile reception?"

Croft's only answer was to raise an eyebrow as he drew his blaster and opened the hatch to the outside.

Outside, a half dozen Graftonites stood there, with blasters raised.

"All right," said Croft. "Get moving!"

The Clapper and Red Sally, looking surprised, headed down the ramp.

The Graftonites looked confused.

"Surrender," their leader said

"No," said Croft. "I'm not surrendering my prisoners. I won't let you take the bounty for them."

The leader did a double take. "Who are you?"

"Plo Lake," said Croft. "Zarias Company."

The leader checked a datapad. There was indeed a Plo Lake in Zarias company. Croft knew it too; that was one of the names he had taken from the stolen datapad.

"Identification."

Croft handed over a datapad. The leader checked it, nodded, and handed it back.

"What happened to you?" said the leader. He thought it a bit odd that this Graftonite was all alone, separated from his unit.

"I was taken prisoner," said Croft, saying as little as possible.

The Graftonites looked surprised. "The sheep took you prisoner?"

"They hit me from behind," said Croft coldly.

"All right," said the leader. "That's more understandable. What happened then?"

"I escaped," said Croft simply. Again, the less said, the better. He abruptly changed the subject. "These sheep are senior diplomats. There should be a good bounty on them."

"These are diplomats?" said the leader, eyeing Sally and the even more eccentric looking Clapper.

"Yes," said Croft. "And I want to take them in myself."

"All right," said the leader. "You can turn them in at our division HQ. It's moved. I'll give you the new coordinates." He punched in a set of coordinates in Croft's datapad, and handed it back.

"Thanks," said Croft cooly. That was nice of the Graftonite, to let him know the location of their headquarters. "All right, you two, get moving!"

"Just one more thing," said the leader.

"Yes," said Croft, getting a chill down his spine.

"When you were captured, did you see this man?" said the leader. He held up a datapad, which displayed Croft's face.

Croft looked at the face closely. "No," he shrugged. "Why, is he important?"

"He is a wanted spy," said the leader. "The award for his capture, dead or alive, is now 50,000 credits."

"Dead or alive?" said Croft.

The leader nodded.

"Then I'll be on the lookout for him," said Croft.

Croft marched Sally and the Clapper off at gunpoint. When they had gotten far enough away, Croft said to the Clapper, "You don't think I look so ridiculous now, do you?"

"I didn't know you were trying to disguise," said the Clapper. "I just thought you were trying to look better."

"Speaking of faces, the next time we're surrounded by Graftonites, can you try not to look so happy at the thought of being captured?" Croft said.

The Clapper put on an exaggerated weepy face. "Better?"

Croft sighed. "I suppose anything is."

"When are we going to stop skulking around and fight?" Red Sally asked.

"Uh, I don't know if you were paying attention during the mission summary, but we're here to gather information, not fight," said Croft. "Or have you forgotten how fast these Graftonite reflexes are?"

"They can't shoot if they're on fire," said Red Sally smugly.

"What a team," Croft sighed again.

They went to the administrative HQ. Croft figured that either some of the prisoners were being held there, or someone there would know where the prisoners were being held. All he would have to do is be officious and ask for directions.

And if Croft had encountered an ordinary Graftonite, he might have succeeded. Unfortunately, Croft ran into Billy Kanner.

Billy was a 17 year old Graftonite who hadn't quite grown up yet. He loved shootings, and competitions, and challenges, and it was just pure luck that he hadn't been killed in a duel yet. He considered fighting a game, a sport to be enjoyed, which is why, had he stayed on Grafton, he probably would've been dead within a year.

As chance happened, Billy signed up with Quandry's mercenaries to get action on other planets, channeling his aggressive energies away from challenging other Graftonites and probably saving his life.

His superiors had quickly noticed Billy's frivolous attitude and penchance for picking fights, and had placed him on administrative duty, figuring he was more of a danger to their own troops than the enemy. Billy hated administrative duty; it made him restless for action.

So when Croft went up to Billy and asked him where the prisoners were kept, Billy was primed for action.

"Did you capture these yourself?" he said eagerly.

Croft nodded.

"Do you mind if I have fun with one of them?" said Billy. "The blonde, maybe?"

Red Sally boiled with rage. Her hair started to turn a light red.

"No," said Croft quickly. "Which way to the detention facilities?"

Billy looked at Croft. "They don't look so tough. What's the matter, can't capture any of the tough ones?"

Croft looked coldly at Billy. He had no idea what kind of game this kid was playing.

"Come on," he said, gesturing for Sally and the Clapper to walk away with him.

"Don't turn your back on me!" Billy yelled.

Croft slowly turned around. Several other Graftonites, attracted by the volume of Billy's voice, were gathering. A fight seemed to be in the offing, and Graftonites loved to witness fights.

"You seem awfully soft for a Graftonite. Turn your prisoners over to me!" said Billy.

"I don't have time for this," said Croft coldly. He looked to the other Graftonites for support, but they weren't getting involved. That was the Graftonite code; one-on-one, a fair fight.

"Didn't you hear me?" said Billy. He suddenly stood up. "I'm challenging you!"

Croft stood speechless for a moment. He didn't know what to do. There was no way he could take Billy. His only chance was to bluff it out.

"Come on," said Croft, gesturing for the Clapper and Sally to go.

Suddenly, moving almost quicker than Croft could see, Billy reached over and plucked the blaster from Croft's holster.

"You're no Graftonite!" said Billy. "He's an imposter!"

Other Graftonites, already coming to this conclusion, raised their blasters and closed in. There was no way they could escape now.

Croft, sighing, raised his hands. So did Sally. So did the Clapper (though even above his head, he clapped his).

"So you are the Clifford Croft spy," said his interrogator. "I have heard a lot about you."

Croft picked the remaining bits of plastiform from his face. His disguise hadn't been meant to stand up to close inspection. The Graftonites evidently had been impressed by his reputation; his interrogator was Colonel Chapman, one of the senior leaders of the Greenfields invasion.

"I can't say I've heard anything about you," said Croft. "Maybe you need a better publicist. Would you like the name of mine?"

"You have caused us a lot of trouble," said Colonel Chapman. "There is a general liquidate on sight order concerning you."

"You're going to put me into a juice machine?" Croft asked.

"Joke all you like," said Chapman. "You won't joke when you're in front of the firing squad."

"Why aren't I in front of one now?" said Croft.

"First I wanted to find out something about you," said Chapman. "You are the first worthy adversary we've encountered."

"Worthy non-Grafton adversary, you mean," said Croft. While he idly fenced with the Colonel, his mind was racing, thinking about possibilities for escape.

"Yes, that's what I meant," said Chapman. He gave Croft a steady look. "I was... curious. I can't help but wonder if you have some partial Graftonite genetic heritage that explains your abilities."

"Sorry!" said Croft. "I hate to put a crimp in your eugenics theory, but genetics have nothing to do with your abilities. Anyone who goes to Grafton and spends enough time there gets the speeded up reflexes. If they ever figure out how to export whatever's in the air or water that does that to other planets, everyone will have the ability."

"Yes, well, those who are actually born there seem to have a higher level of ability," said Chapman. "I thought perhaps your bloodline—well, never mind." He paused. "What of your grotesque companions?"

"What about them?" said Croft.

"The woman, and the retarded anorexic?" the Colonel asked.

"Oh, you mean the Clapper," said Croft. "He's just a little slow."

"What purpose do they serve?" Chapman asked.

"Mostly, comic relief," said Croft.

"You know, I could turn you over to one of our real interrogators," said Chapman.

"You could," said Croft. "But that wouldn't be nice to do to an adversary you respect, would it?"

"No," said Chapman. He poured himself a drink. "Don't get me wrong, Croft. We're not equals. But you do seem to have a superior ability, for your race. It is just a pity for your side that there are so few of you."

"You think you're going to win, do you?"

"It is inevitable," said Chapman.

"Are you quite sure? It might be merely evitable," said Croft.

Chapman looked confused.

"You are few, and we are many," said Croft. "What would happen if we cluster bomb the entire surface of the planet Grafton?"

"Our population is very spread out," said Chapman. "It would require a tremendous amount of ordinance."

"Give us the incentive and we'll do it," said Croft.

"By the time you act we will be spread out on all your planets," said Chapman.

"Yes," said Croft. "Actually, I'm curious how a few hundred of you can control a planet of millions."

"It's not so difficult," said Chapman. He paused. "It will not reveal any special secret to let you know that we have recruited mercenaries in support positions."

"Mercenaries?" said Croft. "You mean, more Graftonites?"

Chapman shook his head. "Non-Graftonites. We have already recruited thousands on the planets we have acquired. They are maintaining law and order."

"Why don't you just use Graftonites?" Croft asked.

Chapman grinned. "Graftonites are more expensive."

"Meaning you still have supply problems," said Croft. "Is that how you conquer these planets? Using these non-Grafton mercenaries? When you invade a planet, our sensors show that you send in just a few hundred at a time."

Chapman smiled again, but said nothing.

"Unless… the non-Grafton mercenaries are already in place before you land on the planet," said Croft. "Is that how you do it?"

Chapman continued to smile enigmatically and sip his drink.

"No," Croft decided. "Even a few thousand non-Graftons couldn't take over an entire planet. And you said before that you were forming these non-Grafton units on planets after you had already taken them over."

"Did I?" said Chapman. He gave a small smile.

"So how do you do it?" Croft asked. "How are you conquering these planets?"

"I'm afraid there are some secrets that must be kept even from you, Mr. Croft," said Chapman.

"Why?" said Croft. "If I'm about to be executed, what does it matter?" He was pressing the matter as best he could.

Chapman paused, as if considering, weighing the possibilities, and then shook his head in the negative.

"Why not?" Croft persisted.

"If I tell you, there are only two possible outcomes," said Chapman. "Either you'll die with the knowledge, in which case there is no harm done. Or else you'll escape, and tell your sheep friends, in which case there is harm done. I don't see what I have to gain from either outcome; therefore, I decline to tell you."

"Do you really think I can escape from here? Surrounded by Graftonites?" Croft tried to sound reasonable.

"Probably not," said Chapman, checking his chrono. "And you are scheduled to be executed in less than an hour. But still, it's not good to take even small chances. Guard!"

A Graftonite entered. "Take Mr. Croft to a cell." He turned to Croft. "The safest thing to do would be to execute you right now, of course. But I'm recalling some of my troops in the field to witness your execution. It's for the morale, you understand. But don't worry, you won't have to wait more than a few minutes."

"You're very comforting," said Croft.

Chapman turned to the guard. "I want him physically guarded, and I want him behind a secure force field. If you fail, I'll call you out myself."

The guard nodded.

Croft slowly let himself be marched to the detention area. Each step marched him to an area that would be difficult, if not impossible, to escape from.

Sure, Croft was an expert infiltrator. Given enough time, he could escape from any prison. But could he escape from behind a force field, guarded by a Graftonite with super reflexes, in the space of only a few minutes? That was expecting a lot, even from him.

Could he try to overpower the guard marching behind him? It was chancy under normal circumstances; the guard had a blaster pointed at him. But this wasn't just any guard; this was a Graftonite, with super reflexes. His chances of overpowering him were... small.

They had stripped him of most of his devices. That was one of the reasons he was barefoot; they had discovered the needle gun in his boot.

As Croft marched closer and closer to the detention area he realized he was running out of options.

He felt a little cheer, however, when he saw several cells sealed behind force fields. There were several civilians in one cell, and in the second were Red Sally and the Clapper.

The Clapper gave a squeal as the field was lowered and Croft was shoved into the cell. The field was immediately raised again. A guard stood watch over them.

"So how do we escape, how do we escape?" the Clapper yelled.

Croft glanced at the guard. "A little louder please, in case he didn't hear you."

"HOW DO WE ESCAPE?" the Clapper screamed.

Sally said, "Quiet!" and the Clapper shrank back. Sally turned to Croft. "What do we do now?" She asked, in a low voice. "I warn you, I'm getting restless."

"I'm sorry you're uncomfortable," said Croft. "But I've got bigger problems. I'm scheduled to be executed in a few minutes."

Sally made a dismissive noise.

"What?" said Croft.

"You're not really going to let them do that, are you?"

Croft looked at Sally. For just a split second, her degree of confidence in him astonished him. They were locked behind a forcefield, surrounded by Graftonites, and Sally expected him to escape. Not just escape, but escape easily.

Did she expect too much of him? Had she overestimated his abilities?

Croft gave Sally a withering look. She was still awaiting an answer to her question.

"No, of course not," said Croft. The old bravado was back.

Even before they had been captured Croft had anticipated the possibility of capture, and had roleplayed through the permutations in his mind. He knew that he might be searched for his devices. Therefore, he needed another method of escape. That's why he had rehearsed one such scenario with the Clapper before they had left the Glory.

Croft turned to the Clapper. "I need you to act normally," he said, in a low voice.

The Clapper acted confused.

"I mean, to act like you're not doing anything," said Croft.

"I'm not doing anything," said the Clapper.

"You will be, ok? I just want you to act like you're not," said Croft.

Looking confused, the Clapper nodded.

"Now you see that force field control? There, against the wall?" Croft asked.

The Clapper nodded.

"You see the second blue button?" Croft had been watching when the force field was activated; and the controls resembled others he had seen in the past.

"Yes," said the Clapper.

"Get ready to press it," said Croft. "But before you do, do you remember the thing we rehearsed?"

The Clapper nodded.

"You think you can do it?" Croft said.

The Clapper shrugged. Whether that was a yes shrug, a no shrug, a I-don't-know shrug, or a shrug for a completely different question he had asked yesterday or last week, Croft couldn't be sure.

"Very inspiring," said Croft dryly. "All right, press the button."

Reaching out, the Clapper used his ability to press the button.

Immediately, the forcefield blocking their cell dropped.

The Graftonite on guard noticed this immediately and had his blaster out. "What's going on?"

"One of my friends dropped the force field," said Croft, gesturing into the room beyond the cell.

"What friends?" said the Graftonite, quickly looking around while keeping his weapon pointed at Croft.

Croft took a step out of the cell.

"Don't move another step!" said the Graftonite.

"Give up," said Croft. "You're surrounded."

"By whom?" said the Graftonite.

"Invisible troopers," said Croft. "Elite League Commandos."

"Invisible? I never heard of such a thing," said the Graftonite.

"Of course you haven't; they're top secret," said Croft. "They're using a new form of cammo armor that renders them invisible."

"I don't believe you," said the Graftonite. "I'm going to call for assistance." He reached over for the control panel.

"Halt!" said Croft, giving the Clapper a meaningful look.

The Graftonite froze in midstep. Something had just jabbed him in the back.

"Don't move," said Croft, taking another step forward. "He has a blaster on you."

The Graftonite slowly started to turn around to see who had a gun on him, but the jab came stronger this time.

"If you move again, he'll shoot," said Croft. He moved forward to the nervous Graftonite. Would the Graftonite be so nervous as to shoot?

Time to find out. Croft plucked the weapon from his hand. He reset the blaster to stun.

"Tell him not to fire," said the Graftonite.

"Don't fire," said Croft, to no one in particular. Then he fired on the Graftonite, who slumped to the ground.

"All right," said Croft. "There are still guards beyond this room, and we have to figure a way out of here."

"Croft," said Red Sally.

"They're going to come for me in a few minutes, and we have to be gone from here," said Croft.

"Croft," said Sally.

"I have to think of a plan-"

"Croft!" Sally yelled.

"What?" said Croft.

"One of the men, in the other cell," said Sally. "I think he's important."

"How important could he be?" said Croft irritably.

"He told me he was the President of Greenfields."

Oh.

Croft focused on the four men in the other cell. The President? He would certainly know how his planet had been conquered so quickly. Croft dropped the forcefield.

"Thank you!" said one of the men. Croft wasn't sure which was the President. There would be time to sort that out later.

Croft considered the possibilities. He could try to cut through one of the walls. But the chances were good that there would be a Graftonite on the other side. No, the only way out was the way they had come.

"All right," said Croft. "We're going out the way we came. Sally, I want you to handle everything in front of us."

"Handle?" said Sally, her eyebrows raised.

"Burn," said Croft. "You do know how to burn things, don't you?" Without waiting for the obvious answer he turned to the Clapper. "You handle anything behind us we miss."

The Clapper opened his mouth-

"Push them off balance. I'll do the rest," said Croft. He turned to the four men. "You! Politicians! No talking, no speeches, just stay in the middle of our little convoy, and keep up if you want to live."

They started walking. As soon as they entered the next room, they saw two very surprised looking Graftonites.

"What-" one of them started to say.

Red Sally sent forth a burst of flame that burned them where they stood. There wasn't time to be gentle, and they had to get out of there. Her blonde hair started to turn red.

They went through another room and ran down a corridor. Sally launched bursts of flame to send Graftonites ducking for cover. That's what worried Croft. Graftonites who ducked into side rooms could come back out when they had passed and shoot them from behind. So Croft kept concentrating on the rear. When two Graftonites emerged from rooms behind them, he shouted, "Now!"

The Clapper looked tense and both Graftonites went spinning to the ground as if pushed by an invisible force. Croft shot them and moved on, always keeping an eye in front of him to make sure that Sally was going in the right direction. She was perspiring heavily now, her hair color a solid red.

Although the Graftonites had faster reflexes, Croft and his people had the advantage of surprise. The Graftonites had never seen a woman shooting bursts of flame, and the sight of it sent them running for cover. They moved quickly in the narrow enclosed space of corridors where Sally could focus her flame it could work.

But Sally was getting tired. Her hair, now a bright red, was steaming.

As they made it to the entrance, they saw a squad of Graftonites running towards them from a few hundred feet away.

"Come on!" said Croft, running in the opposite direction. He looked up at a nearby building, and saw something that caught his eye. Perfect.

They entered the adjacent building; Sally had to give a blast twice to get people scrambling out of the way, but generally this building seemed less populated then the Graftonite administrative HQ. Croft headed for the stairs.

"Up?" gasped Red Sally. "Do you know what you're doing?"

"Come on!" said Croft.

They started climbing. They had only reached the third flight, however, when the politicians, huffing, said they couldn't go anymore.

"Would you rather die?" said Croft sharply. "Come on, it's only two more flights, come on!"

Luckily, it was a low lying building. But that wasn't the reason Croft had picked it.

They got up to the roof, even as they could hear sounds of pursuit on the stairwell.

"Why didn't we take the lift?" Sally gasped.

"Too dangerous," Croft snapped, running to the edge of the building.

Good. Exactly as he thought.

This was the downtown area of Greenfields. There were a network of elevated forceways that connected buildings to each other. This building connected to another building which in turn connected others. They would use these forceways to escape.

"Come on, get over the forceway," said Croft.

The others started scrambling over. Below them, on the ground, Graftonites fired up at them. But their blaster bolts, while accurate, only scattered under the forcefield underneath their feet.

Just as they crossed over to the other side their pursuers broke out onto the roof they had just left.

Croft rapidly looked around for the controls to terminate the forceway. But they weren't there.

In a split second that made sense; they had just left a government building; surely the controls for the forceway would be on the other side, for security reasons. The side they had just left.

Croft had planned to cut the force field to prevent their pursuers from following. This would put a minor crimp in his plan.

Or maybe not. Croft grabbed the Clapper, who squealed. "See those forceway controls?" he said, pointing to a small panel on the edge of the rooftop they had just left.

"Uh…"

"Press the button to shut it down!"

The Graftonites were scrambling towards the edge of the roof where the forceway was.

"Which button?" The Clapper asked.

"All of them!" said Croft.

The Graftonites, four of them, were scrambling over the bridge. In seconds they would be on the other side. On the same roof, with them.

The Clapper scrunched his face. Nothing visibly happened.

"Hurry…" said Croft, just as the first Graftonite was seconds away from crossing their end of the forceway.

Suddenly, the forceway flickered and faded. The expression on the face of the closest Graftonite turned into one of amazement. Both his arms and his feet started to flounder. The last thing they saw was a shocked look he gave them as he fell to the ground.

"He he he, he tried to fly," said the Clapper.

"It's only five stories, maybe they survived," said Croft. What was he saying? Why should he care—those Graftonites were coming to kill him. He turned to the others. "Come on, rest time is over. Let's get going."

They crouched under a pile of bushes in a small city park.

"Why don't we head back to the transport?" said Sally.

"Undoubtedly that's the first place they'll be waiting for us," said Croft. "No, I think we need to be a little less predictable." He unrolled the cuff of his sleeve, revealing a small electrical device. One of the few things the Graftonites had missed.

Croft pressed a button, and said exactly one word. "Pickup."

He waited, then there was a staticy reply. "Location."

Croft pressed another button, sending a quickburst that would enable the Glory to lock onto their location, but hopefully not sustained enough to enable the Graftonites to do the same. The Glory was expecting it; the Graftonites weren't.

"What do we do now?" said Sally.

"Now, we wait," said Croft. He said it nonchalantly, but Croft hated waiting. He wasn't any good at waiting. He was fidgeting already.

"If you had that device, why didn't you call for help when we were locked up?" said Sally.

"I wasn't sure that help could reach us in time," said Croft. "Or even if the Battle Admiral's troops could shoot their way in without getting us all killed." He turned to the four politicians, who looked exhausted. "All right, which one of you is the President of Greenfields?"

One of the men nodded slightly. "I am Zun Buchot."

"Nice name," said Croft. Politicians didn't impress him. "Would you mind telling me how a few hundred Graftonites conquered your entire planet in a few days?"

Buchot nodded. "They took over!"

"Uh, can you be any more specific?" Croft said, working hard to keep the sarcasm out of his voice, at least until Buchot gave him the information he needed.

"They took us hostage."

When he saw a similar lack of comprehension, Buchot elaborated, slightly. "They sent undercover hostage takers."

"Undercover hostage takers?"

"They disguised themselves as common citizens, or even as our own soldiers, and took our senior government officials and military officers hostage. Then they forced our surrender."

"That's it?" said Croft. He had been hoping for something more elaborate. "No super weapon? No fifth column activists?"

"They used their skill and speed to defeat our security. Since they could get in anywhere, they could capture us with ease," said Buchot.

"And your troops?"

"Disarmed, and confined to barracks," said Buchot. "They have started bringing in non-Graftonite mercenaries to replace them."

"They must have done the same to the marines we sent in," Croft mused. "Well, that's an important piece of information, to be sure. Our only remaining task now is to survive long enough for pickup and to live to tell it."

Chapman paced back and forth furiously. Seven men were dead, four seriously injured, and he had already commed Quandry to let him know that Croft had been executed! Now Croft had escaped with the President of Greenfields, one of their most prized prisoners. The information he had could never be allowed to make its way back to the League.

"Sensors detect a transport," said one of his officers.

"Where?"

"Looks like… three miles south of the capital."

"Deploy all available forces there! I want that transport taken!" Chapman said. It seemed they were coming to pick Croft up. Well, Chapman would have a surprise in place for him.

They could hear the sound of the transport heading over the city park and then moving farther away.

"They're going the wrong way!" said President Buchot.

"Quiet," Croft hissed. "There may still be patrols in the area."

The transport settled down in an abandoned lot just a few miles south of the city. In just a few minutes a squad of Graftonites arrived.

"Looks like we got here ahead of the spy," said the squad leader. He drew his blaster. "All right, let's take the transport." His men moved forward cautiously. The minute the Graftonites came into contact with the transport, an internal sensor bleeped, and-

The transport blew up.

"What happened?" Colonel Chapman snapped.

"I don't know… sensors are registering an explosion," said his officer.

"Verify!"

"I can't," said the officer. "I've lost contact with the squad. Wait, I'm getting a connection with new troopers who just arrived on the scene." The officer listened for a moment.

"They say the transport is totally destroyed."

"Good," said Chapman with satisfaction.

"Sir, but I'm reading a shuttle, coming in fast."

"Where?"

"Several miles north of us."

And his forces were clustering south of the city. Suddenly it became clear to Chapman. The transport had been a decoy. "Redeploy the troops! And get me air command."

The shuttle touched down on a lawn just feet away from their concealed location. The ramp opened and four heavily armed troopers jumped out, weapons at the ready.

"Run!" said Croft.

They sprinted for the shuttle. It seemed to take forever for them to get fifty feet. The troops held their fire as they ran forward.

Croft was the first in the shuttle, followed by Red Sally, the Clapper, and the politicians. The marines efficiently closed the hatch behind them.

"We made it!" said President Buchot.

Croft turned to the pilot. "Get us out of here, fast."

The shuttle lifted off.

Even as they were clearing the atmosphere they could detect signs of pursuit. More than fifteen enemy starfighters. The Graftonite starfighters were faster than the shuttle. Quick calculations showed that in two minutes they would be firing range.

And it would take ten minutes to get back to the Glory.

Croft signaled the Battle Admiral from the shuttle. "We're in trouble," he said.

"Help is on the way," said the holoimage of the Battle Admiral.

Even as he spoke, two squadrons of Wildcats streaked past them, heading deeper into the atmosphere. But the Wildcats would be no match for the Graftonites.

"Battle Admiral, in case we don't make it, they're using hostage taking teams to decapitate the leadership and force their troops to surrender," said Croft.

"Acknowledged," said the Battle Admiral.

Whatever the Wildcats were doing, they did it quickly. Thirty seconds later, the Wildcats were streaking in the other direction, retreating back past the shuttle, heading back into orbit.

"They're running away?" said President Buchot incredulously. He saw that Croft had felt compelled to report to the Battle Admiral immediately. Maybe the Battle Admiral, now having the information he needed, had decided that they were expendable.

"We'll be in enemy weapons range in 60 seconds," said the shuttle pilot.

Croft said nothing, studying his fingernails. One of them needed a little trimming.

"Can't you go any faster?" said Buchot.

"No," said the pilot. A few seconds later he studied the sensors and said, "30 seconds." And then, "Wait. They're veering   off."

"What?"

"I'm detecting new sensor blips."

"Homing mines," said Croft. "But they won't hold them more than a minute or two. Just enough for us to get a good lead again. Gun it as fast as you can."

"I am," said the pilot. He noticed several new blips on the sensors, coming from the fleet. "What are those?"

"Don't worry about those," said Croft. "Just get us back. The Glory is coming in on a low orbital approach."

After about two minutes of silence the pilot reported, "They're coming after us again."

"They've destroyed the homing mines," said Croft. "Still, we've bought another two minutes."

"We're still four minutes from the Glory," said the pilot.

Suddenly, several large shapes flew past the shuttle. "What were those?" said the pilot.

"D-34 shipkillers," said Croft. He turned to the passengers. "I suggest you hold on to something."

"They'll shoot them down," said the pilot.

"No they won't," said Croft.

The D-34's detonated just before they came within weapons range of the Graftonite fighters. They weren't close enough to destroy the fighters, but were close enough to shake them up. Even the shuttle, which was farther away from the impact, was quite rattled up.

"That should buy us another two minutes," said Croft, feeling the lesser shockwave of another explosion."

"We're still three minutes from the Glory," said the pilot.

"Then it will be a race, won't it?"

The Wildcats had reformed around the shuttle to protect it, trimming their speed to match the shuttle's.

Croft watched a speck grow bigger on the screen. It was the Glory!

"They're closing in again!" said the pilot. "Interception in thirty seconds!"

The Glory was larger on the screen now. But all a Graftonite would need was a shot or two to take out the shuttle.

"Twenty seconds!" said the pilot.

The Wildcat escorts veered off to intercept the Graftonite fighters. But the Graftonite fighters didn't even react.

"Ten seconds!" said the pilot.

Suddenly, they heard/felt a big rumble around them. From behind them came a huge ship. The Battleship Majestic! It had positioned itself between the shuttle and the approaching Graftonite fighters, guns blazing.

That was something even the Graftonites had to notice. They veered off to avoid crashing into the battleship, and scrambled to reorganize themselves.

In those remaining seconds, the shuttle touched down in the Glory's landing bay.

For a moment, the shuttle was silent. Then, over the comm, they heard, "Croft? Croft?"

"Just like clockwork, Battle Admiral," said Croft. "Exactly as we planned it."

"So now we know their secret, we can deter future invasions simply by putting increased security around our political and military leaders," said the holographic image of the Chief. Her image flickered slightly as the descrambler worked to keep up with the decoding of the secure transmission.

"It won't be that easy," said Croft. "Remember, it's Graftonites we're talking about. But if you put your Presidents and Generals in a room with a hundred guys with guns, yeah, I think that will effectively put their invasion plans out of business."

"What about the planets they have invaded?" said the Chief. "Five, by our current count, four of which are League planets."

"I guess we don't care about Grafton IV because it's not in the League," said Croft, with more than a bit of sarcasm.

"Croft!"

"We can send in the troops," said a new voice. It was the Chief of Staff himself, who like other senior officials was involved in this holomeeting. "Now that we know what to expect, we can protect the troops we send in."

"It won't be quite that easy," said Croft. "From what I've learned, you're not just facing a few hundred Graftonites on each planet; I think they've hired non-Grafton mercenaries to shore up their ranks."

"Nothing can match the might of the League armed forces."

"I'm sure," said Croft, unconsciously falling back into liespeak. "Mr. Chief of Staff, if you'll excuse me, I'm exhausted and need some rest. If everything is well in hand...?"

"Of course," said the Chief of Staff. "Good work, Mr. Croft. Your name will figure favorably in my report to the League President."

"Very nice, sir," said Croft.

The holographic link faded.

The Battle Admiral turned to Croft. "Of course, it's not going to be that easy."

"Of course not," said Croft.

And it wasn't.

The League sent in troops to try and liberate its four planets, but the mercenary and Graftonite forces resisted bitterly. Losses mounted on all sides. The League had an enormous population advantage over the Graftonites and their allies, but with advances in technology the League had shifted to a smaller, more professional force; that was why a planet like Greenfields, with millions of citizens, had an active armed forces of only 40,000.

Still, the League armed forces vastly outnumbered the Graftonites; but there was a limit as to how many could be transported to a planet at any given time. All this meant that the League could wage war, but victory would be slow, and bloody.

Two weeks later the League had beachheads it was slowly expanding on two of the four planets; but the Graftonites responded by reinforcing their garrison of non-Graftonite mercenaries.

"Where are they getting the resources to hire thousands of mercenaries?" the Battle Admiral asked.

It was a good question; Croft wondered that too. He went back to his quarters to review the datapads he had collected from various Graftonites during his expeditions to Greenfields. He had noticed something before that had briefly caught his attention; now he returned to it.

In a few minutes he was convinced he had found something of importance. He got Levi on the comm. For once Levi was actually at work in his lab.

"You have my meat recipes?" said Levi eagerly.

"Sorry, Levi, I've been busy with this little invasion thing," said Croft.

"You always make excuse."

"I need your help, Levi," said Croft.

"You always ask for help," Levi grumbled.

"Levi, I promise, if you help me just one more time, I will get you your Graftonite meat recipes." Croft knew how to handle Levi.

"Promise?" Levi peered out at him as if measuring his reliability.

"Have I ever lied?" Croft asked. "To you?" he quickly amended.

"What is it you want?" Levi sighed.

"I've been reviewing the datapads of some of the Graftonites I encountered," said Croft. "The Graftonites were all paid from off-planet accounts."

"Off which planet?" Levi asked.

"Off of Graftonite," Croft said.

"So?"

"So their leader, Mo Quandry, is a Graftonite. Why would he pay them from off-planet accounts?"

"Maybe he get better rate of return with off-planet account," Levi shrugged.

"Levi, you're a genius but you don't understand the Grafton mind," said Croft. "Graftonites trust non-Graftonites about as far as they can throw them. There's no way a Graftonite like Quandry is going to keep his money off-planet unless...."

"Unless someone else is supplying the money."

Croft transmitted some data. "I want to find out who, Levi."

Levi opened his mouth.

"As soon as possible," said Croft.

Levi tried to speak.

"Today, Levi," said Croft

"All right," said Levi. "But you owe me recipes."

"How can I forget?" said Croft.

It didn't take a day; indeed, with Levi's computer skills, it only took two hours, after which he immediately reported to Croft. And then two hours and ten minutes later, Croft established a holocontact with the Chief.

"The Chief is unavailable, Mr. Croft," said a functionary.

"Tell her it's important," said Croft.

"I don't think that will have any effect."

"Then tell her Clifford Croft says it's important."

The functionary sighed and left the screen. When he returned he said, "She'll see you. But she's not happy."

"Who is, in these troubling times?"

The Chief appeared on the holo, looking drowsy. "Do you have any idea what time it is here, Mr. Croft?"

"No, and I don't really care," said Croft. "Listen, I have an important piece of information for you."

"Speak."

And when he did, her eyes widened.

When he was done, Croft said, "Worth waking you up for?"

"An acceptable judgment call, this time," said the Chief. "Just don't make a habit of it." She paused. "Investigate, and get back to me."

"Croft out," said Croft. He terminated the connection. He wondered whether he should take the Clapper and Red Sally with him. No, he wouldn't need them. Not for this. They would whine, of course. Maybe he could slip away without telling them.

"This meeting of the Whenfor division of the Claritan Corporation will come to order," said the Whenfor Division President, Kenson Manding, sitting at the head of the board room.

The Claritan Corporation was the largest multiplanetary corporation in the galaxy. It sold almost every variety of product. There wasn't an industry that the Claritan corporation wasn't involved in, not a planet where it didn't have some sort of corporate presence. The Claritan Corporation had only one agenda, and that was to make money. Lots of it. Unfortunately, that often meant squeezing the competition or the consumer. And sometimes the Claritan Corporation did some not so nice things in the process.

"Marketing, report," said Manding.

"We've done a special push on our new five ounce action pack flavor juice," said Marketing. "But we're still getting flack from the government that we call it 'juice' when we don't have the requisite 2% of real juice in the mix."

Manding sighed. "We've been over this before. Can't we find some cheap crap to squeeze into the juice? Isn't there something cheap we can use? Lemons? Mutated oranges?"

"Too expensive," said another corporate officer.

"We must have something," said Manding.

"We have found a juicy moss on one of the recently discovered planets that might fit the bill," said the logistics VP. "The moss is plentiful and cheap to collect."

"What does this moss taste like?" Manding asked.

"A little like furniture polish," said the logistics VP. "But we can add more flavoring to cover that."

"Wait a minute," said Manding. "Moss isn't a fruit."

"I think I can reach the right person in the government to get it classified as such," said the governmental affairs VP.

"Oh," said Manding. "Problem solved. Next?"

"We're still getting complaints about the ground cars we manufacture with the faulty accelerators," said another VP.

"Faulty accelerators?" said Manding.

"Remember, we saved money by using those Slurian components... in one out of ten cars, they sometimes cause uncontrollable acceleration when one presses on-"

"I remember now," said Manding. He turned to the Legal VP. "You should have the solution."

"I should?"

Manding sighed. Had seven years of law school been wasted on him? "Include a disclaimer on new cars saying that there can be acceleration problems. If they're aware of the problem, we're not responsible."

"What about existing cars we've already sold?"

Manding rolled his eyes and considered. "Tell owners to bring them to their dealerships. Put the cars in the back for the day and then return them two weeks later, and tell them the problem is fixed."

"Begging your pardon sir, that won't fix anything."

"But it will postpone the problem," said Manding. "What's next?"

Suddenly, the door burst open and none other than Clifford Croft stepped in.

"I told him he couldn't go in, sir," said a functionary, following him in.

"Shut up and sit down," said Croft, pulling a blaster.

The functionary yiped and quickly took a seat.

"Everyone put your arms on the table. If I see anyone reaching for your hidden panic buttons, I'll shoot the offending digit," said Croft.

The officers complied. Manding smiled. "You seem familiar with our standard procedures. Do we know you?" It would only be a matter of time before security or some other assistant checked up on him. In the interim, he would stall for time.

"I know you," said Croft. "I've had... interactions with your company before."

"Who are you, and what do you want?"

"The name is Clifford Croft," said Croft.

Manding looked puzzled. "Croft... Croft.... Were you the one who interfered with our-"

"Probably," said Croft. "But that's not why I'm here. I have a certain objection to one of your corporate operations."

"If you have a problem you should talk with our customer complaint hotlines," said Manding.

"I've decided to speak directly to the supervisor," said Croft grimly. "Now, what are you doing with the Graftonites?"

"Graftonites?" said Manding. "What Graftonites?"

Croft shot a fist-sized hole in the desk next to Manding. "If you lie to me again, my aim will only improve."

Manding gulped.

"Now, I know you've been making payments to Mo Quandry's little army. The question is, why," said Croft. "You already operate on many of the planets that were attacked. What do you get out of it?"

Manding looked nervous.

"Now would be a good time to answer," said Croft, taking aim with the blaster.

"We get... certain concessions," said Manding.

"Can you be more specific?" said Croft.

"We have... contracts for administration," said Manding.

"To administer?" said Croft. "To administer what?"

"The   planets."

"The planets?" said Croft. Suddenly, it made sense. The Graftonites weren't interested in administration; only action. So they hired the Claritan corporation to manage the captured planets for them. By totally controlling a planet's economy, the Claritan corporation could make a thousand times whatever revenue they had been previously making in their various industries. They could tax competitors at any rate—indeed, they could even shut down competitors and build monopolies! The possibilities were almost endless.

"And let me guess—you pay for the invasion up front, and in return you get to keep all the goodies once you start 'administering'," said Croft. "Maybe you pay the Graftonites a percentage off the top."

"Something like that," said Manding faintly.

"Doesn't it bother you that you're helping a dictatorship take over the galaxy?" said Croft. "Haven't you ever considered that they could one day turn against you?"

"It seemed like a good deal at the time," said Manding lamely.

"I see," said Croft. His mind was racing. This could blow things wide open. But he needed proof. "All right, where is it?"

"It?"

"The contract," said Croft. "The contract between you and Quandry."

"There is no contract," said Manding.

Croft fired again, blowing off the right armrest on Manding's chair. Manding grabbed his arm, which felt the edge of the impact.

"There is no contract!" Manding repeated. "No contract here!"

"What do you mean?" said Croft.

"Do you really think a deal of this magnitude could be negotiated by a branch office?" said Manding. "It's all done through the home office. All of it!"

Croft considered. He raised his blaster. "If you're lying...."

"I'm not!" said Manding earnestly.

"All right," said Croft. "I guess I have to pay a visit to your home office. Can I rely on your discretion not to warn them in advance?"

"Of course," said Manding.

"And your associates here?" Croft asked.

"Yes, them too," said Manding, trying to sound reassuring.

"Good," said Croft. He turned to the stunned board members. "Please, don't let me interrupt you any further. Feel free to go about your business."

He turned and left.

Manding immediately called security.

But by the time they got there, Croft had disappeared from the building.

Roger Balit, President of the Claritan Corporation, sat in his office reading the daily datastream when he heard a knock at the door. He didn't even look up as Zilcho Tun, his executive aide, entered the office.

"I'm still reading the daily report," said Balit. "What is it?"

"It's Quandry," said Tun. "He wants money."

"Quandry always wants money," said Balit, continuing to read the daily report.

"He says that under the contract he's entitled to another twenty million credits now," said Tun.

Balit looked at Tun, who seemed to wince slightly when stared at. "On what grounds?" Balit asked, turning back to his morning report.

"Paragraph 7(k) of the contract," said Tun.

"7(k)," said Balit, frowning. "7(k)? There is no 7(k)."

"Perhaps we should examine the contract, just to be sure," said Tun.

"All right, I'll get it out of the safe, in a minute," said Balit. He rapidly scanned the rest of the daily report. As he scrolled down the page he stopped, and then scrolled up. Reading closely, he said, "When were you going to tell me about Croft?"

"Sir?"

"It says here that corp intel indicates that Clifford Croft is on his way here," said Balit. "Don't you think that's just a little more important than Quandry blathering about another payment?"

"Sir, I'm already on top of it," said Tun. "I've increased security all around the building.

"The lobby?"

"Yes."

"The roof?"

"Yes."

"The exterior walls?"

"Yes," said Tun. "And I've doubled the guard around and inside the building. Trust me, sir, no unauthorized person can get in."

"I hope you're right," said Balit. "I've heard of this Croft. He's a Column Eight agent and one of their top infiltrators."

"I'm sure his reputation is inflated," said Tun.

"Never underestimate your enemy," said Balit. He sighed. "All right, where were we?"

"The contract."

"All right," said Balit. He got up, went to a wall, and slid a picture aside, revealing a safe with a keypad combination. He turned to Tun. "You know, just in case, I think it would be better if we had a few security guards here when I opened this up. I could easily see this Croft character lurking around somewhere waiting for us to open the safe."

Tun said nothing.

"Call security and have them send two men."

Tun did nothing.

"Didn't you hear me?" said Balit.

"I heard you," said Tun, drawing a hidden blaster.

"What are you doing?" Suddenly, it became clear. "You, Tun? A traitor? How did they get to you?" said Balit.

"No one got to me," said Tun.

Balit looked confident. "Put down the gun," he said, taking a step forward.

"If you take another step in my direction there will be a nice view between your ears," said Tun.

Balit stopped, and frowned. "You won't get out of here alive."

"You're probably right," said Tun. "But I will."

"What are you saying?"

"I said, you're right, that Tun has no chance to get out alive. But I won't find it particularly challenging."

Still keeping the blaster on Balit, Tun carefully removed his plastiform mask.

"Croft," said Balit, his eyes widening.

"Tun decided to sleep in and take a sick day today," said Croft. "He'll wake up in a few hours with no ill effects. I can't say the same for you, however, if you don't open that safe."

Balit said coldly, "You'll never get out alive. We'll do a special shareholder resolution on you, Croft."

"Right now I'd be more worried about my blaster giving you an impromptu audit," said Croft. He shoved the blaster into Balit's side. "Well?"

Balit said, "Even if I open the safe, you won't be helped by getting the contract."

"Then you should have no objection to giving it to me," said Croft. He pointed his blaster more firmly. "Decide."

Without a further word Balit opened the safe. Croft had him move back and reached in and removed a group of papers.

"Only one of them is the contract, you shouldn't need the rest," said Balit.

"But it's always fun to have something to read on my trip home," said Croft. "And now I must take my leave of you. I'm afraid I'm going to have to stun you so I can make my getaway."

"You've made a powerful enemy today, Croft," said Balit.

Croft shrugged. "You'll have to stand in line." He shot Balit, who fell to the ground.

When Balit returned to consciousness, Croft was long gone. A very apologetic Tun attended to him.

"I'm so sorry sir he took me by surprise-"

"Shut up," said Balit.

"But the contract, sir, what do we do-"

"We do nothing," said Balit.

"Nothing?" said Tun.

"Nothing," said Balit. "It's a minor embarrassment, at worst. But there shouldn't be any harm done."

"No harm? But what when the Graftons learn of our deal with Quandry?"

Balit shook his head. "It won't change a thing." He changed the subject. "But a subject that does concern me is building security. An intruder managed to get both inside and out of the building. Where was our chief of security during this time-"

"Ah, he was-"

"Terminate his employment contract," said Balit. "Immediately."

"Ah, yes sir. But what do we do with-"

"His body? Leave it in the main security office for a few days. As a reminder to those who fail me," said Balit.

Even before Croft had returned to August the information he discovered had been relayed to the Chief; it was only a matter of hours after that that the information was rebroadcasted to Grafton, on every communication frequency. In a matter of minutes, the news was out.

The Claritan corporation was bankrolling the invasions. A holocopy of the contract showed that in return for certain concessions on the conquered planets, the Claritan corporation would pay a large sum to Quandry and his soldiers.

The news hit Grafton quickly. This should be the beginning of the end of Quandry, or so Croft thought.

But only a non-Graftonite was surprised by the response the news got.

Quandry didn't bother to deny the contract. In fact, he acknowledged it. Furthermore, he was lauded by the other Graftonites, who considered him a good businessmen.

As Quandry himself put it in one of his broadcasts, "Yes, I got the sheep to finance the invasion of their own planets, and arranged for a hefty payment for all of us! What could be wrong with that?"

Apparently, none of the Graftons thought there was anything wrong with that. It was, after all, all about money.

"So what do we do now?" said the holographic image of the Chief.

Croft, sitting in his transport, shrugged.

"You are not paid to shrug, Mr. Croft," said the Chief. She obviously was not happy.

"I don't have an answer at the moment," said Croft.

"You spent so much time researching the culture on Grafton," said the Chief. "Didn't that give you any insight?"

"Not really," said Croft. But even as he said it he knew it wasn't true. Actually, something he had been told seemed to percolate in his mind, as a half-finished thought. If he could only figure out what it was….

"I have an idea," said Tane.

"Yes?"

"The Graftonite reflexes are at their peak when they are on Grafton," said Tane. "But when they leave Grafton, they gradually lose their effectiveness."

"That's true, but that takes years," said Croft.

"Well, someone is going to have to occupy those planets," said Tane. "We can play on that fear."

"How?" Croft asked.

"By broadcasting propaganda into Grafton," Tane said. "Tell people that if they invade other planets, they'll slowly lose their reflexes and become no better than what they call sheep," said Tane.

"It might work," said the Chief slowly.

"And it might not," said Croft.

"Let me clear this with the Chief of Staff," said the Chief.

"Of course," said Tane deferentially.

"Of course," Croft parroted.

A few days later the first transmissions began.

"Why risk your life off-planet? All you'll succeed in doing is lose your edge. Each day you spend off Grafton degrades your reflexes. Imagine what your reflexes will be like in a year, or two years? You'll be no better than the sheep!"

Transmissions like that were blanketing the Grafton airwaves for several days.

It didn't take long to judge the response, from the monitoring of the domestic Graftonite networks.

Much of the response was simply laughter. By hiring non-Graftonite mercenaries to keep the order, and the Claritan corporation to manage the economy, only a handful of Graftonites need remain on their conquered planets, and even they could be rotated off-planet at regular intervals.

It was obvious, in just a few days, that this propaganda blitz had failed.

"So it didn't work," said the holo of the Chief.

"That's correct," said Croft. Sometimes he admired her insightful analysis.

"Any other suggestions, Ms. Tane?" said the Chief, and her voice had an edge to it.

Croft casually turned his gaze to Tane.

"I... I...," Tane stammered. Then, "I'm sorry, Chief."

"This is simply perfect," said the Chief. "I have a meeting with the Chief of Staff in 30 minutes. What am I going to say?"

"Not very much, apparently," said Croft absentmindedly. But his mind wasn't really focused on the conversation. He was thinking of something else. The fighting. The fighting was the key. Or rather, the culture of fighting. But how could that be used in their favor?

The Chief glared at him. "Mr. Croft, this is not the day for your lame attempts at humor. I'm warning you, I'm running out of patience. Normally, I can tolerate your kind of foolishness, but given the enormous pressure, you're pushing me over the limit-"

"Of course!" said Croft, sitting upright.

"What?" said the Chief.

"Why didn't I think of it earlier?" said Croft.

"What?" said the Chief.

"You gave me the final piece of the puzzle!" said Croft.

"I did?" said the Chief.

"We all know what a kind, loving, sweet nature you normally have," said Croft. "But circumstances have driven you to a short fuse. You yourself just said so."

"I fail to see-"

"It's the same with the Graftonites. They're normally a sensitive bunch of bounty hunters and guns for hire," said Croft. "What turns them into an interplanetary army bent on conquering the league?"

"It's Quandry. He's stirred them up," said the Chief.

"Let's be specific. He's stirred them up with that sham story of the executed bounty hunter," said Croft.

"So?"

"So why can't we do the same thing, in reverse?" Croft said.

"I fail to follow," said the Chief. She looked really confused.

Croft sighed. "Why don't we stage our own incident, showing a Grafton bounty hunter executing an employer, and broadcast it?"

"How will broadcasting that incident to the Grafton population help us?" The Chief asked.

"No, I understand now," said Tane, realization dawning on her face. "We don't broadcast it to the Graftonites, but everyone else. To all the other planets that hire Graftonites."

"That means-"

"People will stop hiring Graftonites," said Croft. "Already this invasion has put somewhat of a chill on new hires, I imagine. But if we show a Graftonite executing an employer, that will really put a stop to things."

"I think I see," said the Chief. "Once Graftonites stop being hired for off-planet work-"

"You'll have a base of dissatisfied people, who will put pressure on Quandry to stop," said Croft.

"Really quite ingenious," said the Chief. "If it works, that is. What is it you need, Mr. Croft?"

"Merely the offices of a holoproduction facility," said Croft.

It took a week of work before it was ready. When it was broadcast, it hit the League worlds with the impact of a D-34 shipkiller missile.

The following holonews broadcast was typical: "-and security cams actually caught the murder as it happened."

The image shifted to a bounty hunter facing his employer. The positioning of the camera prevented the audience from seeing the Graftonite's face.

"I'm here for my payment," said the Graftonite coldly.

"You've already been paid," said the employer.

"This?" the Graftonite laughed, holding up a stack of currency.

"That was the agreed upon amount."

"I'm changing the agreement," said the Grafton.

"What do you want?" said the employer.

"Everything," said the Grafton. "I want you to sign over all your savings to me."

"All?" said the employer. "Are you out of your mind?"

The Grafton gave the employer a small push. "It's going to be ours soon enough anyway."

"What... what do you mean?"

"If I don't get it, our people will when they take over your planet. So you see, it's better to give to someone you know," said the Grafton. His tone hardened. "Now get on that terminal and start typing."

The employer, looking very nervous, nodded and moved slowly to the desk. But as he sat down he pressed something under the desk. An alarm clanged.

"Not smart," said the Grafton. He fired his weapon, blowing the man's head off.

"Did you have to make it so graphic?" Tane asked.

"Yes," said Croft. "People aren't going to stop hiring Graftons if all they have to fear is a little flesh wound."

"It looked very convincing," said Tane. "Did you use experienced actors?"

"There were no actors," said Croft. "There were no rooms, either. It was all virtual."

"Well, I hope it works," said Tane.

"We'll see," said Croft.

Two weeks later Croft was back on Grafton. He would have liked to come back sooner, but Croft couldn't make his plan work more quickly than this. When he showed up at the Silencer's ranch, he was unsurprised to find that the Silencer was in.

"You again," the Silencer growled.

"Don't mind John," said Annie. "He's just in a bad mood."

"It's that idiot bounty hunter who killed his boss," said the Silencer. "It's causing all the bounty hunting work to dry up. Everyone's afraid to hire Graftonites."

"That's a shame," said Croft. He tried to sound as sincere as possible.

The Silencer looked sharply at Croft for any sign of irony or sarcasm.

"Of course, the bounty hunter isn't entirely to blame," said Croft. "I imagine if Quandry weren't invading planets left and right that people wouldn't feel so threatened."

"That may be," said the Silencer. "But there's not much I can do about that."

"Actually, there is," said Croft.

"Don't start again," said the Silencer. "I'm no politician."

"No, you're just one of the most respected men on Grafton," said Croft. The Silencer started to reply but for once Croft was faster. "I'm not asking you to do anything for me, Silencer. Do it for yourself."

The Silencer paused. "What do you expect me to do?"

"Hold a gathering. Tell people that these invasions are causing business to dry up," said Croft earnestly.

"They'll never listen," said the Silencer, apparently rejecting the idea out of hand.

"You won't know until you try," said Croft, on a cautiously positive note.

The Silencer sighed, looking away for a moment. Then he looked up at Annie, who had been silent all the while. She nodded slightly.

"All right," the Silencer growled. "But I still think it's a dumb idea."

"What is it?" said Quandry, not even bothering to look up as Rocco entered his office.

"Trouble, boss," said Rocco.

Quandry looked up and glared at Rocco. "Can you be any more specific?"

"The Silencer is holding a gathering to turn people against the invasions."

"The Silencer?" said Quandry, frowning.

"He has known links to the sheep on August," said Rocco.

"The Silencer is a mercenary like everyone else; he works for pay," said Quandry. "Do you think he's being paid for this?"

"I don't know," said Rocco. He paused a moment. When Quandry didn't say anything, he said, "What do you want to do?"

"I'm thinking," said Quandry, weighing the alternatives. Then, finally, he said, "I want him taken care of."

"The Silencer????" Rocco sounded incredulous.

"Do it," said Quandry, returning to his data screens.

The gathering was held in a local sports arena. And to top it off, Annie, with a little prompting from Croft, had arranged for the event to be broadcast on all available comm networks.

"Do you think we'll have any trouble?" said Croft, nervously watching the crowd gather. Several hundred people had already showed up, and more were at the gate. The Silencer could really draw them in!

"Trouble?" the Silencer asked.

"From Quandry's people."

Croft eyed the crowd nervously. One shot from a long distance sniper rifle could take the Silencer out.

The Silencer made a derisive noise. "Let them be dumb enough to try." He turned to Croft. "You'd better stay out of sight."

Croft nodded.

When the crowd had entered and taken their seats, the Silencer strode out onto the platform at the center of the stadium. There was suddenly a spontaneous applause in the bleachers. The Silencer acknowledged it calmly, even as it lasted for more than a minute. Many of the people here were his fans.

"Thank you," he finally said, which was an uncharacteristic phrase, for him. He paused and then continued, speaking into his throat comm. "I'm a man of few words, so let me get to the point. These invasions are cutting into-"

He read the speech, much as Croft had written it for him. When he was done, the crowd was silent. The Silencer stared at the audience. "Well? What do you think?"

The silence didn't last more than a second. There were a babble of voices all around.

Some people were clearly against the invasions, and wanted them to stop. But others felt that it was irrelevant what the "sheep" thought, and that if money from bounty hunting dried up, there would still be more money to be made from the invasions. The debate raged back and forth for nearly two hours, with the Silencer saying little. Finally, at the end, the meeting broke up without agreement.

"Well, we tried," said the Silencer philosophically, when they had returned to the ranch.

"That's it?" said Croft. "That's all you have to say?"

"What more can we do?" said the Silencer.

"We persuaded some people," said Croft. "It's a start."

"What would you suggest?" said Annie.

"Hold more gatherings. Try to persuade other people."

The Silencer looked at Croft distastefully. "I'm not a politician, or a big talker. There's a reason I'm called the Silencer."

"But we can't just give up," said Croft.

"Sure we can," said the Silencer.

"But what about your work?"

"I can still get work," said the Silencer. "I'll just have to work a bit harder to get it."

Croft tried to think of something to say to counter that. He looked at the Silencer, who was now ignoring him, and then at Annie. Annie just shrugged her shoulders helplessly.

They were interrupted by a knock at the door.

"Tell them I'm not joining anything, Annie," said the Silencer, heading into another room.

Annie went to the door. When she opened it up, she found herself faced with an unfamiliar Graftonite. She also noticed two Graftonites behind the newcomer, both looking grim.

"Yes?" said Annie.

"I'm here to assess your house, Ma'am," said the man.

Croft listened curiously from within the house. As he had already learned, real estate taxes were one of the few taxies levied on Grafton. Under the system set up by the locals, assessors came and assessed the value of each property, and the higher the assessment, the higher the taxes. But another curious factor that came into play was the quality of the gunfighter who owned the house. Since the property owner could challenge the assessment by threatening to shoot the county assessor, counties typically charged lower assessments on homes owned by superior gunmen, to reduce the likelihood that they would challenge the assessment by shooting the assessor. A gunman, even a superior one, might risk a gun fight if he were assessed high taxes; but if the taxes were kept low, even a crack gunman was unlikely to start a fight.

Annie frowned. "Our ranch isn't due to be reassessed for another year."

"The county supervisor has issued a proclamation," said the man.

"And I don't recognize you," said Annie. "You're not the regular assessor."

"I'm specially deputized by the county, Ma'am," said the man. "My name is Clem Arnot."

"I recognize the name," said Annie. "You're a silver medalist, are you not?"

"Yes, Ma'am, Olympics of '04, I'm flattered you recognize my name," said Arnot.

"Very well, would you like to come in to look at the house?" said Annie guardedly.

"Not necessary, Ma'am," said Arnot. "I'm ready to provide an assessment now."

"Without even looking in the house?"

"New rules, Ma'am," said Arnot.

Annie paused, suddenly feeling tense inside. She heard footsteps moving very softly in the background behind her. "Very well, then. What is your assessment?"

"We're assessing your ranch at 50,000,000 credits," said Arnot. "That will lead to a tax of 1,200,000 credits."

"50,000,000 credits? 1,200,000 credits!" said Annie. "Not only is that nearly quadruple our last valuation, but that's more than seven times the rate we were taxed at last time."

Arnot swallowed hard. "I realize that, Ma'am. But the amount is supposed to be paid in full, immediately on assessment."

Annie stared hard at Arnot. His hands hadn't moved, but were down by his sides. His two men, however, had tensed up.

After a moment's pause, Arnot said, "Ma'am, are you going to pay, or do you want to challenge your assessment?"

Annie looked at him, and then at his two assistants. "Surely you're not proposing to make me fight three of you at once."

"If you choose to challenge your assessment, I'm afraid so, Ma'am."

"The rules have always been that it's a one on one fair fight, with the owner versus the assessor alone," said Annie.

"The rules have been changed, Ma'am," said Arnot. He tried to resist tensing up. "What is your decision, Ma'am?"

The door, which had been halfway open, was pulled open further from the inside.

"I'll handle this," said the Silencer coldly.

He stared at Arnot for a moment, and Arnot withered in his gaze as if he were slowly being burned where he stood.

"So," said the Silencer slowly. "It's not enough to put a ringer in the place of the assessor, a silver medalist ringer, but you have to go three on one, is that it?"

"Your prowess is well known, Silencer," said Arnot.

The Silencer spoke to Annie, without turning his gaze away from Arnot. "Annie, get inside."

"I'm not going anywhere, John," said Annie.

"Wives," said the Silencer, giving a rare smile. He stepped in front of Annie. He looked at the two men accompanying Arnot. "I don't recognize either of you. Are either of you senior medalists?"

The men shook their heads slowly.

"It seems you didn't come prepared," said the Silencer.

"Yes I did, Silencer," said Arnot.

Two more men stepped out of the bushes.

"Meet John Lancing, distance shooting bronze medalist, '54," said Arnot. "And Saw Maran, motion shooting silver medalist, '48 and '57." He looked at the Silencer's face for any sign of fear. Now the Silencer would have to take on five of them, and three of them were senior olympic medalists.

"A double silver medalist, hm?" said the Silencer, addressing Maran. "But you never could be number one, could you?"

Maran stared at him coldly. "Test us and see."

"So it's not enough to have five against one," said the Silencer. "And it's not enough to have three medalists against one. I also see you have those zip guns on the back of your hands, so all you have to do is point to shoot. I assume Mo Quandry sent you; my only question is, is he so short of men that he wasn't able to send anyone else?"

"Are you challenging your assessment, Silencer?" said Arnot, taking a slow step back.

The Silencer nodded. "I'm about to. But first, Annie, get back in the house."

"No, John."

Croft watched intently from the edge of a window frame, keeping himself out of direct view of the others. He knew he didn't have the reflexes to help here, but was fascinated to see what would happen next.

The Silencer paused, as if considering what to say next, and even half turned his head to say something, and then, almost faster than Croft could see, his blasters zipped out, one in each hand, and was blazing away. Annie's gun was out too, though Croft couldn't say exactly where in the chain of events it left her holster.

There were several flashes of light, and then silence.

In the time it took Croft to turn his gaze away from the Silencer and Annie to the ground outside, he saw five bodies, sprawled on the ground.

The Silencer casually stepped out onto the porch to make sure they were dead.

"You could have coordinated better, John," said Annie. "I almost didn't draw in time."

"Nonsense," said the Silencer. "You know my half turn move better than anyone." He kicked the bodies each in turn, observing no sign of life. Then he casually walked back to the porch, and eyed something on one of the beams. A scorch mark.

"Another one. We'll have to get that fixed too," said the Silencer calmly.

Croft came out onto the porch. "That was incredible!" he said.

"Really?" said the Silencer.

"You took out five of them!" said Croft.

"It wasn't like any of them were even gold medalists," said the Silencer. "And I let Annie take one of them."

"Two of them, John," said Annie. "I also got Maran."

"He was dead before your shot hit him," said the Silencer.

"We can argue about that later," said Annie.

The Silencer turned to face Croft, and his expression was cold. "I'm not very happy with you," he said, looking hard at Croft.

Croft resisted the urge to run away. "What do you mean?"

The Silencer slowly approached Croft. "You got me involved. If I hadn't gotten involved, this wouldn't have happened. You've forced me to kill people without getting paid. And they're going to only send more and more people that I'll have to kill, also without getting paid." He now stood almost face to face with Croft. "I don't work for free; how do you plan to compensate me?"

"John!" said Annie, getting between him and Croft. "Don't blame him. You decided what to do for yourself. Clifford didn't make you do anything."

The Silencer turned away for a moment. He didn't say anything. One moment passed into another.

Croft looked wordlessly at Annie. She motioned him to keep quiet.

What was the Silencer thinking? Was he really debating whether to shoot Croft?

The Silencer let himself be bathed in the wind outside his home for a moment. They heard the low rustle as the wind swept by the trees. Then, when the wind had passed, he turned around.

"All right," he said, clutching one of his blasters.

"All right, what?" said Croft, gulping.

"It has to be done," said the Silencer.

Annie moved in front of Croft. "John, what are you talking about?"

"I'm going to kill Mo Quandry."

"Are you sure this is a bright idea?" said Croft.

"What do you mean?" said the Silencer.

"I mean here we are, you, me, and Annie, in a lone ground car, approaching Mo Quandry's stronghold on Grafton," said Croft. "Who's to say that a group of his men won't just wipe us out?" He had an image in his mind of the ground car being surrounded by gunmen. The gunmen would open fire, raking the car with blasterfire before even the Silencer could move   or   react.

The Silencer snorted derisively, and the image in Croft's mind vanished.

"Well?" said Croft.

"You don't understand, Clifford, that's not the way things are done," said Annie. "Fighting other than one-on-one isn't honorable."

"But that's exactly what they did at your ranch," said Croft.

"We were all alone there," said Annie. "Quandry wouldn't do anything like that in public, even in front of his own men."

"I'd just feel more comfortable if we had brought some allies of our own."

"If you're feeling uncomfortable, we can let you off here," said the Silencer.

Croft said nothing.

They approached the sentry gate. The Silencer stopped the ground car and lowered the window, to face a pair of sentries.

One of the sentries looked at the Silencer, then, looking obviously startled, gave a second look to confirm what he thought: this was the Silencer?

"Do… do you have an appointment?" said the sentry.

"I'm here to see Quandry," said the Silencer, his voice low and deadly.

"Ah, uh…"

"I suggest you let me in," said the Silencer.

The sentry looked nervously at the second sentry, who also looked nervous, confused, and dazed, all in the same instant.

"I'm not going to ask again," said the Silencer calmly, making no move towards his weapon.

The sentry, who was standing up with easy access to his blaster, had an advantage over the Silencer. But he didn't feel lucky. "Opening the gate, sir."

The gate opened. The ground car moved forward.

"So far so good," Croft muttered. He eyed the Graftonites in the compound. What was there to prevent a group of them from ganging up and shooting them all dead even before they stepped out of the ground car?

If the Silencer was concerned, he didn't show it. He parked the ground car in front of what looked like a main building. When he got out, another sentry said, "Sir, you can't park   there."

The Silencer just looked at the man; recognition dawned on the man's face, and he took a step back.

It was like that with everyone they encountered as they walked into the building. The Silencer stopped twice to ask for directions. Even though he didn't identify himself, answers were quickly forthcoming.

They shortly found themselves in a large office. A Graftonite sat behind the desk.

"Where is he?" the Silencer asked bluntly, not bothering to identify himself or even to explain further who he was referring to.

"I'm in charge," said the man. "He's not here."

"Where is he?" said the Silencer.

The man said nothing.

"I'm not going to ask a third time," said the Silencer. "As I suspect you're not the only one who knows where he is, I consider it fair warning to let you know that you're quite expendable."

The Graftonite shifted uncomfortably in his seat. "He'll kill me if I tell."

The Silencer's blaster was out and in his hand and pointed at the man's head. "Even if that's true, you'll live a longer life than the alternative."

The man sweated, staring at the blaster pointed at him. He made no move for his own weapon; he knew who the Silencer was.

"August," he whispered.

"What?" said the Silencer.

"He just left a few hours ago for August," said the Graftonite. "That's all I know!"

"If you're lying, I'll be back for you," said the Silencer coldly.

They went back to their groundcar. Croft expected some kind of ambush before they left the compound. But, much to his surprise, there was none.

"I guess I'll never understand you Graftonites," said Croft.

The Silencer said nothing.

"We should have stayed and sweated out the full truth from him," said Croft. "We don't know what Quandry's plans for August are."

"That doesn't concern me," said the Silencer.

"Why not?" Croft asked.

"I don't need to know what he's doing in order to kill him," said the Silencer coldly. He didn't like all these questions.

"But how will you know where on August to find him? It's a big planet."

"He'll make his presence known," said the Silencer, sounding annoyed. "Now keep quiet."

Annie turned to the backseat and put a finger to her mouth. Croft nodded.

Croft angled his starfighter behind the Silencer's as they headed towards August. He saw the tinny holo of the Chief on his miniholodisplay.

"Quandry's coming here?" said the Chief. "Where specifically? What is his plan?"

"Ah, I didn't get full details on that."

"What can he possibly accomplish here?" said the Chief. Then a thought struck her. "He can't... no, he can't be planning to invade August, can he?"

"The orbital blockade tracked a group of twenty fighters that slipped out of orbit several hours ago," said Croft. "That's not enough for an invasion force, even for Graftonites."

"Still, I'm going to put our ground forces on alert and seal up the airspace above the planet. We'll have the skies filled so tightly with our ships that no one will get through."

"Chief, do you really believe there is any blockade that these people can't get through?" said Croft wearily.

The Chief blinked. "You're quite right, of course, Mr. Croft. Well, we'll just have to do the best we can. You say that your Silencer friend is going to kill Quandry."

"That's the general plan, yes."

"How will that help us? How will that prevent Quandry from being replaced by a deputy who will carry out his policies?"

"Well, it won't," said Croft.

"Then why are you planning to have him killed?"

"I'm not," said Croft. "Perhaps I wasn't clear. This isn't exactly my plan. It's the Silencer's idea."

The Chief looked surprised. "Well, you should dissuade him from it. We can't eliminate Quandry until we have fully thought out the consequences."

"I'm afraid I don't have much influence in this area," said Croft. "The Silencer's pretty upset with Quandry."

"Why?" said the Chief.

"He didn't like the taxes," said Croft bluntly.

The Chief looked confused. She didn't understand that at all.

Croft thought of the bodies of the five dead gunfighters. Then he thought of something Annie had said. And then, at that moment, it came together.

"Chief, I have it," said Croft.

"What?"

"I know how to stop the Graftonites in their tracks. I know how to stop the invasions, and how to make Quandry lose all his support. I also know exactly how to do it," said Croft.

"How?"

Croft checked to make sure the channel was scrambled. It was. Still, he didn't want to risk having the transmission intercepted and decoded. "I can't explain right now. But trust me. I think I know how we can discredit this entire invasion movement."

The skies around August were indeed sealed up by the time Quandry's two squadron of fighters reached orbit—there were all varieties of battleships, monitors, cruisers, and fighters crisscrossing the planet, eagerly on the alert for intruders.

Quandry and his men slipped through the blockade effortlessly. League fighters zoomed down in pursuit, but they arrived too late; Quandry's fighters zoomed over their destination; and when they got there, each Graftonite pilot ejected, sending their fighters crashing harmlessly into the sea off the east coast of August. It was a measure of skill that Quandry's men sent their fighters out of harm's way; for even they appreciated the beauty and majestic construction of Sarney Sarittenden.

The capital.

Quandry and his men drifted downwards on portable gravitators. In moments they were on the grounds of the capital. In the distance they could hear the first sounds of the pursuing fighters. But they would be too late. Way too late.

President Lo Rareen was just sitting down to lunch with some of his cabinet when the door burst open. A palace guard ran in. "Sir, we've got to get you out of here."

The sound of blaster fire could be heard in the distance.

Rareen dropped his electronapkin. "What is it?"

"We're under attack!"

"Here, in the capitol?" said Rareen.

"Yes," said a new voice.

Several men in denim stood at the door. The guard turned, his gun raised-

And was shot. He fell to the ground.

The Graftonite who had shot him stepped forward. "Allow me to introduce myself, Mr. President. My name is Mo Quandry."

"I'm picking up some kind of alert," said Croft, adjusting the comm in his fighter.

"Listen to channel 42," came the Silencer's voice.

Croft turned to the channel. A holo of a broadcaster appeared. "-just moments ago Graftonite terrorists stormed the palace itself. Gunfire was heard inside. There is no word on whether League President Rareen is-"

"I told you he would tell us exactly where he is," said the Silencer lazily.

"What can he hope to accomplish by this?" said Croft. "Does he really think he can get the League to surrender by grabbing the President?" It didn't make any sense to him.

"It doesn't matter what he thinks," said the Silencer.

"Why not?"

"Because in two hours he'll be dead," said the Silencer, in a tone that didn't tolerate any argument.

By the time they had landed their fighters at Sarney Sarittenden Spaceport, they heard the rest of it. Mo Quandry was holding the President and several cabinet members hostage. He wanted a ransom of 200,000,000 credits. If he didn't get it, the President and the cabinet members would be killed.

"He can't seriously believe the League will pay such a large amount," said Croft.

"It doesn't matter what he believes," said the Silencer.

"Because you're going to kill him, I know," said Croft. "But I am still wondering what he's attempting to do. Does he really expect the League to pay?"

"Of course not," said Annie. "It should be obvious." And it was, to a Graftonite. So she explained it to him. "He plans to execute your President to get your League to take harsher measures against Grafton. That in turn will turn even more of the population against the League. I think perhaps John's gathering was not quite the failure that you might've thought it was."

"Oh," said Croft. "But if he kills the President, does he really expect to get out alive?" They were close to the capital now. The area was swarming with troops. It didn't seem to Croft that even Graftonites could escape such a tight net.

"Yes," said Annie simply.

At that moment Croft's comm beeped. It was the Chief.

"Croft, where are you?"

"In a ground car close to Sarney Sarittenden."

"I'm on the way there myself," said the Chief. "The Graftonites have the place sealed off. Does your Silencer think he can get in?"

Croft looked at the Silencer. "I imagine so."

"You must impress on him that the number one priority is to save the President," said the Chief.

"He doesn't impress easily," said Croft.

"This isn't a joke, Mr. Croft," said the Chief. "If you go in there, I am holding you personally responsible for the consequences."

"Personally? I'd like to keep our relationship on a professional level," said Croft.

"Croft-"

"Chief, I have to go. The Silencer is about to go in, guns blazing, and I have to make sure he doesn't shoot the wrong people," said Croft. He cut the comm even as she started speaking again.

Croft raised his voice. "Did you hear what the Chief said?"

There was no answer from the front seat.

"We want the President alive," Croft said.

There was silence again.

"Well?"

The Silencer slowly spoke. "If he doesn't get in front of my target, I won't shoot him."

"Why don't I find that very reassuring?" Croft wondered.

"You can't seriously believe that they're going to pay you," said President Rareen.

Quandry turned to Rareen. "You'd better hope that they do."

"What are you really trying to accomplish here?"

Quandry paused for a moment, as if he were considering whether to reveal his plan. On the one hand, it was important to keep it secret; on the other, he never liked passing up an opportunity to show how clever he was.

"All right, I'll tell you," said Quandry. "We're going to kill you."

"What?" said Rareen. "You mean, if they don't pay?"

"Pay, don't pay, whatever," said Quandry. "You've got to die."

Rareen was speechless for a moment. Finally a single word came out of his lips. "Why?"

"I'm having some recruitment problems at home," said Quandry. "I need your military guys to take some action which will help rally support to my cause."

"So you're going to kill me, the President of the great League of Planets, all for some petty political maneuvering?"

"That's about right," said Quandry. "Except I don't consider it so petty. The only reason you're still alive right now is that I may need proof you're still breathing until the deadline passes."

"If you're going to kill me, why didn't you simply do it without a hostage ransom?" said Rareen.

"Don't you know anything about politics?" said Quandry. "I need to look like I was forced into it. What kind of politician are you?" he said, disgustedly.

Rareen started to answer.

"Don't say anything," said Quandry. "You're starting to annoy me."

"Listen, I can help you in other ways," said Rareen. "If your hardliners are pushing you into this-"

Quandry drew his blaster and pointed it at Rareen. "Not. Another. Word."

The Silencer got as close as they could get to the palace at Sarney Sarittenden and then they got out of the ground car. Croft's ID got them into the security perimeter but not through it. A major in charge refused to let them go any further.

"I've already sent a platoon in, and none of them came out," said the Major. "What does one guy think he can do?"

The Silencer just looked at him.

"Let us go in and see, Major," said Croft. He tried to sound persuasive.

The Major looked apologetic. "I'm sorry, but I don't have the authority-"

The Silencer, moving in a blur, took the Major's blaster from its holster and pointed it at him. "We've wasted enough time."

"You—you're one of them!"

"If I were one of them, you'd be dead," said the Silencer. "I suggest you escort us to the perimeter before I decide to switch sides."

The Major, gulping, nodded.

He walked them through to the forward sentries. They all saw the Silencer had a gun on the Major, but he nodded, ordering them to let the Silencer, Annie, and Croft through.

When they had gotten to the forward post the Silencer handed the Major back his blaster. The Major looked at it as if he were considering turning it on the Silencer.

The Silencer simply looked at him.

The Major holstered his gun.

"A wise decision." said the Silencer.

"You won't get in," said the Major. "They have marksmen at every entrance."

"He has a point," said the Silencer. He turned to Annie. "I know better than to ask you to stay behind."

He turned to Croft, who he noticed for the first time was carrying a briefcase. "I can't guarantee your safety."

"In these crazy times, who can guarantee anything?" said Croft philosophically.

"You can't do much fighting carrying that."

"I'm not planning to fight," said Croft.

The Silencer said nothing.

They entered Sarney Sarittenden. One way or another, it would end here.

Chapter 12: The Final Battle in Sarney Sarittenden

"I can see you," said the Silencer, staring off into the gloomy corridor. Bodies of League marines littered the ground all around them.

There was no response.

"Just because you're peeking out from 100 feet away doesn't mean I can't see you. Or shoot you," said the Silencer calmly. "Come out now or I'll demonstrate it."

Slowly two figures stepped out of the gloom. Both had rifles. They cautiously stepped forward.

"Who's there?" they said gruffly. Their hands tightly gripped their rifles. They were still ready to fight.

The Silencer didn't answer, but stepped forward, followed by Annie and Croft.

The sentries' eyes widened when they saw the Silencer. "Silencer! What are you doing here?"

"I'm here to see Quandry," said the Silencer.

"About what?" said one of the sentries.

The Silencer looked around. "This is a mighty expensive looking place he's living in. I'm here to reassess his taxes."

What did that mean? "We can't let you through, Silencer," said the sentry. "Our orders were to let no one through."

"But I'm not no one," said the Silencer ominously.

The sentries didn't respond. They seemed unsure what to do.

That told the Silencer that he needed to push harder. "There are two ways of doing this," said the Silencer. "But either way, I'm going in."

The sentries glanced at each other. Then, they slowly nodded.

"Thank you," said the Silencer coldly.

The Silencer, Annie, and Croft walked by. As they passed Croft looked behind them, to see if the guards would shoot them down from behind. They didn't.

That only confirmed his theory. It was their code of conduct. His plan could work.

"They're probably being held in the central rotunda," said Croft. "Go straight and then right, you can't miss it." He started to turn towards a set of stairs.

"Where are you going?" asked the Silencer.

"You know, that's the first sign of genuine curiosity I've seen from you in some time," said Croft, purposefully being evasive. For once let the Silencer guess what he was up to.

The Silencer looked at Annie, shrugged, and started forward.

When they reached the entrance to the rotunda they heard someone shout, "Hold it!"

The Silencer stopped.

Four guards stepped out of the entranceway.

"You're not allowed here."

"I'm going in," said the Silencer.

The guards looked at each other, silently conferring. They looked at the Silencer, weighing their options. Finally, they said, "All right. But just you."

The Silencer considered this. Then he slowly nodded.

"No way am I letting you go in there alone!" said Annie.

The Silencer spoke as if he hadn't heard her. "Just be aware, gentlemen, that this is my wife; and if anything happens to her, I'll find you and make you wish for a quick death." He stood face to face with them. "Do we understand each other?"

The guards, some of them trembling, nodded.

The Silencer turned away from them and entered the rotunda.

There were a dozen of Quandry's handpicked men there, standing guard over the prisoners, a very worried looking bunch who were sitting on the floor. One of them was the League President, Rareen.

Croft could see the whole situation very clearly. He had climbed four flights of stairs and was looking at the room through a small window built into the side of the ceiling of the rotunda. None of the Graftonites had noticed him. Croft rapidly opened his briefcase. It contained two devices. He rapidly assembled the smaller one. It was a holorecorder with a boom mike.

The Silencer recognized Mo Quandry. Quandry stepped forward, flanked by two of his men.

"You must be the Silencer," said Quandry. "It's quite an honor to meet you."

"I wish I could say the same," said the Silencer coldly.

Quandry smiled, letting the comment slide. "I'm afraid you've been misled."

"Have I?"

"Yes, you've fallen into bad company," said Quandry. "You're here to save the sheep." His eyes flickered to Rareen, who was trying his best to be invisible.

"I don't care about the sheep," said the Silencer. "I'm here for you."

Quandry said, "So the sheep have hired you to kill me." He raised his voice. "No Graftonite lets a sheep tell him what to do."

"It wasn't a sheep that made me want to kill you," said the Silencer, never taking his eyes off of Quandry. He raised his voice as well. "It was the five men you sent to kill me."

There was a murmur among Quandry's men. They didn't like the sound of that. Was that really true? Had Mo sent five men to kill the Silencer? Even those aligned with Quandry didn't like the thought of it.

"I'm going to offer you one better," said the Silencer. "A fair fight, you against me. I challenge you."

The murmuring grew louder.

"I don't think so," said Quandry. "That doesn't sound very fair to me. I'm a gold medalist, but I'm no Olympics champion many times over."

"Then I suggest you surrender," said the Silencer.

"I don't think so," said Quandry. He snapped his fingers. The two men at his side stepped forward. "Do you recognize these gentlemen?"

The Silencer said nothing.

"Cal Carpan, who took the gold in race shooting in '24," said Quandry. "And Mar Topogican, a quadruple gold medalist in distance and precision shooting."

The Silencer noticed now that all three were wearing zip guns. They wouldn't even have to spend time drawing their weapons, all they would have to do is point their fingers and fire.

Croft recognized the dangerousness of the situation immediately. Back at the ranch, the Silencer had faced down five opponents, but he had had Annie to help them, and none of those had been gold medalists. Now there were three gold medalists facing him. This could be beyond the Silencer's ability to handle.

Croft rapidly assembled the second piece of equipment in his case. In seconds he had assembled a very nasty looking sniper rifle. He held it up and aimed it. At the very least, he could take out one of them.

"So maybe you want to reconsider," said Quandry.

"Maybe you want to reconsider," said the Silencer in a chilly voice. He looked towards Quandry's other men. "Three against one!" he said, raising his voice. He looked at Quandry's other men. "How is that a fair fight? Do any of you have a problem with that?"

Even Quandry's handpicked commando squad looked very uncomfortable. One of them started to speak up.

"Mo-"

Quandry shot him a glare, and the man stopped in midsentence.

"So this is the new Grafton you're building, where three or five against one is considered a fair fight," said the Silencer.

"We do what it takes to win," said Quandry. He suddenly tensed. "Either join us, or leave, or pick up your weapon."

The Silencer considered for a moment, as if weighing whether he could take on the three of them. One moment grew into two, and two moments grew into three.

Croft's grip tightened on the sniper rifle. He aimed at one of the gold medalists on the right. He had no way of knowing who the Silencer would aim for first, but he had to try to help. He kept his aim as steady as he could.

The tense silence continued, but as time wore on Quandry grew less tense. He even gradually started to break out into a smile. The Silencer was scared! He was actually scared! He opened his mouth to make a witty comment, when there was an explosion of light.

From the gallery, Croft instinctively pressed the trigger. He only had time for one shot, before everything became quiet again.

They were all standing there. The Silencer, and his three opponents.

Then one of Quandry's gunmen fell to the ground; then another; and then Quandry himself.

The Silencer shuddered, clutching his side. He pulled his hand away, and felt blood. He staggered forward, unintentionally dropping his weapon.

The rest of Quandry's men in the room simply watched him.

When the Silencer was face to face with one of them, he spoke slowly. "Get out of here."

The Grafton turned towards his fellow commandos, nodded, and they left. Croft didn't bother wondering if they could slip out past security; he was running down to the rotunda.

But by the time he got there Annie was already there, slapping a bandage against the Silencer's side.

"You fool, I told you not to handle this alone," said Annie.

Croft heard the sound of rushing footsteps, and saw out of the corner of his eye that League soldiers were entering the room. The captive politicians cried out for them like children who had been separated from their parents.

The Silencer, lying on the ground, said, "I didn't think it would be any problem," he said.

"Three gold medalists?" said Annie.

"Topogican was the only real threat," said the Silencer. "As for Carpan, anyone can win an award in race shooting."

"And Quandry?"

Croft looked over at Quandry, who had was lying on the ground with a big gash in his chest.

"A politician," said the Silencer dismissively. He coughed, and pain wracked his face.

"Lie still," said Annie. "We'll get you to a doctor."

"It's a scratch," said the Silencer contemptuously. "Just a zip gun hit." He turned to Croft. "Thanks for trying to help. But I had everything under control."

"What do you mean, trying to help?"

"Your beam hit Carpan about a half second after mine did," said the Silencer.

Croft stared wordlessly at the Silencer.

"This place must have a security holo, you can check it out," said the Silencer.

"I have something better than a security holo," said Croft.

League President Rareen was on his feet, slowly being escorted from the room. "Wait, wait," he said. He turned to the Silencer, who was still on the floor.

"Thank you, thank you," said President Rareen.

The Silencer looked coldly at President Rareen.

"You saved my life!" said Rareen. "If there's anything I can do-"

"Money would be nice," said the Silencer immediately. "Maybe, forty or fifty million credits."

The President looked speechless. Behind him, the Chief of Staff rolled his eyes.

"I assume your life is worth that much," said the Silencer. "Annie, give him our bank account number."

Annie handed the President a pre-printed card. He numbly took it.

"It was a pleasure saving you, Mr. President," said the Silencer.

The President nodded numbly. And then he was hustled away.

"You think he'll really pay?" said Croft.

"Either that, or one of your agencies will," said the Silencer. "I don't work for free, you know."

"I know," Croft sighed. He stood up, looking at the ornate rotunda around him. So it had all ended here. Quandry was dead.

But his army and movement lived on, at least for the moment.

But little did anyone know that this movement was about to be unraveled. Only Croft knew that the end of Quandry's movement was very near.

The holo was broadcast onto Grafton and all the other worlds the Graftonites had taken over. The effects were almost immediate; within a day, many of the Grafton occupiers were flying back to Grafton II. Within two weeks, only a handful remained on the other planets, and, seeing their position was untenable, they also left for home.

"Don't believe it," said Levi Esherkol, reclining in an easy chair. "Seem too easy. Like simply turning a switch on and off."

"That's because you don't understand the Grafton mind," said Croft. He and Levi and a number of others were reclining on the roof of the Column HQ. A number of Gamma Operatives were running around, shouting, and making odd noises.

"Then maybe you explain," said Levi.

"The Grafton code of honor prized fair fights above all else," said Croft. "Think about it. It was rooted in practicality. With no law to speak of on Grafton, each Graftonite had to survive by his ability with a gun. That equalized things for one on one combat. It deterred senseless attacks, because a Grafton considering attacking another Grafton knew he could get shot in the attempt."

"But think about what would happen if groups of Graftons banded together and attacked an individual Grafton. Gangs of criminals would terrorize the planet. The Graftons realized this, and created their code of conduct for a 'fair fight'," said Croft.

"Ah, I see," said Levi. "When Quandry refused to do fair fight-"

"and the entire Grafton population saw it, his movement was discredited," said Croft. "It also helped that his senior underlings stood by and let it happen; that helped discredit even more of the movement."

"But still, Graftons in this for money, not honor, and that not really changed."

Croft smiled. "The Graftons were never really into this in the first place. They had to be maneuvered and manipulated by Quandry to start their war of conquest, so it didn't take that much to turn them against it. Our gathering on Grafton started the ball rolling. Why do you think Quandry was here? He knew he was losing support and had to goad the Alliance into making another attack to shore up his base of support. Since the Graftons were never really interested in wars of conquest in the first place, it didn't take much to get them out of it."

"But Graftons like to fight."

"As individuals, yes. But not in groups, not in large armies (aside from small mercenary teams), and not to take over territory. What would Graftonites do with a planet once they took it over? I suspect most of them were clueless. No, most of them wanted to operate on their own to make a quick buck. That's their nature."

"You were smart to record battle," said Levi.

"Thanks," said Croft. "Of course, I had to do some retouching of the holorecording. The image of my laserbolt, for example, had to be painted out. We didn't want it to look like the Silencer had any help from some outside sheep, did we?"

"With Graftonites out of business, I presume blockade lifted?"

"Yes," said Croft. "For once the Chief persuaded the Chief of Staff to take my advice and leave well enough alone. If we demanded reparations that could just restart the troubles we had."

"And what about Claritan corporation?"

"What about them?"

"They cooperate with invaders, have many interests on League worlds. How were they punished?"

Croft frowned. "To my knowledge, they haven't been."

"Not punished?"

"Oh, there's an investigation in the legislature; they'll report back in ten years or so, and then maybe Claritan will have to pay a small fine."

"Small fine, for trying to take over League."

"They are quite an important corporation with many interests in League worlds, remember," said Croft. "Disrupting their operations would disrupt planetary economies."

"And politician bankrolls," said Levi.

Croft watched the gamma operatives walking, yelling, and playing around the roof. One of them walked by Croft, and hissed, "Yes, Croft is very pleased with self, always congratulating, self-congratulating."

In the background Croft could see the Clapper clap.

Red Sally was at a grill, apparently cooking food from her fingers.

Croft turned to Levi. "What are they all doing here?"

"They don't get out much," said Levi.

"And why are you letting Red cook? Is there something wrong with your grill?" Croft watched flame spout from her fingers, cooking a hamburger. Sally chuckled with delight.

"Nothing wrong with grill," said Levi. "Which remind me, what about Grafton meat recipe you promised?"

"Levi, I, ah,"

"You promised!"

"Levi, I was a bit busy," said Croft. "You know, saving the League from invasion, preventing a presidential assassination, that sort of thing."

"Oh," said Levi, pouting.

Croft reached over into a carrier bag, and took out a datapad. "Here," he said.

Levi's eyes brightened. "Recipes?"

"200 of them from among the best chef databases on Grafton," said Croft.

"You remembered!" said Levi.

"I know how to take care of my own," said Croft.

"So what you do now?" said Levi.

"I'm up for some vacation time," said Croft. "The Silencer and Annie have invited me to stay with them on their ranch while the Silencer recovers. I think I'll take them up on it."

"Silencer not know that you responsible for fake holographic murder scene and reduced bounty jobs, no?"

"No," said Croft. "And I think that bit of information is best kept between us."

"You think it safe to go back to Grafton now?"

"I don't think there will be any trouble," said Croft. "After all, it was a fair fight."

Croft got up and looked at the view of August around him. The buildings glittered in the morning sun. He smiled, and stretched. Who knew what tomorrow would bring?

The End

Author's Notes, August 28, 2002

So ends "Attack of the Bounty Hunters" (originally "Attack of the Graftonites"). As I write more and more books, I find I produce them in segments. I started writing this book, stopped in the middle for a few months, wrote "Rise of the Standard Imperium", and then came back and finished this book. Furthermore, when I came back and wrote the second half, I wrote the last chapter first, followed by the second to last chapter, and so on until I moved back to the middle of the book. I find I enjoy writing more and more of my books this way, and

since I have an outline to work with, I always know where I'm going (or coming from). You can find more of my books available at www.CliffordCroft.com
--Steven Gordon

Read an excerpt from "The Invasion of August"

Chapter 1: The Fall of August

They were incredible.

One of them could shoot fire from her hands.

One of them could move objects with his mind.

One of them could see into the future.

One of them could create illusions, see through walls, and turn his right hand into almost any object he wanted.

They were also, in many ways, neurotic or borderline mentally retarded

The one who could shoot fire from her hands was named Red Sally. She had the power to burn enemies, but also a constant urge to burn things, which, combined with a hair trigger temper, made her almost as dangerous to allies as to enemies.

The one who could move objects with his mind was called The Clapper. He had the intellect of a ten year old, and had the constant urge to clap his hands, far from ideal in missions requiring stealth.

The one who could see into the future was named Mongo. But he could only see possible futures, and his predictions were far from certain. Furthermore, he was very difficult to deal with, because of an anti-social complex that led him to feel that everyone around him was ungrateful for his services.

The one who could create illusions, see through walls, and turn his hand into almost any object was not one but three separate and totally opposite personalities, each with their own skill. The primary personality was known as Crazy Rob. He could create illusions. But he was also paranoid, and was convinced that everyone was out to get him.

Another personality was Matt. He could see through walls. He was actually the easiest to get along with, although he was kind of dreamy, which made it difficult to get him to focus on things such as work.

The third personality was Bender. He could turn his right hand into objects, but the object he usually chose was a large spoon. With coaxing he could turn it into other things, but Rob, who was clinically depressed, was not the easiest person to work with. Or should I say easiest personality?

And the master of ceremonies in this four ringed circus was none other than myself, superspy Clifford Croft.

I'm a spy.

A spy.

A SPY. S-P-Y.

That means I spy on people. Sometimes, I commit espionage. Occasionally, and this isn't my favorite part of my job, I have to shoot people, usually ones shooting at me.

Nothing in that job description even remotely relates to mental counseling, does it? And yet here I am, in Column HQ, running a discussion during "community time" for the Column's "gamma operatives", those with special abilities.

The Chief picked me. He said that the doctors were having trouble getting through to them, and that they might listen to someone they respected.

That still doesn't explain why he picked me.

"Stop hitting me!" Mongo squealed.

"You tripped me!" said the Clapper.

"You're making me hot!" said Crazy Rob, sweating.

"Stop putting snakes in my lap!" said Red Sally, frantically brushing away empty air.

"Stop!" I said. They continued to argue. "STOP!" I shouted.

They still ignored me, arguing among themselves, seated in a circle while white clothed orderlies watched from a respectful distance.

I sighed, and drew my blaster. I adjusted the setting. To maximum.

I fired at the ceiling. There was a tremendous noise, and large chunks of plastiform fell around me.

That got their attention.

"Hello!" I said. "Let's handle this one item at a time, shall we?"

I turned to Mongo. "What's your problem?" I noticed two guards standing behind him. Mongo was currently confined to the detention center, and had only been let out temporarily, under guard, for this "therapy session". I idly wondered what he had done to wind up in detention.

Mongo pointed a bony finger at the Clapper. "He is hitting poor Mongo! Ow" He said, his head jerking to an imaginary slap.

I turned to the Clapper. "Stop that."

"He tripped me!" said the Clapper, clapping. (Clap clap!)

"No," said Mongo. "Mongo only tells him he sees a future where he trips."

"Yes, and when I actually tripped, it was because you tripped me!" said the Clapper.

I turned to Mongo. "You can't expect to hurt people without getting some kind of negative response."

"He never appreciates Mongo," said Mongo accusingly.

"Well, now you can appreciate how he can hurt you," I said.

I turned to Crazy Rob. "What's your problem?"

"This heat is sweltering!" said Crazy Rob, and I saw he was sweating. He glared at Sally. "She's doing it!"

I felt the air around him. It was hot. I sighed. "Sally, stop."

Sally was still brushing imaginary objects off of her lap. "I will when he gets rid of these snakes!"

"Rob?" I said. "You want to do something about the snakes?"

"They're not really there," said Crazy Rob defensively.

"And I have no reason to really be here," I said. "But if you stop, perhaps I can persuade Sally to."

"It's all a conspiracy!" said Crazy Rob, glaring at me. "You put her up to it! You're making her do it!"

"Yes, Rob," I said, playing into his conspiracy theory.

"You--what was that?"

"Yes, you're right, I conspired with Red Sally to make you feel hot. Now that you've exposed the conspiracy, can you lighten up on the snakes?"

Crazy Rob looked startled, as if he hadn't been expecting the conversation to take this turn. He nodded, and Sally suddenly relaxed and stopped brushing away the air around her.

"And now, Sally?" I asked.

"He deserves it," she said glaring at me. Her hair was now blonde with a slight pink ting to it. The more she used her power, the redder her hair became.

"Yes, but he uncovered our conspiracy, and there's no sense in continuing," I said.

"What conspiracy?"

"Sally."

"All right," Sally sighed, and the air around Crazy Rob suddenly cooled.

"I want to know more about this conspiracy," said Crazy Rob. "Were you all in on it?"

"We can get back to that later," I said. "Does anyone have any idea why I'm here today?"

"To entertain us!" the Clapper squealed, clapping.

"To show appreciation," said Mongo.

"To annoy us," said Red Sally.

"This is all a diversion for something else," Crazy Rob said.

"I'm here because you're all having some difficulties with interpersonal relations," I said diplomatically.

"And they sent you?" said Red Sally contemptuously.

"I don't light people on fire when I get angry," I said.

"You just shoot them," said Sally.

"This isn't about me," I said. "I'm here to help you."

"Chief orders it," said Mongo, getting a far reaching look. "I sees it yesterday. Chief says to Croft, she says, Croft, you must do this. Croft protests, he protests he does not like us-"

"That's not true," I said. "Whatever future you were seeing, that wasn't the real one. It's not that I don't like you, but...." I paused, momentarily lost in liespeak. They looked at me, awaiting my response. I changed the subject. "Let's get back to you. Wouldn't it be nice if you could deal more easily with other people?"

"If other people were nice, yes," said Mongo.

"Let's start with you, Mongo," I said. "You feel that you're underappreciated."

"Yes, yes!"

"But maybe if you appreciated other people more, they would do the same for you."

"Why would Mongo appreciate others?" Mongo asked. "Can others see the future too?"

"Well, no, but seeing the future isn't the only nice thing a person can do for someone else," I said. "Take your food, for example. If someone goes through the trouble to prepare a special meal-"

"Is nothing compared to seeing future," said Mongo.

"-so you do see the similarity," I said, doing my duty in a purely perfunctory way. How could the Chief really think that I could help these people?

I turned to Red Sally, who was next. "Sally, I think you could get along better with people if you didn't light them on fire."

"You TELL me to light people on fire," said Sally.

"Enemies, in combat, yes," I said. "I was referring to people here, like the orderlies in this room. Orderlies, those of you who have been burned, at one time or another, raise your hands.""

Two orderlies in white slowly raised their hands.

"Raise your hands, don't be shy," I said.

All the other orderlies raised their hands.

Sally said, "Well, I don't mean to, but.."

"Exactly. You need to control your temper," I said.

"I'll try," said Sally. "But people have to try not to get me so angry."

I turned to the Clapper. "And you have to learn not to push people around with your mind."

The Clapper clapped, giving an idiotic grin.

"People don't like being slapped, even if by an invisible force."

The Clapper, still grinning, clapped again.

"And don't think they can't figure out who's doing it, because they can."

The Clapper kept clapping.

"And if you get them angry enough, they might glue your hands together."

The Clapper stopped smiling, and his hands, clasped together, suddenly stopped moving.

I turned to Crazy Rob. "Causing hallucinations won't win you many friends either."

Crazy Rob, his head drooping, said, "Why should I care?"

I suddenly noticed that his right hand had changed into a large metal spoon. He had changed from his Crazy Robert personality into his Bender personality. Bender was merely depressed; he didn't actually bother anyone. There was no sense in talking to Bender about Rob, since there was no connection between the two.

I was actively debating how to fill up the rest of the hour when the building-wide alarm sounded.

Want to read more? Check out our books on our website....

Clifford Croft Press, New York
www.CliffordCroft.com

Clifford Croft Press, New York
www.CliffordCroft.com

The Clifford Croft Series

Attack of the Bounty Hunters
The Invasion of August (Attack of the Insects Book 1)
The War Admiral's Fleet (Attack of the Insects Book 2)
Death to the Insects! (Attack of the Insects Book 3)
Nightfall on August (Attack of the Insects Book 4)
Rise of the Standard Imperium (Attack of the Insects Book 5)
Still The Most Dangerous Game
Infiltrator
The Essential Mindreader
Escape from Altera

The Invasion of August

The "Insects", a race of giant intelligent bugs, have destroyed the human fleet and invaded August, the ultra-futuristic capital of the League of United Planets with skyscrapers that extend for miles in every direction.

Leading a ragtag resistance is as follows: Superspy Clifford Croft; Red Sally, a tempermental woman who can start fires with her mind and a major cause of friendly fire incidents; the Clapper, a telekinetic who can move things with his mind, even as he claps his hands all the time; Mongo, a bitter, hissing viewer of futures who is firmly convinced he's never appreciated; and the Silencer, a gunman with super reflexes.

The War Admiral's Fleet

The Insects destroyed 95% of the human fleet at Vitalics; but it's that 5% they have to worry about, because it's under the command of the legendary War Admiral Norman North. The War Admiral gathers what survivors he can and heads out into deep space, in search of an ancient weapon that can push the bugs back and save the League.

Death to the Insects!

Superspy Clifford Croft is on the run as the Insects have invaded August, his allies are scattered, and his friend the Silencer has been captured and is forced to fight gladiator games against monsters in front of jeering insect audiences. Croft must gather together his allies--the fire starter Red Sally, the telekinetic Clapper, the future-teller Mongo, the mysterious advisor Inspir, a blue Capybara with unimaginable mental powers, and others to eliminate the Insects from August.

Nightfall on August

The Insects have been pushed back, but at a tremendous cost. At the last minute as they were retreating they launched a devastating weapon at League planets, one which created an energy draining mist that prevented all electricity from working. Advanced societies that were dependent on power suddenly reverted to the stone age. Food and shelter, concepts that were taken for granted, suddenly disappeared. Superspy Clifford Croft finds himself in a different role as he and former resistance fighters try to stitch society back together. But they discover that the Insects have not quite been defeated....

Rise of the Standard Imperium

Clifford Croft remembers a futuristic alien spaceship, floating in space, which held the key to lifting the energy mist and restoring power to August. But this ship was one where he barely escaped with his life, where a 1000 year old monster floats in the darkness, waiting....

Infiltrator

Imagine a planet where everyone is under the direct mental control of the state, and plotting to put the rest of the galaxy under mind control as well. In one of Clifford Croft's toughest assignment, he has to infiltrate this society, which is so orderly that everyone is brainwashed, everyone wears an ID number, and the entire society is under constant surveillance. Can he penetrate this society without getting caught, and brainwashed like everyone else?

The Essential Mindreader

Someone is attempting to kill the President of Paley Paratus. But that's not what interests superspy Clifford Croft; his number one witness is a man who can apparently read minds, and Croft is in a race to protect him before the other side gets him.

Still The Most Dangerous Game

Ernst Manheim Studt has a new hobby: hunting people. He kidnaps them, brings them to his uncharted planet, and hunts them. If they can survive three days in the wilderness, they are free to go. So far, no one has left. Bored with killing Graftonites with their super reflexes, he settles on a new target: superspy Clifford Croft.

Escape from Altera

Space Pilot Idaho Took has been shot down and placed in a brutal Slurian labor camp, where he endures terrible hardships in his struggle to survive. It will take the combined efforts of superspy Clifford Croft and the legendary Graftonite gunman the Silencer to rescue him.

Attack of the Bounty Hunters

The Graftonites had super reflexes, making them superior bounty hunters and almost unstoppable gunmen. They could draw and fire a blaster in a blink of an eye, before an opponent had a chance to even go for a weapon. Grafton II had evolved into a planet with no government--a purely libertarian society where all services were privatized and civil disputes were mediated with one-on-one gunfights.

For hundreds of years the Graftonites hired themselves out for individual jobs requiring their unique skills. Until the day Mo Quandry came along and organized them into an army with the intent of conquering the galaxy. No opposing army of any size would be able to oppose them.

The League of United Planets sent their best agent, Clifford Croft, to investigate, along with the Clapper, an eccentric telekinetic who liked to clap, and Red Sally, a constantly angry woman who can literally start fires with her mind. As Croft becomes a target for Quandry's assassins, he'll learn he will need the help of the legendary bounty hunter known as "The Silencer" to stop the Graftonite march towards conquest.

Other novels by Steven Gordon

Clashik Cube
A band of adventurers--a coward, a schemer, a barbarian, a scientist, and an expert tactician--set out to find an artifact of great power. But in order to get it, they must pass progressively more and more deadlier tests, until only one remains.

Unexpected Wizardry
A New York lawyer bored with his job gets transported to another world and finds he has the ability to use magic. Can Whyse the Wizard teach him before enemies, attracted by his magical ability, rip him to pieces?

Future Park
Imagine the amusement park of the future, where you can actually live inside an entirely self-contained spaceship combat simulator for several days, and go on missions just like in the movies!

Redweld Warrior
Jane Sommers is an ivy law school grad who inadvertently gets a job at a scummy New York law firm where she is degraded and sexually harassed. Read as she takes it, and then how she fights back. This book shows what life is like at many New York law firms, with just a bit of parody.

Finish Line

Candidates will lie and cheat to become governor of New York, but only one will kill. Read the coldly calculating political memoir of Governor Powers.

Check out these titles at
Clifford Croft Press, New York
www.CliffordCroft.com

About the Author

Steven Gordon is many things to many people. To some he is an inventor--he invented Allexperts.com, the first large scale question and answer website on the internet, and he currently runs Allreaders.com, the only search engine which lets one search for books by discrete plot, setting, character and style elements. To others he is an author, having so far written 17 books. To a very few he was a lawyer, a graduate of Yale University and Harvard Law School. Steven Gordon lives in the very dirty New York City with a beige Pomeranian named Beaver. You can contact him by using the feedback form at www.CliffordCroft.com.